I'm coming, Griffin, *she thought.*
Coming for you.

With renewed purpose, Camille felt her way along the rock. Soon, the path widened considerably, allowing the team to gather together and help each other to safety. Good—all accounted for.

Something stirred behind her, rattling the leaves of a bush. Camille spun around, found nothing. She checked her wrist tracker. Silent.

Then quiet steps, shuffling over rock. A snuff. A growl. No one moved. Slowly, she started to take out her dart gun. Started to turn around.

Eyes. Six pairs of preternaturally shining orbs glowing from the skulls of wolves. A huge gray one—the alpha female—slunk forward, flashing teeth. Fangs.

Camille grabbed her guns. "Watch out, wolves. I'm no Red Riding Hood."

Dear Reader,

What do you plan to accomplish in 2005? Let Silhouette Bombshell jump-start your year with this month's fast-paced lineup of stories featuring amazing women who will entertain you, energize you and inspire you to get out there and get things done!

Author Nancy Bartholomew brings on the heat with *Stella, Get Your Man*. P.I. Stella Valocchi is on a missing-persons case—but with a lying client, a drug lord gunning for her and a new partner who thinks he's the boss, Stella's got her hands full staying cool under fire.

The pressure rises as our popular twelve-book ATHENA FORCE continuity series continues with *Deceived*, by Carla Cassidy, in which a computer whiz with special, supersecret talents discovers that she's on the FBI's Most Wanted list and her entire life may be a lie.

Reality isn't what it seems in the mystic thriller *Always Look Twice* by Sheri WhiteFeather. Heroine Olivia Whirlwind has a unique gift, but delving into the minds of crime victims will bring her ever closer to a ruthless killer and will make everyone a suspect—including those she loves.

And finally, travel to Romania with Crystal Green's *The Huntress*, as an heiress with an attitude becomes a vampire hunter on a mission for vengeance after her lover is captured by those mysterious creatures of the night.

Enjoy all four, and when you're finished, please send your comments to me c/o Silhouette Books, 233 Broadway, Suite 1001, New York, NY 10279.

Sincerely,

Natashya Wilson

Natashya Wilson
Associate Senior Editor, Silhouette Bombshell

Please address questions and book requests to:
Silhouette Reader Service
U.S.: 3010 Walden Ave., P.O. Box 1325, Buffalo, NY 14269
Canadian: P.O. Box 609, Fort Erie, Ont. L2A 5X3

the HUNTRESS

CRYSTAL GREEN

Published by Silhouette Books

America's Publisher of Contemporary Romance

SILHOUETTE BOOKS

ISBN 0-373-51342-9

THE HUNTRESS

Copyright © 2005 by Chris Marie Green

This edition published by arrangement with Harlequin Books S.A.

® and TM are trademarks of Harlequin Books S.A., used under license.
Trademarks indicated with ® are registered in the United States Patent
and Trademark Office, the Canadian Trade Marks Office and in other
countries.

www.SilhouetteBombshell.com

Printed in U.S.A.

CRYSTAL GREEN

lives in San Diego, California, where she writes for
Silhouette Special Edition, Silhouette Bombshell and
Harlequin Blaze. When she isn't penning romances, she
loves to read, overanalyze movies, pet her parents' Maltese
dog, fence, do yoga and fantasize about being a really good
cook.

Crystal loves to travel whenever possible. Her favorite
souvenirs include journals, the pages of which reflect everything from taking tea in London's Leicester Square to wandering the neon-lit streets of Tokyo. She'd love to hear from
her readers at: 8895 Towne Centre Drive, Suite 105-178,
San Diego, CA 92122-5542. And don't forget to visit her
Web site at www.crystal-green.com!

To Shine, my partner in vampirology, movie analysis and saber wielding. Thank you for all your ideas and scientific genius. Now go out and continue saving the world.

Chapter 1

Camille Howard tried to control her heartbeat as she shifted under the sweating, beefy man who was straining on top of her.

She was on her back in a Transylvanian meadow, surrounded by wildflowers, thighs wrapped around the thick, vein-strung neck of a local peasant.

Choking and gurgling, the man clutched at her form-fitting khaki fatigues as she squeezed her legs together. His eyes bulged, watering. A tear dropped onto her chest from the slope of his cheek.

Good for him. He'd lasted longer than the other four guys she'd wrestled so far.

But he still hadn't proved he could be of any use.

Infinite seconds passed as he huffed. A burst of wood

smoke darkened the spring sun, then cleared. She had enough time to turn her head, to survey the crowd of Vasile village men watching the match.

All of them looked about ready to wet their pants.

Their fear—her own hovering fear, too—concerned Camille. None of them had the luxury of being afraid. Not if they were going after the *strigoiaca.*

Strigoiaca. Camille clenched her thighs even more at the thought of them. Five female vampires who'd survived hundreds of years on the blood of Romanian men. They roamed the countryside, looking to sustain themselves once every year, when their pet males died and the female creatures needed to replenish their food supply.

Nine months ago, they'd stocked up in the village of Juni. Now Camille wanted to take back what was hers.

Damn the *strigoiaca.*

The peasant gave a tiny catlike yowl between her legs.

All right. So he'd had enough of her Brazilian jujitsu, a martial art that didn't depend solely on strength. A lot of it was technique.

Hell, even a five-foot-five-inch, 124-pound scrapper like her could take down the Hulk with her training. As she was now proving.

Camille held back a resigned sigh when, after a last-ditch grunt, the peasant tried to pry her legs apart. She reacted by calmly grasping her shin, levering her leg farther downward.

"Opri!" Stop. His plea was a desperate wheeze.

Dammit. If any of these Vasile men were going to be of any help whatsoever, they were going to have to grab their sacs.

Frustration—bitterness—roiled through her veins. Instead of letting the man free, she held him steady.

He let out an anguished groan. Wuss.

"So you want me to stop?" she asked in pretty flawless Romanian, if she said so herself.

Well, her accent had better be perfect. She'd been in Romania for most of the past year studying the language…and more. The doc, Beatrix Grasu, would throttle her if she heard even a trace of American pie creep in.

"*Opri!* Yes!" The peasant's face was the color of a plum that'd been crushed under an 18-wheeler's tire.

Finally, she loosened her grip a little, but didn't let go. She needed to prove a point to these guys, these men who thought that their village women weren't strong enough to hunt vampires.

She shot a glance at the rest of the male crowd. Their friend's indignity had collected some perspiration on their brows, right under their fur caps.

Just you wait, she thought. This is nothing compared to what we'll go through out in the wilds.

"Ah!"

Camille's captive pounded at her thighs. Oh, brother. She hated when she made men cry.

Not to be cruel, but…

She allowed her fingers to linger on her ankle, almost as if she was intending to snap the guy's neck off with one more wrench southward.

The crowd pulled in a shocked breath.

Another flex of her fingers. Ready to jam down, to cut off air with more viselike pressure.

The peasant's eyelids fluttered.

It was a good thing she didn't have fangs, she thought. This peach would've been drained three minutes ago.

Just as one of the peasant men stepped forward—right, as if he was really going to take her on—she released her victim, rolled to a sitting position, then to a stand, in one fluid motion.

She made a point of looking pissed off, of drilling a stare into each and every male in the front row. They all glanced away, clearly embarrassed to have been manhandled by a whippet-thin, pale chick who wasn't much to inspire thoughts of superheroine beauty.

"You think that was harsh?" she asked in their tongue. "I've seen what those vampires can do."

She held out her arms in invitation to the men as her victimized peasant balanced himself to his knees, grabbed his tumbled cap and slunk away.

"So who's next? Who's quicker?" She lowered her chin. "Who can tear me apart before I can do it to you?"

No answer.

Killed hope tumbled through her, lost before it'd even been found.

Could she go after the vampires all alone?

Without thinking, she touched the ever present good-luck charm around her neck. A baby ring.

Griffin.

She clamped her fingers around the smooth circle of the totem.

I'm coming for you no matter what.

Sustained by the thought of what she had to do, Camille raised her gaze, dropped her fists to her sides.

"Isn't there anyone?"

A hank of her red, arrow-straight hair escaped her braid and caught the wind, covering her view of the men. With a curse, she cuffed aside the offending strands.

The spectators hadn't moved during her challenging silence. At least not physically. But they'd retreated just the same. It was in the way the men looked at each other from the corners of their eyes. The way they kept their shaggy heads bent.

A fragile female voice said, "There is no one."

Camille turned around, finding her mentor, Dr. Beatrix Grasu, a silver-haired matron decked in a tweed skirt suit, horn-rimmed eyeglasses and a pair of Ugg boots.

Camille's heart melted a little at the sight of her. Bea—the woman who had taken Camille in, cared for her, given her strength after the most terrifying night of her life.

"An entire population of Dracula snacks." Camille switched to English while striding away from the circle. No use announcing her defeated faith to these men. "We should've hired those female bikers in Bucharest. Even untrained, they'd last longer than these guys."

"Random women," the doc said. "They have no personal issue in this. The people of Vasile have much more at stake. They *want* to fight at your side, these men do."

"Their good intentions aren't enough."

The elderly woman rolled her eyes at the irony of it all, then lifted her face to the sky, sniffing. "There are more charms decorating doorways, darling girl. Garlic and wild roses. They are ready for an attack, even more so than yesterday."

"Superstition. Right." Camille stood by her friend's side, shook her head and glanced over her shoulder at the gathered males. They shuffled their *opinci,* rough pigskin shoes, and withstood her withering inspection.

She lowered her voice. "Catering to male egos has cost us an entire morning. No matter how much these guys protest, let's get the women out here. We can't screw around anymore."

Bea smiled sweetly, making Camille think that maybe everything *would* be okay. The ever-optimistic doc had always told her so while educating Camille in the ways of vampires and science, giving her a sense of wary hope.

"And how will you select your females?" the old woman asked. "Your prey—they do not wrestle. Why you are practicing a triangle hold on these men, I do not know."

"Yeah, yeah." Camille's natural impatience returned, in spite of Bea's calm. "You'd rather recruit a mob and just give them our toys, but I need people who think on their feet, too. People who can get themselves out of a fix. They have to be speedy, just like those creatures, or they'll be token sacrifices. We'd be in a situation like I found myself in at Juni—"

Her voice caught.

She'd tried so hard to forget about it—a nightgown flapping over moon-pale skin, Griff yelling her name and reaching out for her….

Camille closed her eyes, fighting the memory, hurting too much to continue talking.

The clang of a goat's bell filled the silence as she steeled herself. She opened her eyes to find Bea watching her with familiar concern.

"Aunt Bea," Camille said, using the Mayberry nickname that reminded her that, somewhere on earth, there was a place that felt like home, "any male who can't take me on is going to die within the first second of a confrontation with those bitches. I can't let that happen."

Bea's gaze softened in sympathy and, even though Camille just wanted to fold herself into the doc's safe arms and pretend she was a real aunt who'd just baked gingerbread in the kitchen, she couldn't.

Weakness wasn't an option. Wiping all feeling from her body, she walked back to the crowd, switching to Romanian.

"Are your females any tougher?" she asked them.

There was a ragged laugh from the back, near the faded planking of the inn walls.

Camille waited for the designated smart-ass to step forward. She loved knocking the piss out of people who didn't take her seriously.

The peasant men turned around to see who was stupid enough to be ticking off "our huntress"—a moniker they whispered behind her back. As the crowd parted, it revealed a tall, muscle-honed man clad in army-green fatigues, combat boots and a wicked machete sheathed by his side. He had hard-edged features: squinting eyes that still echoed his mocking laugh, a pugilist's often broken nose, a cleft chin with a day's worth of beard stubble. His light brown hair wasn't exactly cut in military fashion; it was too long. The style smacked of the way his type—army assassins—singled themselves out as more than soldiers by refusing to conform to the basic grunt shave.

And then there was the ugly scar decorating his neck.

Without being introduced, she knew exactly who he was.

The man called Sargent leaned against the inn and extracted a Marlboro from a box in his T-shirt pocket. A thorny cross positioned by the side door lingered above his head. Two men framed the notorious mercenary: a platinum-haired guy dressed in white hippie wear, and a time-wrinkled peasant wearing a hand-embroidered shirt and a sheepskin-lined vest. He seemed fascinated by Sargent.

"Gee, I knew my luck would run out sooner or later." Camille tweaked a sarcastic smile to Bea. Translation: Just what we needed, more vampire munchies.

Holding back a grin, the doc shook her finger at her student, lowered her voice. "Be nice to the man."

When Camille glanced back at the notorious killer-for-hire, the old man next to him stared longingly at Sargent's ciggie. The commando shrugged and gave him one. Then he lit a flame to his own, the furious shade of red bathing his face. An instant later, the nasty glow subsided as he handed the match to the old guy.

"Women have no place in war," Sargent said in Romanian, the cigarette bobbing between his lips. "Especially rich heiresses who think this is some kind of spat."

Camille had known he'd speak the language. In fact, when she'd discovered that Sargent had been hired by

Flora Vladislav and the other Juni peasants to go after the *strigoiaca,* she'd learned a lot of other things about him, too. How he enjoyed slaughtering just for the hell of it. How he was relentless in his pursuit of anything remotely associated with fangs.

She absently touched her baby ring.

Sargent stepped away from the wall and walked toward her, a drift of cigarette smoke curling from the side of his mouth. His hippie friend shook his head, then entered the inn, abandoning the scene.

The mercenary saluted her with the cig. "You got here before I did."

So Flora Vladislav had told him about her, too. "Get used to second place."

He didn't find that funny. "Word travels fast out here. I understand you're on some kind of mercy mission."

"From what *I* hear, I doubt you'd understand anything that has to do with mercy." Her pulse started thudding at the thought of what he'd do to Griff if he found him before she did. What he'd do to all the captives and vampires.

According to Flora, Sargent had killed his first vampire years ago. He'd been on some secret military mission and attacked by a female vampire informant during an ambush she had orchestrated. Supposedly, Sargent had snapped. Robbed of trust and his perception of the world as he knew it, he'd made a name for himself as a preternatural terminator.

As he sauntered closer, Camille's gaze lingered on his neck scar. The web of dead skin.

What, exactly, had turned *him* into a killer? What

deep instincts had changed him from a soldier to an animal with the worst of reputations?

He came to stand right in front of her, forcing her to lift her chin to meet his glare.

Right. *Make* me back down, she thought.

With an amused lift of the eyebrows, Sargent grinned, sucked on the cig until it burned into a crackling column of ash, then tossed it into a patch of dirt. He ground it to gray matter beneath the toe of a beaten combat boot and puffed out a cloud of smoke.

This time he used English. "You can pack up the carnival now. Time to go back on home to the States."

His own American accent turned some heads. The peasants eyed him with a measure of relief and caution, probably because he'd saved them from further mortification at her hands. Or probably because of that white-hot badge of violence on his neck.

"You don't trust women enough to fight?" she asked, taking one step closer to him, bringing them chest to chest. "If the men I'd hired to take care of this situation in the past had been successful, I wouldn't be here myself."

The peasants shifted, no doubt sensing the tension.

"Never send a man to do a woman's work, huh?"

"Are you here to join the team or what?" She made a please-don't-make-me-ill face.

"Let me see if it's worth my effort." He took two steps back, then ran a slow gaze up her body.

His attentions left a running trail of reluctant awareness over her legs, her belly.

"Done yet?" she asked. "I'm on a schedule."

Much to her chagrin, he continued his easy inspection until he got to the baby ring on her chest.

Griff's ring.

The wheels were turning in his head: *why would a crankbuster like her be wearing a sentimental trinket?*

He didn't need to know. No one did.

"I suppose you're next in line for some roll-in-the-dirt schooling," she said, gesturing to the ground.

"Thought you told your great-aunt that you're in some kind of hurry." Sargent winked, probably thinking he'd rattle her composure. "When I get you rolling in the dirt, we'll want lots of time."

Automatically, her spine straightened, and she berated herself for allowing him to chalk one up for his team.

They continued to stare at each other. Hell, she'd be damned if she looked away first.

Knowing Camille's stubborn streak quite well, Bea cleared her throat, then addressed the crowd in their language, thanking them for their courage. Asking them to send out their women since it was their best bet against the threat to this village.

The vampires.

Everyone scattered, including the doc, who came over and pulled her student's face toward her, making Camille lose the staring contest.

"Hey, Bea—"

"Prepare."

With that, Doc cast a considering glance at Sargent, then left him alone with Camille.

"I'll give this to you," he said, grinning because he

knew he'd won. *By default.* "That wrestling show was spiffy. But if you get a vampire between your thighs, it won't beg you to stop squeezing. Not like our friendly Vasile peasants. The *strigoiaca* will dine on your femoral artery. You know, it's the one near those balls of yours."

"Oh, score for you, Mr. Sargent. Impressive work upholding your reputation. You truly are an ass."

Sargent maintained his condescending demeanor. From what she'd heard from Flora Vladislav, he'd spent years developing that battle face. Years wearing the paint of war, moving through deserts and cities without sound or error.

That was the rumor, anyway. Flora and the Juni women, the ones who'd lured Sargent here with their life savings in order to cleanse the area, had told Camille all about him when she'd gone back to Juni and announced her intention of saving the captured men herself.

"So," she said, still stinging from the way Flora had rejected Camille's own rescue plan. The villagers hadn't believed in her. At all. "You don't mind being a murderer? Killing living creatures for blood money?"

"Someone's got to be the exterminator around here."

His offhand comment ripped at her. Goaded her into resorting to her least favorite form of persuasion.

Using her Howard family fortune to make him go away.

"Flora and her village couldn't possibly be paying you as much as I could," she said.

"To kill vamps?"

"To leave."

For a second, his rigid toughness evaporated. It looked as if he couldn't believe what he was hearing.

But, true to form, he recovered quickly, reverting back into egomaniac mode. "And what're you planning to do with those beasts? Sweet-talk them into being good little bloodsuckers and playing nice with the nearby villages?" He held up a finger. "Or maybe you're going to jujitsu them into wholesome, upstanding citizens."

Jerk. In order to keep control, she intentionally backed off, sighed, checked her state-of-the-art, rocket-science watch. "Lecture completed?"

"I've got a lot more to say."

He was starting to look as angry as she felt.

"Frankly," he said, "it's people like you—simple, naive newcomers—who make my job harder."

To emphasize his next point, he reached out, grasped one side of her neck. She didn't panic. Instead, she forced herself to watch him with what she hoped was removed detachment, daring him to go further.

And he did.

His thumb threatened the tender center of her throat, but she stood her ground, actually smiling in his face.

He smiled, too, and not very nicely.

Her ring shifted, brushing against Sargent's hand.

"You know what vamps do," he said softly. "They go for your pretty little necklace holder here. They feed on you, sometimes out of hunger, sometimes out of boredom. Depends where you run into them, what their culture is, what their needs are. But there's always one constant."

He pressed against her windpipe, not enough to hurt her, but enough to stress his meaning. She'd be damned if she allowed herself to start choking.

Sargent continued. "Uh-huh, one constant, Miss Bleeding Heart. You *never* give vamps a chance."

By now, adrenaline was singing through her body, the blood in her neck veins kicking under the pressure of his grip. Her breathing quickened, but she wouldn't give him the satisfaction of hearing her voice falter.

"The vampires don't need to be killed in order to neutralize them." There. Strong as steel. Bastard. "Beatrix and I know they can be turned."

"Holy—"

His reaction allowed her enough time to windmill her arm over the one he was using to captivate her throat.

Zinging that arm up, then downward, she caught him in the soft inside of his elbow with a chopping motion, breaking his hold. With her other hand, she planked his arm away. In the next instant, she backed off, taking up a defensive stance, punch ready.

Sargent casually peered at the resulting red mark on his arm. "I suppose I deserved that."

"Don't pull it again." She was still on guard.

"Relax. I'm done." He held up his hands, palms outward. "Damn, you're jumpy."

"'Jumpy' doesn't cover it. Touch me again and you'll sing like Frankie Valli in 'Walk Like a Man.'"

He laughed. Actually *laughed*. "All right. Just tell me why you're so sure you can save our fanged friends. Why would you even *want* to save them?"

Although she kept her distance, she lowered her fists. "If you take a step, I'm going to practice my science experiments on you."

"I believe it. And I'm actually sort of curious about what you have up your lab coat."

"Heh. My sides are splitting with laughter."

"Come on, Howard. Coddle me a little. Spill."

How much could she tell him without seeming as if she was on a one-way trip to failure? She'd been told she was crazy enough times to make her wary of explaining.

She paused, then said, "Dr. Beatrix Grasu—who is, by the way, a professor at the University of Bucharest and not my great-aunt—"

"Then why do you—?"

Camille held up a hand. She wasn't about to detail her emotional attachments. Not to someone who wouldn't comprehend the term.

"As I was saying, Dr. Grasu was able to get one of the *strigoiaca* on an autopsy table."

"So I heard. Question. How does the university feel about her slicing up vampires? Doesn't that cause some unrest?"

"Dr. Grasu now works in the lab I fund. And we've learned enough about the *strigoiaca* that we can contain them…and recapture their prey."

Griff's voice floated into her head, soothed her as it always did in her most hopeless moments.

I love you, Lady Tex.

"So," she said, "what's your price? How much money will it take to get you out of here?"

Sargent's lips drew into a single line of determination. Still locking gazes with her, he rubbed his cheek against a shoulder—the side with the neck scar.

"There's not enough currency in the world to send me away," he said. "Ever."

Something fisted in her gut, squeezing, pulling her inside out.

"There's something else I've been wondering…." he said.

Camille went into protective mode once again. He sounded way too human this time. He wanted something. Information. The upper hand. Whatever it was, he wasn't going to get it.

He must've taken her silence as a go-ahead. "Flora said you were an anthropology student who asked way too many questions last year in their village. That for almost a year, you've been hiring mercenary after mercenary to track those female vampires that attacked Juni. She said your friend is missing—"

"Not your business."

"Ah, short. To the point. You know, I don't care much about your personal details, even though I do feel sorry for you, what with your parents dying like they did…."

Camille cut him off with a sharp look that hid her anguish. She'd been practicing the expression—the avoidance of the reminder—for years.

Sargent cleared his throat.

"I need particulars about the vamps. Having an eyewitness account could only help me, and according to Flora, you saw them take your…friend."

"I'm not here to help you. Remember? I'm here to bring the hostages and the vampires back alive."

He shot Camille a pitying glance. "You're asking for trouble if you don't slay them. Believe me. These things are fast, like vipers. Lethal. I know from experience."

"We're not underestimating them. We have devices that'll keep everyone safe while we transport their prone bodies."

He chuffed. "You're not serious."

"We know where they are. I'm sure Flora told you that a hunter from the last team I hired stumbled into nearby civilization a month ago and talked to an innkeeper before dying from blood loss. The *strigoiaca* are in the forests near the Borgo Pass. Five female vampires, including one woman who was converted that night in Juni, and two male captives of the five that they took last year. Bea—Dr. Grasu—and I have spent all this time studying their kind."

She didn't mention all the physical training she'd put herself through—the months of sharpening her mind and body until she'd been deemed suitable by Bea to go after the vampires herself.

"So," Sargent said, "if you bring all of them back breathing, you'll have *seven* monsters on your hands. Not five. You know that, right? And that's only if the male captives truly survived this long. It's said that those beasts feed off the men until they're worthless. Killing those guys would be doing them a favor—if they're alive."

"A month ago there were two men left," she repeated. It was a comforting mantra. Something to keep faith blooming. "They could still be alive. There's a chance to recover them. I've trained and studied for the past nine months, banking on that, knowing that a female hunter can succeed where the men haven't."

"They'll kill you as fast as they will me."

"Oh, no. Not as fast. I'm just a nuisance to them. Something to get past. You're life."

Sargent looked at her as if she was ten kinds of bonkers. And maybe she was.

"What's life to you, Miss Bleeding Heart?" He narrowed his eyes. "The scientific lure of discovering a new classification of killer animal?"

"You threaten those vampires…or their prisoners," she said, taking a step toward the village inn, "and I'll neutralize *you*. For a long time."

"Flora hired me to avenge her husband and son, not to preserve their kidnappers in the name of science."

Explaining her deeper reasons wouldn't do any good. This man was as thick as timber.

She lowered her voice. "Just get the hell away from my mission and hightail back home. You're not needed here."

As she stalked toward him, the sunlight flashed over her. It captured the metal of her baby ring, throwing the glare onto Sargent's face. He held up a hand and turned away from the light.

At the same time, Camille bodychecked him, her shoulder to his chest. He swung around with the momentum of her aggression.

That's when she aimed a middle finger high in the air.

"Ah. Glad to be wanted," he said as she retreated.

She ignored him and disappeared into the dark, garlic-laced doorway of the inn, blocking out the smoke and low chatter by resting her head against the wood wall.

How was she going to get rid of this buffoon? She could just imagine how the search for the vampires would be: him tailing her. Her having to fight him off.

As if racing Griff's death clock and dealing with monsters who preyed on men weren't enough...

Camille straightened, hands against the wall.

Men. The strigoiaca. *Sargent.*

If she used a male lure, could she bring the vampires to *her,* thus saving time?

A bolt of self-doubt ripped through her. Oh, God, no. What was she thinking? Using Sargent as bait was immoral. Unthinkable.

Still...

No. No way. *Never.*

She hated herself for even coming up with the idea. The old Camille wouldn't have acted like this; she respected life so much that she couldn't bear to see it extinguished.

But that girl hadn't lost everything. Not like the new Camille had.

Nothing's going to stop me, Griff.

Nothing.

As she leaned against the wall, torn, the room seemed to darken around the new Camille, eclipsing the girl she used to be.

Chapter 2

London, approximately one year ago

Camille contained a rush of embarrassment as a cheeky guy checked her out from across the room.

As she sat on a bench in the National Gallery's East Wing, she adjusted her headphones and spiked the volume on her CD audio tour. Pretending not to notice the gaper, she stared straight ahead at Van Gogh's *Sunflowers,* listening to the monotone announcer talking about *impasto,* thick brush strokes, and how the technique affected the painting's texture. At the same time, she blocked out the surrounding post-Impressionist paintings by Cezanne and Seurat.

And she almost—*almost*—escaped the gaze of that nosy clod across the room.

This morning, after rolling out of her hotel bed, she'd thought that a good, relaxing spell at an art museum would massage her jet lag. Camille wasn't in the mood to walk the city streets with the spring-vacation tourists and their camera-happy smiles, their gaping boy-howdy-look-at-that expressions, their excited babble about "doing" the Tower of London or Madame Tussaud's.

That's right—this was a hide-in-the-headphones type of day for this temporary world resident.

Strange, how she'd hoped to disappear among the puzzle pieces of other people. In spite of the room's quiet shift of activity, this was the perfect place to be alone. To stare at artwork and read her dog-eared copy of Thomas Malory's *Morte d'Arthur.* To think about how many countries she could keep running to before having to go back to the U.S.

Back "home."

Back to nothing, really.

Once again, she flicked a glance across the room. The guy was watching her again. He grinned, then scribbled on a pad of paper.

Cute. She'd give him that much. Black hair that curled to the collar of his blue wool sweater, one dimple decorating the side of his smile, the facial symmetry of a classical Greek sculpture.

Too handsome for the likes of her. She didn't mind admitting it.

He looked up again, and she looked away.

Men like him didn't really take to Camille, not unless they knew about the size of her bank account, or they had some kind of sick interest in her morbid past. So why even bother? Her book was much more interesting anyway.

Besides, he was probably just another inevitable member of the paparazzi. A hindrance tracking her, splashing the Howard name all over the gossip columns.

Jerks. Couldn't they just leave her alone? It'd been eleven years since her parents, hotel magnates and the Golden Couple of New York City, had been murdered, and the cameras still liked to follow her, speculating about how the horror of finding their bodies had affected her psyche. Lately she'd been lucky, avoiding them, but every once in a while, when the stories about "The Howard Tragedy" would resurface, someone would recognize her and snap away. Articles with updates and pitying comments about her lifestyle would be written.

And that's when the bitter helplessness would grow. Closer to the bursting point. Closer to the end.

She tried to go back to *Sunflowers*. Tried very hard. But...

Hopeless.

The painting's colors were bright enough to cheer her slightly, but something about the sharp green edges—jagged as knife cuts as they surrounded the yellow blooms—cut into her. Something about how the stems curved away from the other flowers—like two limp bodies staring sightlessly at a ceiling—unsettled her.

Her parents.

Their lives bled short, their murderer gone unpunished. The cops knew who had arranged the hit on the only people she had ever loved, but the culprit—a business competitor—had squirmed out of an arrest. Harry Boston was too powerful, too rich to ever be punished for hiring a kid from the streets to break into the Howard penthouse and do the dirty work for him.

Sometimes Camille just wanted to hunt the killer down herself, force a confession out of him as his eyes glowed with the dawning realization that he'd been caught.

A shudder racked Camille's body, and she turned away from the art.

She wasn't the kind of person who lived for revenge. But, God, if she could just bring the dead back to life, she'd sacrifice everything she owned—all the stocks, bonds, properties and businesses.

She would fight to get her parents back, if it were only possible.

Her gaze refocused and, with a start, she saw that Dimple Guy was still looking, concern etched across his features.

Mortified by the rage he must've seen on her face, she rose from the bench, then speed-walked past the silent, shuffling audience.

Was she running from him? she thought. Or herself?

As she passed the man, she kept her gaze fixed straight ahead. But his flicker of movement caught her attention.

He was silently holding up that pad of paper. On it, she found her image. A lone woman slumped on a bench with a Bugs Bunny scarf all but hiding the studious pout of her lips as she stared straight ahead. Her eyes seemed lost, guarded.

But he'd translated her aloofness into a comfortable dignity, had made her seem even sort of…pretty.

Now she found herself doing the inspecting, curious about his work. About how he'd gotten *this* out of what she saw in the mirror every morning.

She removed one side of her headphones, hearing the drone of the tour guide's voice as he continued, halfway abandoned.

"You want money or something?" she asked, not sure what else to say.

He remained seated on his bench, leaning back to stretch his legs and cross his ankles. Then he reconsidered his artwork.

"Never thought myself good enough to earn a living at this, much less a compliment."

He spoke with a British accent. A local?

Camille merely nodded, said, "Good for you," and started to leave, quickly, before she had to explain who she was or why she wanted to get away from him.

"No, don't tell me," he said, reaching out to tug on the flap of her long, deceptively blasé coat, stopping her. "All of this tortuous labor, and it's for nothing?"

Was he hitting on her? *Him?* Prince Hottie?

Camille couldn't remember the last time she'd had a quality conversation with a man. Or when she'd pulled her head out of a textbook long enough to notice the interest of one.

Sigh. The perils of an eternal student.

"I think," she said, "you drew a different girl on that paper there. Maybe she's still around. Somewhere."

He pulled a charming, addled face, glancing at the picture. At her.

"No. You're one and the same." He flashed the full force of his smile, dark-brown eyes crinkling at the tips, then stuck out a hand. "Griffin Montfort, visual poet and museum skulker."

Tentatively, she accepted his gesture. The audio tour guide talked in one ear, just like her conscience, distracting her from this fleeting meet-and-greet.

"Camille Howard," she said, making quick work out of the shaking ritual. When she'd finished, she stuck her hand in a coat pocket. He hadn't reacted to her name— a good sign. "You make a living at drawing? I thought you said…"

"Looks like you've caught me." He dropped the pad on the bench next to him, by a laptop computer bag and an unopened copy of the *Times*. "It's crap. Really, I'm a layabout. Or so I've been told."

"Oh, no. Your work is really good. It's just…"

Her tongue seemed to wrap around itself again in the awkward haste to be semicool about his attentions.

Maybe she should just seem flattered, then make a graceful exit before he realized that the quiet beauty he'd drawn didn't resemble the one standing two feet in front of him.

"Hold on," he said. "Didn't mean to put you off. I only thought that if I told you I designed Internet sites you'd think I was an absolute git. Artists are much more mysterious."

"Hmm," Camille said again, her flirtatious banter tapped out already.

"And here I thought I was doing a brilliant job of pulling." Griffin shook his dark head. "I'll have to find new ways to meet girls."

"I'm sure it's not a problem for you."

"It depends on the quality of them."

Camille actually felt herself blushing again. He had to be some kind of reporter, sitting here flattering her like this.

How could she get out without being rude?

She aimed herself toward the exit, balancing her body away from him. He must've read her intention to scoot.

"The Death of Arthur," he said.

Swaying back toward him, she clutched her book with one hand, fully taking off her headphones with the other. She hooked them around the CD player's strap and shut off the program.

Now this was something she could deal with. Shop talk. "You've read *Morte d'Arthur?*"

"No. In all honesty, *you* interest me, Camille Howard. Earlier, when you were reading and not looking at those sunflowers like they were ghosts with their hair ablaze, I was taking you in. I fancy how your eyes widened while you followed the story, and how you stood out in this room from all the other zombie-like aficionados. Why don't you sit down with me?"

"I've got to go." Her pulse winged. Nerves. Attraction?

Lifting an eyebrow, he absently traced a finger over

her image on the paper—her face, neck, arm. Camille's skin awakened, tickling against the thin silk of her long undershirt. Reminding her of how long it'd been since she'd been touched by anyone.

Undone, she talked, filling the loaded silence. "Really, I'm meeting some friends. At the gym. You know, working off some of the day's tension."

And the demons. Always the demons.

The stain of blood on her memories, the sight of empty eyes staring through her as she entered her parents' suite that one fateful day.

"Hey." His voice was soft, careful.

Even so, she blinked, donning the mental armor of protection. Hoping he couldn't see past the shield of her gaze.

"See, I'd be boring company." She hugged her book to her chest. "My mind's everywhere these days. Tintagel, Glastonbury—"

"I knew it. You're a King Arthur groupie." He pointed to his temple and nodded.

"Yes, smart boy." She couldn't help laughing. Might as well stay a minute longer, even though she hadn't lied about the gym. But it wasn't as if her friend the punching bag would mind her tardiness.

"College student?" he asked.

"Doctoral candidate. Anthropology with an emphasis on folklore." She allowed the book to slip away from her chest, back down to her side. Her words tumbled comfortably now that she was on firm ground. "I'm here looking for a dissertation topic. I'm interested in how tales and legends shape a modern society, and I thought the Arthurian stories would be a good basis for my research."

"We get a lot of you romantic Yanks."

Camille shrugged. "I know. That's the problem. The more I think about it, the more I believe my idea has been done to death."

"At least you get to prance about merry ol' England." Griffin Montfort gestured to the seat next to him, an adorably hopeful expression on his face. "I can be a hell of a historian—if you'll believe that I'm a decent sort of chap and allow me to offer my expertise."

Panic at the thought of attachment—even one that might only last for a short time—invaded her. It sparked a blinding flash of loneliness, leaving her flailing inside.

"But you don't even know me," she said, realizing how lame it sounded.

Every day regular women met guys they didn't know. They didn't freak out or invent excuses to leave.

Was she that in love with solitude? Why couldn't she step out of her comfort zone, just this once?

"You're a tough one," he said, reaching for the portrait. "And I know when I'm beaten. Here, it's yours. A souvenir. You can go back to your horses and rodeos and tell everyone about the poor Bloomsbury bloke whose heart you destroyed."

"Enough with the melodrama." Camille glanced at him sidelong. "How did you know I've lived in Texas?"

"Your twangy accent. And I've done some traveling. I've been to a steak barbecue. I'm also ashamed to admit that I watch *Dallas* reruns. Besides, isn't Texas the only state in the U.S.?" He held out his drawing. "And it was a lucky guess, Lady Tex."

The quick nickname made her smile. Really smile.

She accepted his sketch, inspected it again. In a burst of something that might've been flirtation, she nodded semiplayfully—well, the most playful she could get, anyway—and pretended to analyze the shading of her hair, the strong, clean lines of her face.

"If I were a princess of England, I suppose this could hang in the National Portrait Gallery."

There. Trying to connect hadn't been so hard, especially since he was grinning at her as she peeked over the top edge.

God, that dimple.

"Then I pass muster?" he asked.

She paused, swallowed. "I suppose you do."

Did he realize she wasn't just talking about his artistic bent?

Heart skipping against her breastbone, Camille Howard took a deep breath, sat down and filled the empty space next to the Englishman.

And that's where it began.

They laughed and talked for the next four hours. He walked her to the tube station and through Hyde Park. Dropped her off at the luxurious entrance of the Dorchester, where she was staying in the Audley Suite with its French Empire opulence. He promised to ring her the next day.

Camille was surprised when he did.

She was stunned when it happened time after time, too, especially after she told him about her glamorous parents and the Howard name, which he hadn't connected to her at first, thank goodness, since he was more into movies than accidental celebrities or tabloids. Gradually, she also told him about the fortune, the fractured family ties that remained after her parents had "passed away." How she had no interest in running any of the family businesses that'd been left to her.

Even though she hadn't told him the ugliest parts, for the first time in her life, she smiled when she stretched awake in the mornings.

She couldn't have predicted that, three months later, she'd take him with her to rural Romania where she would interview the peasants about their legends and contained fears.

Little did she know she'd be confronting her own monsters in this place where vampires were said to roam.

Little did she know that, even though she'd finally rediscovered light in England, she'd battle darkness in Transylvania.

Chapter 3

Present

The next evening, Sargent's Jeep roared over the rough forest road as he followed three military-green Humvees through the Borgo Pass. The sun had darkened over the jagged edge of trees, the crest of hills, the occasional remains of an ancient, skeletal fortress.

The simple wooden crosses lining the fields.

"You might consider backing off," said Ashe.

Sargent spared an unconcerned glance at his friend. Hemp clothing, scraggly platinum hair and Birkenstocks.

A disciple of good, Sarge thought.

He'd hired the Wiccan for his protective talents, his

skill in keeping the vamps away with all those crystals, herbs and candles. Ironically, Ashe—or Todd Crandall, as he'd been known before taking his magickal name— had been the medic attached to Sarge's Delta Force squadron.

Together, they'd gotten to know some vamps.

"Want me to back off?" Sarge relaxed his hand over the steering wheel. "Nah. That woman needs to know I'm right here, dogging her every step. Scientists. Know-it-alls. Just a matter of time before she finds out that vamps won't sit still for experimental prodding and poking."

"I meant for you to back off the Humvee, Sarge. You're driving up their tailpipe."

"Hey, just keeping an eye on the cargo."

Their headlights bounced over the gleam of long, silver items in this last military vehicle. The second Humvee carried the same objects. Coffins. Or—as Beatrix Grasu had explained to him before the convoy left Vasile this morning—"life-sustaining units." The women planned to house their specimens in the specially constructed caskets and deliver them to their lab, where Dr. Grasu, who'd been left behind, would house the beasts.

Crazies. Even the apple-cheeked village women in the lead Humvee who'd been recruited for the mission.

A flash of taillights forced Sarge to jam on the brakes, to focus on his surroundings by wiping thoughts of Camille Howard's delusions from his mind.

"Why're they stopping?" he asked. "I don't feel anything around here."

"Neither do I." Ashe leaned forward in his seat as a Humvee door bolted open in the near distance.

Miss Bleeding Heart appeared to their left, bundled in a body-hugging jacket and a headset that contained a powerful light. She also wore a utility belt that carried some of the nasty items Dr. Grasu had told him about when they'd had a drink—or six—together last night.

A long wand, two pistols, rope and arm restraints.

Another belt dipped over the first, gunslinger style. This one was decorated by strange silver, oval objects that Dr. Grasu hadn't gotten around to explaining since she'd passed out after that final whiskey shot.

As Miss B.H. wandered farther away, she lifted a hand to her ear. The other wrist was raised so she could look at that heavy-duty watch of hers. It was some sort of tracker, he knew.

Ashe spoke. "She's in such pain."

Sarge didn't respond. Even though he didn't have Ashe's empathetic skills, he could've guessed as much. If there was one thing he knew, it was pain.

"She thinks," the witch added, "the only way she'll heal is if she finds those vampires."

"And bring them out of the wilderness to hunt in a much broader field at the same time." Sarge opened the Jeep's door, alighted. "You remember the night those first vamps ripped the throats out of half our team before we knew what was happening? Then there was Barrow and the bayou and—"

"I remember."

"Enough said." Sarge raided his arsenal and loaded up, preparing his flamethrower, his lucky aspen-wood stake, a crossbow that shot holy-water-dipped arrows.

"I've got to stop her before she rattles the food chain around these parts. Dr. Grasu, bless that ivory-tower brain of hers, didn't understand my point of view, either, when we talked last night."

"You should've been resting, gathering your strength, just like our Ms. Howard. And me."

"A good drink does wonders for the soul." Sarge patted his machete. "If you have one."

"Hold up, Sarge."

Ashe took out a bottle of essential oils and meditated over the mixture. Sarge respectfully waited while his partner chanted, then anointed him with the contents.

"'An ye harm none, do as thou wilt.'" The former medic nodded at Sarge. "Do what you want as long as you don't hurt anyone, man. And one more thing."

"What now?"

The Wiccan concentrated, shook his head. "You really need to be careful. I mean it. I've got a feeling, and it's not necessarily about the vamps, Sarge. Watch out."

"Hey, Ashe. Who you talking to here?"

Sarge grinned, hefted up his crossbow and started to follow Howard, knowing Ashe would now light a candle and meditate to see if he could connect with whatever Howard was tracking out here.

When Sarge caught up, she'd frozen at the foot of a steep hill, gaze fixed on her watch. Fallen petals from a hovering plum tree surrounded her, and Sargent stopped, pulse picking up speed just from looking at her.

Why? Who the hell knew. Maybe it was her spirit that kind of stirred him up. Whatever it was, Sarge didn't have time for it.

As her tracker thudded softly, a wolf howled in the distance. A sliver of moonlight shifted. Muted pale moonlight coated her bladed cheekbones, the red of her braided hair.

Much to his dismay, Sarge's blood thudded, making him a little light-headed. Dammit, he'd been trained to control his heartbeat, so what was the deal now?

"Could your heart beat a little louder, please?" she said. "They can't hear it in Bangkok."

And here he'd thought they'd been getting along so much better than yesterday. Granted they hadn't seen each other *since* yesterday, but he thought he'd sensed some tolerance in the way she avoided him.

"That's how your watch works?" he asked, ignoring her curtness. "Heartbeats?"

"Bea theorizes that their blood is a different viscosity than ours. It's thinner, so their hearts don't have to work as hard to pump. My sensor picks up the slower rhythmic vibrations within a certain proximity." She glanced up, her headset beam piercing him with light. "We hope."

Then her hand flew up to her ear again, redirecting the lamp's glare. "What, Doc?"

Sargent paused just as she did, trying to feel the vamps himself.

I'll be damned, he thought. There was something here. Faint, like a change in the hum of air around him. A niggling electricity that disturbed the hairs on his skin.

Maybe the range of her tracker was superior to his own usually dependable intuition. But his inner radar was pretty good about telling him which vamps could be spared and used to destroy others. It was helpful in predicting attacks, too.

Howard was talking to Beatrix again. "I think I have something, but—"

"You do," Sarge said, unwilling to desert his instincts.

They both peered around at the ever darkening forest—the coves of pines, oaks, beeches. A hiding place in every patch of huddled foliage. Too bad they couldn't have hunted by day. If he knew anything about vamps, it was that they were quicker at night—given that they had the ability to face the light at all.

After touching her earpiece three times, she spoke in Romanian. "Load up, ladies."

Then she grabbed one of her small, unidentifiable pistols, checked it and put it up to her neck.

"What the hell?" He reached toward her.

Too late. She'd already fired it with a muted click.

"Adrenaline shot, Sarge. The women are taking them, too. The doc and I came up with a nondegradable formula—"

"The last thing I want to hear is lab babble. You just freakin' shot yourself."

She leaned back her head, blew out a breath, shimmied her body with the awakening energy, probably just to irk him. "Twenty minutes of enhanced strength. I'd ask if you want one, but a manly man like you would be offended. And stow your playthings. We're not going to need flamethrowers or…good God, you're a walking death machine."

"I'm used to heavy equipment." He walked away, then closed his eyes, concentrating.

The electronic thunk of her tracker intensified, meaning she was right behind him. Sarge could discern four more approaching now, as well.

The village women, minus the three who'd volunteered to drive the Humvees.

Blump, blump…went the devices.

She was walking past him, and he followed, eyes still shut, trusting himself.

"Where are you?" he heard her whisper. And he knew she wasn't talking to him.

He could sense the anxiety in her question. The captives couldn't last much longer. That's what she had to be thinking. Time was short.

None to waste.

Sarge only hoped those captives didn't realize they had choices, other means to stay alive. Hopefully, they were as dumb as snail shit and just as easy to terminate.

While being led to the north, Howard's tracker grew louder.

"How do we know we're not picking up on one of your precious victims?" he asked, keeping his voice low.

"I *don't* know." She was slightly ahead of him, breathless. The adrenaline was working. "That's why I'm going to take the lead here, okay? You hang back and don't go all cowboy on me."

"This John Wayne just might save your Girl Scout bacon." He aimed a little to the east, gut clenching. "You've got some moxie, coming out here with just a light-saber to fight evil."

Blump, blump, blump, blump... Four trackers echoed just in back of them.

"My UV wand's a little more sophisticated than that," she said, speech quickening. "It emits enough radiation to kill cell membranes. And it doubles as a...well, I guess the peasants might liken it to a cross."

"Not a bad analogy."

He could almost see her shaking her head.

Blump, blump, blump, blump, blump, blump...

"Superstition. Weapons," she said. "We're hunting nature's mutants, Mr. Sargent. Killing machines. One thing Dr. Grasu has taught me is that vampires as the world knows them are fiction. Garlic and holy water are jokes."

"Tell that to the scar on my neck."

"We all have our jewelry." He could tell she'd turned around to address him. "Hey, open your eyes, you fool."

In response, he kept tracking, turning west, wandering several yards farther.

His skin puckered into itself.

Blump blump blump blump blump blump blump blump...

He opened his eyes.

"Sargent!"

Bracing himself, he raised the loaded crossbow. There was a buzzing sound, then a high-pitched, ghoulish cry. Something rushed out of the dark and slammed into him with the force of a wrecking ball, barreling him into the ground, making him lose hold of his weapon.

No breath. Goddammit, no...

It was sniffing at his neck.

Instinctively, he lashed out with an arm, connecting

with a skull, hair catching his wrist. A whoosh of air—copper soaked, blood laced—screamed past his ear.

Just as suddenly, the body jerked as a boot connected with its head. A spray of white light cut through the darkness, and Sarge hopped into a crouch. He secured his flamethrower, ready.

"I've got it," Dictator Howard said, brandishing her UV wand. "Put that damned thing away."

An angel with a sword of justice. That's what she was—her posture steel straight, her triumphant face glowing in the brightness. A painting in the art books his zealot mom used to show him before she died.

Through a haze of controlled frenzy, he saw that the village women were surrounding them with their lights, also. In their eyes, he could see the fear, the retribution, the fury of saving their loved ones before the vampires came to them.

His neck wound tearing itself apart with a burning agony, Sarge turned his gaze on the creature.

It looked like a primal beast caught in the split-second flash of a camera's bulb, memorialized in statue stiffness.

Howard had been right about the light having the same effect as a cross. The creature was scared out of its gourd. Fascinated and repulsed into a motionless pose of utter horror.

It was different from the others he'd seen in his career, with a once white nightgown shredded to rags, her plump arm stretched above her forehead, shielding herself from the inevitable. Under the shadow of that arm, her eyes glowed red, feral, adapted to night vision. Her dark-brown hair was matted, braided with twigs. Her skin was baby-pink, flushed with the blood of men, and her teeth…

Fangs. Bared at Camille Howard.

The vamp let out another grating, ear-shattering screech, and Howard calmly shoved the wand at her, grabbing the arm restraints on her belt with her other hand.

The monster's mouth froze, lips twisted.

Transfixed by the light.

"I know who this girl is," Howard said. "Her name is Ecaterina. She was a Juni villager. I interviewed her about the vampire legends, and she said she'd heard about a tribe of males who live in the Carpathians, and maybe they'd visit instead, one day."

Sarge knew about that vamp tribe, all right. But did Howard realize that it was made up of the few males who'd escaped the *strigoiaca* over the years?

Easier if she *didn't* know.

He stood, hand on the machete. Clearly, this vamp was all animal, lacking in human intelligence. Worthless, really.

"Let's put her out of our misery. It's easier to handle one than a whole crowd of them."

"Don't." Howard leveled a lethal glare his way, her headset light blinding him. "When the *strigoiaca* attacked Juni, they lost one of their numbers. It was like they all heard the vampire's death scream because, seconds later, they got Ecaterina. Turned her into one of them. She hasn't been a vampire for that long. Maybe she can still talk." She turned to the monster. "Ecaterina?"

Sarge wasn't surprised when all they got was a blank, red stare. A hiss, like a cornered viper. She coiled her body into a protective ball, cowering.

Howard sighed, walked around to the creature's back side. Sarge did, too.

"Look." She pointed to the monster's spine, where clear, gel-like wings fluttered fruitlessly. "Fins, kind of like the ones seahorses have. That's how they get their speed. Bea thinks adrenaline powers the motion. They don't fly, per se, but they can zip around like lightning. Ecaterina's are smaller than the ones on Bea's corpse, probably because our girl here isn't done mutating."

"Interesting. Now let's kill it."

"I wonder if she's out hunting for food or something. Sustenance for the males?" She knitted her brows, checked her watch. "I don't see any other vampires around, but we must be close."

His machete scraped as he pulled it out of the sheath. "Nosferatu 101 is over now, Howard. Let's get this done and move on."

But he never had the chance to follow through.

Her UV wand blinked out.

Sizzle, snap. Darkness, except for the team's innocuous headset beams.

The vamp flinched, scanned the other lights.

"Reveka?" barked Howard, summoning a villager.

The woman, or maybe it was a bear wearing a parka, stepped forward, sternly pointing her own wand at the vamp.

"I need you to keep her here while I bind her."

Mocking them, Reveka's wand lost power, too.

Sarge rolled his eyes. "Real life ain't exactly a laboratory. Is it?"

"Damned batteries," Howard muttered. In Romanian, she shouted, "Dart pistols!"

Two more lights fizzled out until there was only one. *One.*

The vamp hissed, the odds greatly decreased.

Most of the women, including Howard, had by now abandoned their wands, trading them for the sedative pistols.

Finally, thought Sarge, gripping his machete. Some righteous destruction.

The slender dandelion of a villager who held the last UV trembled as Howard beckoned her closer. "Hold steady, Delia," she said in the woman's language.

In the meantime, Howard grabbed her own dart pistol, aimed for the vamp's neck.

Then the last UV zapped off.

Immediately, the whir of vampire fins filled the silence. In the chaos of streaking headset beams, all Sarge could see were trees slashed by strokes of light. All he could hear were Romanian curses.

He knew he'd be the first target. He just had to listen. To focus.

Za-room.

The vamp flew past him, and he raised the machete.

Come on, he thought, moving within five feet of the action. Let's spar a little.

A yelp of rage split the night, and the headset lights bobbed, gathered on Howard and the vamp.

She had the beast against a tree, forearm pressed against her windpipe. It'd been the vamp's cry—that wailing, nails-down-a-blackboard shriek. Howard flicked the dart pistol against her neck, but then the tables turned.

Time happened in something like slow motion. The vamp opened her mouth and, with the slimy grace of an eel slicing through water, her long tongue whipped out, heading for him again. The end was pointed, dagger-like.

As Sarge dived backward, out of range, Howard shoved the heel of her palm upward, blocking the attack, losing her balance in the process.

That tongue had almost gotten him. Would it have speared through his neck? Sucked the blood out of him?

As the vamp grabbed Howard by the jacket and spun her around so the huntress was against the tree now, Sarge sheathed the machete and went for a longer-range weapon.

The crossbow.

He searched the ground, found it.

The other women were helpless, inexperienced, adrenalized, clearly afraid to take a shot with their pistols in case they hit Howard. One of the braver ones, a tall, braided teen, ran at the vamp, weapon extended.

In the instant it took Sarge to lift the weapon to his shoulder, she'd already made his shot unsafe. Dammit.

The vamp merely slapped the peasant away. The woman hit the nearest tree with a sick crunch.

Two peasants sprinted to their friend's aid while the other two backed off, staring, their frozen headset lights giving Sarge a safer chance at hitting his target.

That's when Howard took an elbow and slammed it into the vamp's jaw, not that it did much good. But it bought some time. Enough for her to shove one of those oval things from her second belt over the vamp's mouth. The monster clawed the air, furious, as she latched on to Howard and lifted her into the air, above her face.

Clear, thought Sarge. He pulled the trigger.

At the last second, the vamp angled her body, causing the arrow to zip right past her, into the tree trunk.

Damn. Sarge hadn't missed since his Shooting House training days. Shame boiled through his veins as he reloaded.

"No!" yelled Howard. "She doesn't have a weapon now."

He marveled that she still wanted the thing alive.

Her necklace dangled over the vamp's face, and the monster stopped. Tilted her head. Observed the ring.

Sniffed it.

The moon broke through the trees, revealing a look of naked heartbreak on Howard's face. Then the light rolled over, welcoming the near darkness back.

Without warning, the vamp hurled Howard to the side. She skidded along the dirt, crashed into the two women who hadn't run to the aid of their other friend. They quickly recovered their balance and yanked their boss to a stand.

The vamp slowly turned toward Sargent.

Drawing on all his calm and training, Sarge fired.

With ease, the vamp reached up. Caught the arrow in midair. Found it useless, then dropped it.

Okay. Not his day for projectiles.

He drew his machete again, positioning for the kill.

With her hungry eyes burned onto him, the beast ripped at the device on her mouth, digging the skin around her lips to a pulp.

Now this was the definition of pissed.

She shook her head, again trying to remove the oval restraint. Unsuccessful, she stopped, threw back her head in a silent scream.

Then she exploded toward him, eyes fiery infernos.

But he was waiting.

At least, he would've been if the dart hadn't pierced the side of his neck, knocking him to his knees with the power of whatever Howard had dabbed on the tip.

As a flurry of more darts caught the vamp in midattack, she slumped to the ground, jerked, then stilled.

All the women kept their stances, pistols aimed. Emptied.

He remembered how, yesterday, Camille Howard had lined up the female peasants, tested them with firearms to see who could shoot the apples from a grove of nearby trees. Remembered how Dr. Grasu had told him that many of these women had been raised to use pistols because of the revolutionary turmoil in Romania over a decade ago.

Remembered how Howard had become inexplicably tolerant of his presence today.

I've been used as goddamned bait, he thought.

Watch out, Ashe had told him. And Sarge hadn't. He'd been too careless, just like the last time a woman had screwed him over.

As he fought dizziness, Howard lowered her dart pistol, strolled toward him.

Damn her. Didn't she understand what she was doing?

With the last of his strength, he tightened his grip on the machete, crawled to the vamp. Raised the blade.

One swift strike of his weapon decapitated what was once a girl named Ecaterina.

Worry about removing her heart later, he thought, crumpling to the forest floor, the sweet stench of dirt lulling him to reluctant rest.

But before the void claimed him, he focused on her. The latest woman to betray him.

Surrounded by a fuzzy halo, growing mistier by the second, she bent to a knee. Watched as he grew weaker. "All I wanted to do was stop you," she said, voice soft, gaze filled with something close to regret. Then she leaned in closer. "But congratulations anyway. One vamp down, four to go, right?"

"Damned straight," he whispered. He didn't have the energy for much conviction.

"Wrong." She stood, all hints of remorse gone, a livid figure against the backdrop of night. "When we find the tribe, they're not going to just go after you men—they're going to want to replace the female they've lost, just as Ecaterina was the replacement for the one killed in Juni."

Waves of dizziness washed over him. He wanted to tell her that killing the vamp—all vamps eventually—was the right thing to do. But he couldn't move his lips anymore.

"Well done, stud," she said. "You've just made every woman on this mission a target."

Her image was swallowed by a black hole where nothing existed anymore.

Where he didn't have to think about how a woman with a baby ring around her neck could offer him up for sacrifice.

Chapter 4

London, approximately one year ago
Three months before the strigoiaca *came to Juni*

Camille's chest burned as she ran past the Georgian town houses on Cartwright Gardens, dizzy from fleeing the man at the Euston Station tube stop.

He'd been aiming at her.

Aiming a camera. She'd blinked in the sudden flash. Captured. Knowing, once again, they'd found her.

So she'd fled. Hidden herself away.

She ran and ran and…yes. There it was, straight ahead, across from the quaint neighborhood gardens.

Safety. Refuge from the memories of *that day*.

She darted up the steps to the redbrick building, crashing against the mahogany door, pounding on it.

"Griff?" she yelled.

Then she glanced in back of her, expecting to see the photographer dogging her heels.

It didn't take but a few minutes for Griff to throw open the door, his eyebrows drawn together in confusion.

"Not to be rude, but…" She brushed past him, slammed the door, moved to a lace-curtained window where she could peek at the street.

All she saw was the hint of evening fog. Twilight was a shade away, lending the window glass a spring-in-England chill as she brushed her knuckles against it.

"Usually," Griff said from behind her, "after I'm dating a girl for two weeks, she's bolting out of my flat instead of into it."

Camille's breathing was just now smoothing out, making her responding laugh one big pant. She held a hand over her heart and reached behind her with the other, seeking him. Still, she watched the street.

He slid his fingers over hers, warming them, his body drawing closer as he also looked out the window. The scent of him overwhelmed Camille—Ivory soap and musk. He wrapped his other arm around her waist and nuzzled aside her hair. Then he kissed the side of her neck. The soft pressure of his lips measured the tempo of her fluttering pulse.

"Hey," he said, speaking into her skin.

"Hey." She smiled at the little greeting pattern they'd already fallen into.

Hey. I love seeing you again.

It was so much easier to "hey" than to tell him about her deepest secrets, the paparazzi, her parents. Still too early to scare him off with her horror stories. She was too greedy for these addictive, invading emotions, the mindless yearning to be with him during the day when she was studying and he was at home designing his Web sites. The giddy insecurity of never having felt this crazy about a man before.

Total infatuation.

With a last look out the window, she turned around, skimmed her hands over his shoulders and slipped her fingers into all that dark, thick hair. At the same time, she guided him away from the window.

He seemed to gauge her for a second, taking in the disheveled slant of her long coat, the slight layer of sweat on her forehead. "What made you run?"

"I wanted to see you, is all." *Change the subject.*

She leaned over, rubbed her mouth over his.

Persuaded, he smoothed his hands over her hair. Her face. Then he officially welcomed her with a kiss, sending quiet electric shocks through her body as he pulled her into the parlor. There, sensuous, melancholy music ebbed, flowed, echoing their caresses.

She came up for breath, lazily focusing on the TV.

White silk bedsheets. A brooding, tuxedoed man leaning over a reclining woman, preparing to bite her neck.

Griff's mouth brushed against Camille's jugular vein, and she startled back to the reality of him.

"Any luck at the university library?" he asked.

"No good research today." Teasing, she stretched

against the length of him. He responded, hardening against her lower stomach.

"Griff?" she asked hopefully.

An ache, a slow twisting between her legs, getting her ready. Willing.

"Not that I'm easy, but I'm not a blushing virgin, either. When…?"

"Tex, I'm not in a rush."

She shifted against him, feeling evidence to the contrary. Whenever there'd been a man in her life, she'd wasted no time. Her background—her parents, the paparazzi—normally sped things along because the breakup always came too soon.

Griff stroked his thumbs over her temples. "I'm not sure that what I'd like to say fits into the 'less-than-one-month' rules. But…" He took a deep breath, exhaled.

"Is this one of those bad conversations?"

He laughed, coasted his palms from her head down to her shoulders, underneath her coat and to her hips. "I suppose this might be a good time to let on that I'm not all that brilliant at having a girlfriend."

Oh. Here it came.

"Tex, what I'm trying to say is that…before…my mates and I weren't all that serious about, um, women."

Was he blushing?

"So I'm some kind of record for you?" she asked.

"You could say that. In all truth, you seemed like a bit of a challenge in the gallery."

Uh-oh.

"But then…" He trailed off.

This was suddenly a new Griff.

bluster and was revealing a new side of himself. Camille was touched by his guarded vulnerability.

"I know this is difficult," she said, trying to make light of the situation so it'd be easier for him. But guilt was stabbing her, because she wasn't brave enough to expose anything major to *him* yet.

He assumed a sheepish grin. "I'm trying to say that you're not like the others. There was that soulful look on your face while you inspected *Sunflowers*. Remember?"

Green leaves, red slashes on skin. Wilted stems, lifeless bodies.

"I remember," she whispered.

"That day, I wanted to take you in, make you feel better. I can't say that's ever happened before."

A bright yellow warmth spread through her, burning away some of the deeply seated frustration.

"I should tell you something, too," she said.

Don't forget, she thought. Sunflowers can also cut. They can also make you bleed.

Why was she going to tell him this? Because he'd opened up to her?

"Tell me anything." One of his fingers crept under her sweater to loop into the rim of her jeans. Fingertips brushed her waist, warm and wicked.

The intimacy jolted her system, and she hesitated. *Do it.*

"That first day we met," she said, "we let out just enough of ourselves to retain some distance, didn't we? And you told me more as the days went on."

A shadow passed over his dark eyes. When Griff

was young, his family had been poor. So poor that, when he was ten, his parents had sent him, a third child and extra mouth to feed, from Manchester to London to live with relatives who wanted to open a fish-and-chips shop. They didn't have children of their own, and Griff would work for them, free, in exchange for a new family.

"You never saw your parents again," she said. "Just like me. But for different reasons."

Just say it.

She exhaled. "There's this picture of me when I was fourteen. I'd been in the papers before, because of society functions I attended with my parents. But this photo was different. I was staring at the camera and there's blood all over my hands, my face…"

Tenderly, Griff took off her coat and led her to sit on his overstuffed couch. He stroked her hair while she swallowed, recovered.

Someone on the TV screamed. When Camille turned to see who it was, she found a woman bending over the victim's dead body, slashes of red against white silk sheets. The actress wailed again, withering from pure agony.

Though Camille had spent all her life avoiding such pain, she couldn't tear her eyes away this time.

"I'm the one who found my parents. I'd just come home from winning first place at the science fair." She smiled, recalling Mom and Dad's pride in all the stupid inventions she'd produce daily.

Then the smile disappeared. "I kept trying to wake them up, but… There was blood splattered all over the walls. Some paparazzi managed to sneak into our pent-house while the cops secured the crime scene. And that's when they got me."

On the TV, the woman stood, strolled to a side table laden with food, picked up a long carving knife.

Camille continued softly. "Right away, Uncle Philip took over my parents' hotels and media outlets. I was shuffled off to a nanny who raised me like I was her own kid, thank God for her. She remarried and took me with her to Houston. My uncle was relieved, to say the least."

It was so much easier focusing on the TV, where the woman climbed into a carriage. It traveled away from her mansion, swallowed by mist and darkness.

"All that time," Camille added, "I kept asking Uncle Phillip when they were going to make an arrest. When would I get to testify and see the bastard put away?"

"Did they catch him?"

The TV woman came to a crypt, opened the door. Her shadow pooled over a gaping coffin.

Camille's mouth went dry. "No, they didn't. There were stories about how one of our business competitors hired a street guy to take care of my parents. The detectives on the case thought they had the guilty party—Harry Boston, a competitor—but his money got him off the hook. I believe to this day Boston is the one, because a few months after the murders, my uncle sold our radio stations to the guy, just like he'd been waiting to pounce. He'd been after the properties for years. Uncle Phillip just shook his head and said, 'There's nothing I can do, Camille. No concrete evidence. Nothing.' So I hired an army of PIs and..."

"Still nothing. Tex…"

"I wish I had the strength to go after the killer myself."

Hands fisting, she couldn't look at Griff, couldn't stop watching the woman on TV.

The slayer raised her arms over her head in preparation, screamed in fury, then stabbed the vampire.

But the thing came back to life.

Griff cupped her jaw, angling her back to face him. With wonder, she saw that he was in anguish for her.

Overcome, she held his knuckles to her cheek, trying to make *him* feel better now.

"You know what I'm talking about, don't you?" she whispered. "The impotence at not being able to do anything? Don't you feel just a little of it with your parents? Don't you want them to pay for giving you up?"

His eyes widened at the barely restrained rage in her voice. "I've accepted it. Certainly, I feel the need to hang on to everything I've earned—my auto, my business—because I'm afraid it'll disappear, but…"

"But you never dream of justice?"

He looked surprised.

"Don't worry." Camille tried to laugh, but it was a wasted effort. "All my therapists tell me to play out my revenge scenarios on punching bags. And they seem to think I seek logic and order in all my books, too."

"I can't say I blame you."

"You can't? You don't think I'm going to explode from repressed fury one day?"

"I would hope not. At least, not in the parlor. I'm rather fond of my hard-earned, yet meager, furnishings."

"Cheeky." She nestled against his chest, shivered as his arms enveloped her.

It was only now, at the end of her confession, that she realized her heart was racing.

"If you decide to hang around with me," she said, "you'll have to get used to the media attention. They dog me when they need some lurid copy."

"I like a proper fight now and again."

She hesitated, told him about today's photographer, then added, "I usually leave when they find me."

"Then I suppose it's time for a vacation." He played with a strand of her hair. "Where to? The Algarve coast in Portugal? Or maybe Monte Carlo, since I have a rich girlfriend who can afford such trips."

"Sounds good, but wherever we go, I've got to get started on my dissertation."

When her attention drifted back to the vampire movie, he noticed.

"I can't work without the telly noise," he said. "*Curse of the Blood Count.* A classic. Say, perhaps we could go to some Transylvanian castle. Aren't there some bloodsucker legends you could research?"

From the tone of his voice, she knew he was kidding. They'd only been dating two weeks, after all. Two intense, female-version-of-blue-balls weeks.

But he'd gotten her mind to spinning.

"From a purely sociological standpoint, that would be fascinating," she said, watching as the fanged one was fully resurrected by a drink of the actress's fake blood. "How have vampire legends shaped the lives of the most superstitious people in Romania? Peasants, villagers…"

"You *are* serious?"

Her mouth was running before her brain had a chance to catch up. "Why don't you come with me?"

He froze. Didn't answer. But she knew. Not only had she overstepped their second-inning-of-a-relationship bounds, she'd also suggested studying *vampires*. The dead come back to life—a feat her parents could never manage.

But what if she could find answers about death while still remaining far away from it?

Imagine. This could be the first step out of her perpetual hiding. This could be a new leaf turning over....

Warming to the idea, she rushed on. "It'd be an adventure. You can bring your laptop and work while I interview and research. No pressure, though. But they say you learn a lot about another person when you travel with them. I mean, I know we've barely started seeing each other, but I'd be leaving in a couple of months or so. There's time to think about it."

No response.

"Then again," she added uncertainly, "it's just an idea."

Griff appeared to consider her invitation. "Let's see. Traipse about the globe with a beautiful swashbucklerette or remain in London for the flood of tourists. Impossible choice. But..." He nodded, grinned.

"Really?"

"Really. Yet there's one condition." He stood, gently dumping her on the couch.

"Where're you off to?"

He bounded up the steep town house stairs, then reemerged a few minutes later. Waiting behind the couch, he kept his hands behind his back.

"What do you have?"

After a playful pause, he reached over and spread open his fingers to reveal a tiny ring. A baby ring. Tarnished golden metal, with a fake sapphire in the middle. He'd looped a chain through the center.

"I know you're used to better," he said softly, "but... Put up your hair."

She did, shivering at the rhythm of his breath on her neck as he fastened the chain. "It's beautiful, Griff."

"It's got superpowers, protective properties money just can't buy. This ring will protect you from vampires or nightmares or...whatever might trouble milady."

A flush heated her body. "This is yours?"

"Yeah. I wanted to save the bauble in case I ever had children. And, I have to say, it wasn't seeming too likely." He stopped himself.

Until you came along.

He didn't say it, but she heard it.

She pulled him down for a thank-you kiss. This one embraced all the words she was too afraid to say out loud. All the I-think-I-could-love-you's and lacy endearments that usually chased men away.

This one was slick with passion, urgent with a growing hunger. This one led them both to the couch, then to a floor strewed with sweaters and jeans.

Then to the joining of their bodies, the sweat-steamed emotion of entwined limbs, groans and promises.

Later that night, as he rested his head on her chest,

their legs wrapped together, their heartbeats connected, he whispered to her.

"I'll be where you are, Lady Tex. Always."

And two and a half months later, they arrived in Transylvania.

Chapter 5

"He is coming to," said Reveka's voice from ten yards away.

The volunteer hunter had the honor of watching over Dipwad, as Camille now fondly called the drugged Sargent.

Behind one of the Humvees, Camille was standing under a portable light. Hands gloved, she inspected the tongue in their dead vampire's detached head while Delia, one of the village women, recorded her findings on a video camera.

Camille answered Reveka in Romanian. "Tell him 'Good morning, sunshine' for me."

A grumpy—no, make that a really *enraged* voice—bellowed through the night air, "Where's that bitch?"

"I'm in the kitchen cooking, darling," Camille said.

Actually, a gurney laden with a headless vampire probably wouldn't be something the Iron Chef would cotton to. But, seeing as they were still in the same woods where Dipwad had so conveniently blown her plans, she wasn't complaining. She'd make soup of the situation yet.

Before leaving the village this morning, Camille and Bea had decided that using Sarge as bait would be a good strategy. In fact, though Dr. Grasu liked the mercenary in a drinking-buddy kind of way, she'd supported Camille's idea of using him and his skills until they found Griff and the vampires.

Camille could almost hear the doc's voice early last night: "We knock him cold again when we must capture the specimens. Mr. Sargent will only want the kill, and that presents a problem."

It really had been the best way to deal with Sargent. And it'd worked, drawing one of the vampires to them.

Ecaterina. Sweet, undead—but now dead—girl.

Camille sighed under a surgical mask coated with Vicks to mask the stench of death, then set the decapitated head next to its corpse in a coffin lined with UV bulbs.

If there was one thing she'd learned, it was that these "vampires" weren't undead so much as a different form of life.

But any way you put it, Camille thought, she was still dealing with another corpse.

Her headset fizzled on.

"Can you upload the movies now?" Bea asked from her base in Vasile. "You have told me there are no major differences in the tongue, either, but I would like to see."

"Will do, Aunt Bea." Doc was so cute when she got excited about her job. "I'll send the images shortly and preserve the remains so you can cut her open yourself."

As Camille dismissed Delia, she stripped off the gloves and the mask, placed them in a covered container in the Humvee. "I'm signing off now because your booze buddy is conscious and cranky."

Bea's voice crackled in transmission. "Think on what we talked about."

Knocking him cold, once again, when it came time to capture the vampires. "I will. Sweet dreams, Doc."

From a distance, a wolf howled. Another one answered.

Camille touched her headset three times, changing frequencies, contacting her team to make sure they were still awake and on watch with their trackers. Then, satisfied, she set about getting the autopsy files to Bea via laptop computer.

All too soon, she heard Sargent's slurred voice behind her. "Thanks for the nap, Howard."

Casually, she turned away from the computer. Found him leaning against a pine tree, stripped of his weapons. Ashe, the Wiccan hippie guy, supported him on one side, holding a broom in the other hand.

The witch-medic had already set the broken arm of one of the Vasile women—Irina, who'd been slammed against a tree during the melee. Next, he was supposedly going to bring up some kind of magick circle to protect them. Then, while everyone slept, he planned to work some spells. Camille guessed that the broom was for doing some magickal cleaning or something.

"Don't look so scared of me," she said to Sarge. "I'm not in an aggressive mood. My adrenaline shot's spent."

He merely stared at her.

Ashe let go of Sarge, seeing if he could stand on his own. In response, the bigger man wavered, causing the Wiccan to steady his partner again.

"So can I leave you two alone while I do my work?" he asked.

The mercenary held up a hand, shooing Ashe away, then wobbled until he grabbed the tree. "What was in that dart?"

"Just a stunning agent. If I recall, you probably wouldn't want me to get all scientific about it. And calm down. I was never going to let you die."

"You used me." He turned to Ashe, pointed a finger. It caused him to sway until he caught his balance again. "And shouldn't you've known that I was going to be bait?"

Ashe's face reddened. Against his shoulder-length moonbeam hair, the shade was startling. "My psychic equipment isn't perfect, Sarge."

Camille could tell he was mortified by his failure. Bea had told her what Ashe did for Sarge—how he used empathic and Wiccan skills to help in protecting his old military buddy and himself during vampire hunts. Even if she had more faith in science than hocus-pocus to get them through this nightmare, he instilled confidence in some of her women who *did* believe in superstition, and that could only help.

"So," she said to Ashe, ignoring Sarge, "you think the *strigoiaca* know we're here?"

"I haven't sensed that they've detected us."

Lucky guess. It'd been a trick question. Last year, back in Juni, a dying vampire had used a different cry, one that had another tonal quality, to summon the rest of its tribe for help. Oddly enough, during the *strigoiaca*'s conquest of the village, they had exhibited a hands-off policy when it came to helping each other capture their prey. As a student, Camille had believed this to be ritualistic behavior, a way for each vampire to prove herself worthy of the tribe.

Or maybe not. The *strigoiaca* were still a mystery to her, and that was a disquieting disadvantage.

Even so, the fact that Ecaterina hadn't emitted an alarmlike cry tonight made Camille feel a little better, giving her reason to believe that the other vampires hadn't been alerted yet.

"We're close to them," Ashe added. "I'm feeling where they are. Stone chambers, gargoyles, wolves…"

"Maybe a castle?" Camille asked. "According to our maps, there's a deserted one almost two miles up the road."

Ashe nodded, smiled. "That's it."

"Are you sure you're right this time?" Sarge put a hand to his neck, covering the spot where Camille had shot him with the dart gun. His bite scar stood out on the other side, a map of never-healed skin. "I wouldn't want to go banging on the wrong door in this neighborhood."

The Wiccan tensed. Even under his loose white clothing, Camille could see the bunching of lean muscles.

But Sarge didn't apologize. He was back to dissecting Camille with his baleful glare.

Shutting out his partner, Ashe turned to Camille. "I'll have my circle up soon. You'll sleep in safety."

A pack of wolves cried in the distance, causing them all to pause, to listen. To shiver with a chill brought on by the unearthly sound.

Then, before she could tell Ashe not to bother with the voodoo, he walked off, using the broom like a staff.

"I think you hurt his feelings," Camille said.

"You register feelings?"

If only he knew how sharply. "Don't tell me you're going to pout about the dart. I told you to stay home."

Though his silence stung, she'd done the right thing, dammit. If it saved Griff, the end justified the means.

When Sarge did speak, his voice grated with bitterness. "Let's get something straight. You don't screw with me when it comes to vamps. I know when killing is necessary. Once, in Mexico, I had a run-in with a sucker who killed children for their blood. And in Greece, I had to deal with a group that lured tourists into torture chambers so they could get their jollies while stretching human bodies apart. We're dealing with pure evil with these females, too."

Sarge drew himself up and walked slowly away from his tree. "Your little do-gooder weapons, scientific theories and belief that every creature deserves to live will get *you* killed."

"Not so far." Camille glanced at Ecaterina's corpse, remembering how serendipity had played such a huge part in fighting that first neutralized vampire in Juni. "I held one off a year ago, too. And I didn't have to murder to do it."

Someone else had finished off that first one. Just as Sarge had killed Ecaterina tonight.

"You held one off?" Sarge laughed, then shoved a hand to his forehead. Shook it away. "Holding them off isn't a permanent solution. If I hadn't sliced the noggin off your friend here—" he motioned toward Ecaterina's body "—she'd have gone back for her buddies. Now we've got one less to deal with."

"I think I mentioned how we're all suddenly targets, since they won't want just you men now."

"Hey, equal opportunity, right?"

"Dipwad."

She shot him a disgusted glance as he tamed his wooziness and sauntered by her, toward Ecaterina, ignoring the new nickname. He'd probably heard worse.

"I'm going to have to cut her heart out," he said.

"You've already done enough damage. Besides, that's just superstition. She's dead. Got it? Not moving. Things usually don't function without a head."

"You never know with the undead."

"Sarge, she'll be nicely captured in this coffin. It was designed to bring back hibernating vampires for Beatrix so she could work on a serum that actually might cure the problem. But she'd need a working body for that."

Sarge inspected the tongue that lolled out of Ecaterina's mouth. "I've got a better idea. If we kill them, we've got a cure." When he glanced at her, a deep anguish filled his gaze. He turned away, probably hoping she hadn't seen it.

Was this how murderers acted and thought? Had the man who'd killed her parents used the same form of twisted logic?

And what about Sarge himself? What had happened to make him so bloodthirsty? With the way he talked, she wondered just how hunting them down had become so personal.

Strangely moved by the way he was trying to hide his face from her, Camille opened her mouth to ask all these questions. But before she could, Sarge turned back around, grabbed her arm, intensity taking the place of the pain in his eyes.

"Flora Vladislav had already briefed me about the tongue and said that during the Juni attack the vamps weren't using them to sting women. I noticed that tonight, too. Why?"

His hands were callused, rough. The heat of contact imprinted Camille's skin through the jacket, sending a shock wave through her body.

Stunned, she wrenched her arm away. What had *that* been? Misplaced anger? A stressful reaction to the night's events?

Crossing her arms over her chest, she said, "We think the vampires know that the tongue venom won't stun females. They save up and strike only at men because that's how they disable them for capture and travel."

"How do you know the venom won't work on women?"

"I tested it back in Bucharest."

Sarge shot her a look, half of which said she was crazy while the other half said he admired her courage.

She couldn't handle his respect, not when she was all too aware of him hovering over her. "I took a small shot of the stuff at first, since the Juni corpse's tongue provided us with a sample," she said, taking a subtle step away from him. "Gradually, I upped the dosage. It never affected me or the other volunteers. Of course, a live vampire's venom might be a different story."

Thank God he was back to inspecting Ecaterina's head, not seeming to mind the stench. Earlier, the silver oval had fallen away, allowing Camille to inspect the tongue.

"That was a pretty effective thing you used on her mouth during the scuffle," Sarge said.

"A mouth sealer. It uses vacuum power to keep the vampires' lips closed. It renders their fangs useless. Problem is, it loses power after fifteen minutes." She kicked at a rock on the ground. "When I invented it, I couldn't stretch the time out any longer."

"You made it?" There was that look again, but it was mostly respect now.

"Yeah. I'm a geek that way. When I was a kid I'd spend time in the school lab, messing around. I—"

She'd said way too much, gotten too personal. There was no need to confide in this man, her competitor.

"And how about that UV wand?" he asked.

Her invention, too. "It doesn't matter."

She wasn't about to tell him about how much time she'd had on her hands this past year. Time spent waiting for word from her mercenary teams. Time spent discovering new ways to fight vampires with Bea's advice.

Somehow, she'd always felt in her gut that she'd be going after Griff. That finding him would make all the difference in her life.

While Sarge talked, he liberated a knife from a hidden ankle sheath. "You've got quite a mind on you, Howard. But I'm still going to cut this thing's heart out."

"Oh, come on."

"You said a dead vamp won't be so useful in the lab."

Should she just get him off her back? Besides, they'd have more *live* vampire hearts to study by the end of the mission. "Okay. But don't think I'm always going to give in to your whims."

"That's what you say now." He slid her a meaningful glance and, if he weren't such a scumbag, Camille might've actually thought the look was hot—in Bizarro World.

She called Delia over again to record the process for Bea. When the villager was ready, Sarge twirled his bowie knife into a reverse grip, then sliced into Ecaterina's chest.

Cuts. Slashes. Camille turned away, momentarily shaken.

"What have you and Dr. Grasu found out about this form of vampirism?" he asked.

The metallic buzz of blade against bone turned her stomach. Did Sarge have the right idea? That talking would shut it out?

"More or less, these vampires are victims of a virus that is passed through the exchange of blood mixed with saliva. We haven't been able to trace its origins, but we know that the virus mutates the cells, and the cells multiply like gangbusters and take over the body. Basically, vampirism is cancerous, and it shapes the human body into the perfect vessel for its survival. That's why these creatures have developed small fins for quick movement, superior strength and night vision so they can stay out of the sun."

He was still sawing. "The *strigoiaca* are like other vamps, then? They don't like beach bathing?"

"Only because of the ultraviolet rays, not some symbolically charged reason." Camille concentrated on the treetops, the sudden scatter of a flock of birds.

Anything but the knife. "UV actually kills cells, and the virus can't withstand that. In fact, we think using UV can turn the vampires human again. Like chemotherapy."

A slurping, creaking sound told Camille that it was time to lose her dinner.

Still, she held on. "We'll monitor the curing process to make sure nothing unexpected happens. Remember that serum I mentioned to you? The one Bea won't get to develop without a living vampire? We'd like to use that, too. And, of course, we'd wean the vampires off blood."

There was the sound of a boot clearing leaves. The thump of an object—the heart—hitting the ground.

"That'll be a trick," he said. "You got some kind of twelve-step program for vamps?"

Camille turned around to retort, then paused when she saw the heart. Like the Juni vampire's organ, this didn't look any different than a human one.

While Delia filmed a close-up, Sarge wiped his bloodied knife on some damp leaves and got out his pack of cigarettes, plus matches. With laconic grace, he flipped a death stick into his mouth.

Looked as if Sarge was a fast healer. Back to his old cocky self, except for a slight wobble every few minutes.

Camille dismissed Delia and started uploading the new images to Bea. "From all indications, we theorize that these females choose males for sustenance because they're addicted to the testosterone. It feeds the virus."

Sarge lit a match and spoke, his tone bitter. "Sounds a lot like love."

Then he bent down, lent flame to the heart, used more matches to stoke the growing conflagration. Absently, he dipped his ciggie into the fire, giving it life.

Once again, Camille actually felt something for the guy. A soft, weak chink of pity or... Who knew? He had some kind of story, just like her. Had some slant of humanity. Maybe.

They didn't say anything until Sarge had finished the cigarette and the organ had ashed itself out.

"You think your revenants can be turned by some serum or UV rays, then," he said.

She gave a confident nod. "I'd bet my life on it."

"You already have."

"That's why these coffins contain UV bulbs." She walked over to Ecaterina's unit, closing it over the body and head now that Sarge had gotten his thrills. No need to turn on the UV for this corpse, though. "The coffin's radiation isn't high enough to mutate a breathing vampire's cells, but it's enough to keep them frozen in fear."

As Sarge used his bowie knife to dig a hole in the ground, Camille rolled the coffin into the Humvee.

He buried the ashes as she closed down the computer and bolted up the vehicle.

The wolves started up again, their cries mixing with a mist that shrouded the trees.

He cleaned the knife one more time. "Think those howlers have anything to do with vamps? Maybe protectors?"

She couldn't tear her eyes off his weapon. "That's all a bunch of nonsense. Remember, we're dealing with real life. Diseased beings. Not mythical figments."

"So you say." He held up a finger—*Wait*—and ambled to his Jeep, digging inside the back storage area.

Had Sarge been like her, once upon a time? A normal person who hadn't believed in bloodsucking creatures at all? Sure, she'd found out eventually that they were merely mutants, evolved due to a sickness, but…

What, beyond the *strigoiaca,* had Sarge actually seen in *his* life?

She'd learned that killers lived according to their own stories, their own perception of what the world was. They created excuses to murder.

And Sarge's monster-vampires just weren't logical. Did he enjoying stalking and murdering so much that he'd convinced himself that superstitions were true and they all needed to be vanquished?

He had to know that there were reasonable explanations for everything. *Always.*

Sarge came back, covered with a flak jacket and carrying another knife. This one had a six-and-one-half-inch serrated silver blade with a rubber handle.

"It'll work on werewolves as good as a silver bullet," he said, offering it to her.

Camille swallowed. "No, thanks."

Sarge looked it over. "I know it's not as fancy as a mouth sealer or a UV wand, but it comes in handy when you fight mean animals in a forest. What're you going to use if we brush up against those wolves or a mountain lynx?"

"We've got our dart guns."

Again, Sarge stared at her. That steady look was fast becoming his most effective comeback. "Are these cap shooters as good as those wands? You know, the lights that sputtered out?"

"We're recharging those. They don't last very long, so that makes us work quickly to restrain the vampires. The dart guns will work just fine for any wolves though. We've tested them in the lab."

"Great. And that's all you have? You're kidding."

"No." She thought of her parents' bodies, the sick stench of undeserved deaths. "We don't need to kill them."

"Just disable them. I know. *I know.* Listen, sometimes you don't have a choice about killing."

She didn't want to be reminded. Juni had taught her this lesson—one she'd rather forget.

"Then I suppose that's the difference between us,"

she said. "*You'd* walk into that vampire castle with weapons blazing. *I* go in to resolve the situation without wreaking total destruction."

"Hell. You'd bring a knife to a gunfight. Or, in your case, a dart." He paused, a muscle working in his jaw. "Besides, I've been known to discriminate between who needs to stay alive and who needs to die."

Even though she doubted it was true, the tone of his voice hinted at something Camille couldn't pin down, couldn't quite grasp about this man. "All I know is that my silly little dart was enough to take you down."

"Not before I did my job."

Sarge's arrogant smile heated up that damned warm patch of skin where he'd touched her arm.

Anger, she thought. It was only anger.

"Say we drug some wolves," he said, "we go up into that castle, we do some vamp damage and...whoa. What do you know? On our way out, we've got wolves who are a little groggy, but really displeased. Kinda like me."

"Maybe they'll have more of a capacity for forgiveness."

Reaching out, Sarge grabbed her hand and held it steady before she could protest. His touch was warm, vicious, forcing her to block out all the confusion the contact whipped up.

"I don't need that knife," she said.

"I don't have enough real pistols to equip you and the ladies, but if you want one..."

"No."

Gently, he laid the weapon over her palm. Camille drew in a shuddering breath.

"That ain't so bad, is it?" he asked.

Yes, it was. She couldn't say whether it was because Sarge was still touching her, or if it was because she was weighing the instrument of her parents' deaths. She found herself unmoving, caught between fascination and the growing doubt that maybe dart guns wouldn't be enough to tame those wolves after all.

"Here." He folded her lower three fingers tightly around the base of the handle. "Then your index finger, lightly."

His thumb gently guided it around the handle, too.

He stepped closer, his voice warm in her ear. "Now extend your thumb, parallel to the blade."

His tone was low, as soft as the brush of his jacket against her back. For a second, Camille was lulled, wanting so badly to feel cared for again. The need blurred her thoughts, making the knife feel okay in her grip. A little powerful.

I'm going to get Griff back, she thought, warring against those stirred-up emotions. He'll make me feel alive again.

"This is what they call a Filipino grip." Sarge slipped his palm under her free arm, her hand, turning her forearm to face the outside and lifting it in front of her body. "I've noticed that you know a thing or two about boxing."

"I've dabbled," she croaked, then cleared her throat, creating distance from Sarge—even if it was more mental than physical. "Okay. I think I've got the arm position now."

He laughed, probably because she sounded so eager for him to back away. "Take a boxing stance."

She did, and he made a few adjustments: knife hand forward, hands lower than usual.

"Tuck your chin more," he said, using his thumb and forefinger to slowly angle it down. "You walk around like you've got a chip on your shoulder."

His easy gesture had given her one of those dizzy shivers again. She whipped away from his touch, straightened up. It didn't feel right to be giving in to the knife.

"This isn't my style." She held it back out to him.

Sarge walked in front of her, stalking, gauging her fears. Then, without warning, he pulled his own knife, preparing to slash diagonally from her waist up.

Grateful to be back on familiar ground with him, her instincts spun into motion, causing her to step forward, angling her body away from the attacking cut and to his outside.

"Stop." He grabbed her wrist. "That was a good reaction. Now just meet me—" He placed her blade against his knife arm. "Then do a safety check." He forced her free hand to push his attacking arm away. "Then—" he pulled her resisting arm, making her thrust to his throat, stopping as the knife point just nicked his skin "—I'm a goner."

The feel of the blade against his neck made her pulse race with giddy speed, made her realize that she could do more harm than good.

She dropped the knife at his feet, her hand shaking. It stabbed the ground, quivering between the both of them.

Sarge shook his head. "You're going unarmed into a

world where your darts can only go so far. You'll be sorry if you think you're prepared."

"But I'm not like you, Sarge. Not at all."

I'm like Griff—gentle and normal.

He measured her with a gaze, then turned around, walked away. Still, she could hear him clearly.

"Coming from a woman who was all too willing to use me as a fishing worm, that's funny. You *are* me, Howard."

And as she watched him retreat into the thickening mist, she told herself she'd never become like Sargent.

Even if she was already halfway there.

Chapter 6

Juni, approximately nine months ago
Three days before the strigoiaca *came*

Camille squinted at the sting of cigarette smoke and surveyed the village inn as she tipped a glass of *palinca* past her lips.

The brown-haired girl sitting across the rickety wooden table for her interview beamed with approval.

"Este regular?" she asked.

"Mmm." Camille ignored the burning sensation in her throat and gut, compliments of the potent plum beverage. Regretting that she'd ever accepted the drink in the first place, she deposited the half-full glass on the table. "Yes, it's okay. *Multumesc*. Thank you."

It rested next to her plate of *sarmale,* stuffed cabbage leaves that were a staple of the Romanian diet. Even if she and Griff had already spent a few days in northern Transylvania while she interviewed folks in another village, too, she'd never get used to this hearty food.

Salads were more her thing. Wow. Her stomach really missed the light grub.

At any rate, she'd accepted the meal from the innkeeper's wife, Flora Vladislav. According to Camille's research of the local beliefs and superstitions, she knew that failing to finish the beverage would supposedly bring Mrs. Vladislav bad luck.

Heck, from what she'd seen of Juni so far, they needed all the luck they could get. A tiny village located near Roman ruins, all Juni really had to offer was a wooden Orthodox church, a dark neighboring forest and surrounding farmland stacked with hay. Most of the inhabitants watched her and Griff with barely concealed distrust—something Transylvanians felt for Westerners, Camille had been told.

During this latest pause in Ecaterina's interview, Camille must've been pursing her lips or something because, even from across the low-lit, hazy room, Griff was grinning at her. As was his habit after putting in his work for the day, he was yukking it up with the friendlier locals: dark-eyed men fresh from the fields and eager to practice their English.

Camille couldn't help smiling back at her boyfriend, couldn't help flushing a little, just knowing they belonged to each other. Just knowing that, every passing day, she was falling deeper and deeper for him.

A woman's heavily accented voice interrupted, mid-blush. "Ms. Howard?"

It was Eva Godea, the guide and interpreter Camille had hired at the University of Bucharest. Young and capable of relaying the subtleties of Camille's intricate questions, she wore ambition in the guise of a career-minded, olive-toned suit and auburn hair that was twisted into a severe chignon. The difference between her and Camille's subject, Ecaterina, a local Juni girl wearing braids and a traditional embroidered blouse, was startling. A time warp.

"Okay, next question," Camille said, grabbing her pen and smoothing the page of her bulging notebook. "Ah, here we go. I've noticed that folklore for this area refers a lot to female vampires, not men, or even Vlad the Impaler."

"Bram Stoker's fiction," sniffed Ms. Godea.

"Vlad Tepes is a historical figure, but most of the other stories are fantasy to some extent."

"As you've learned, not to many of these people."

Across the table, Ecaterina was watching, wide-eyed, their English meaningless to a girl who'd already revealed that all she wanted to do was marry a local boy and cook him proper meals for the rest of his life.

Camille glanced at her notes again, then back up. "In the other village we've been to, the literature is the same. Now…how can I phrase this?" She paused, wanting to know if the stories had empowered Ecaterina as a female in any way. At the same time, she didn't want to offend.

Leading up to her point, she asked, "Ecaterina, how

do you feel about women being the aggressors in these tales?"

While Ms. Godea efficiently translated, Camille followed to the best of her abilities. She had a talent for languages—Latin, Spanish, Italian, Portuguese, French, German—and was interested in mastering this one, too.

Though Romanian is Latin-based, she definitely wasn't fluent enough to be interviewing in it yet.

In the meantime, the innkeeper's wife strolled by, blue scarf on head, tucking her veined hands in her apron pockets. She shot a pointed glare at Camille's *palinca,* then wandered away.

Ecaterina was taking a moment to formulate her answer, so Camille picked up her beverage again, determined to finish. To distract herself, she glanced around the common room—the rough wooden walls, the simple furnishings, the medieval weaponry stored in glass cases behind the bar.

Interesting. Did Mr. Vladislav threaten to use the mace or the battle-axes when a patron got nasty?

Triumphantly, Camille drained her glass and thunked it on the table. Whoo, doggie. That was some stuff.

Now, for the cabbage.

She finished the food as Ecaterina finally spilled out her answer, cheeks stamped with rosy excitement. Griff's laugh sounded from across the room, and Camille tried to concentrate on understanding the Romanian while holding back her silly smile.

"'Women should not be taking lives,'" Ms. Godea translated. "'Females are made to create, not destroy.'"

Using shorthand to record the answer, Camille said,

"Same feedback as most females in the other village. In spite of mass communication, media and education, they're still clinging to superstition and tradition. There's a real divide between the old ways and the need to move on, isn't there? Especially in Juni. It hit me right away, yesterday, when we got here and Ms. Vladislav automatically put me and Griff in different rooms."

"There was the revolution in 1989." Ms. Godea's stoic, librarian-in-need-of-hot-sex expression didn't waver. "Life changed, Ms. Howard. But morals didn't."

Camille had already studied all about the executed Communist dictator Ceausescu, so she didn't need a history lecture. Instead, she turned back to Ecaterina.

"Do you believe the females, the—" she leafed through her pages, wanting to pronounce the word correctly "—the *strigoiaca*, will ever come to Juni? After all, it's said that they visit different villages every year."

After Ms. Godea posed the question, the girl answered with a firm *"Nu,"* then proceeded to give a long response.

"'No,'" Ms. Godea translated. "'Even if there are those who do not believe in the old tales, there are enough believers to keep the *strigoiaca* away. It is the villages who have lost faith and become lazy who will suffer attacks.'"

"Dang, Ms. Godea." Camille shook her head. Was it her own disbelief or the plum drink that was spinning her mind? "When I came here, I expected to hear about legends and fireside tales. To see people laughing about what used to be accepted as truth. Vampirism used to explain sickness and death, certain corpse conditions that medicine can now justify."

"We all have our science, our reasons for how the world works."

She was right. The Greeks used to explain the change of seasons with the story of Persephone. People used to believe that frequent baths were bad for one's health. Every day, perception changed according to new discoveries. Maybe even her own accepted version of science was a myth that would be refuted one day.

Still…vampires? They were fantasies, horror flicks, reasons for attracting tourists to Castle Dracula and making an easy buck off the hunger for entertainment.

Ecaterina and Ms. Godea couldn't be serious.

The village girl started talking, and Ms. Godea nodded.

"Our silly little miss wants to speak about male vampires," the translator said. "She is talking about a reclusive male tribe in the Carpathians."

"I haven't heard about this group from the other village, or in my books." Camille scribbled more notes. She'd have to ask additional villagers about the males. Maybe the legend was unique to this location. If so, how had it developed? And why hadn't she read about this in the literature yet?

Excitement bubbled in her veins. Could this be her big break? A discovery to be published, making her something more than "that Howard girl"?

"Ecaterina hopes the male tribe comes to Juni instead of the females." Ms. Godea said, censure in her tone.

Did an educated woman like her believe in these tales, too? Or did she think Ecaterina was a dimwit for another reason? A more modern, women's-lib-type concern?

The translator continued. "She thinks they'll be very romantic. And…" Ms. Godea stopped, rattled off a question.

Ecaterina merely batted her eyelashes in response.

Ms. Godea huffed out a long-suffering sigh, then said, "There are stories of male vampires who visit women in the night and impregnate them."

"I've heard, but… Don't tell me she wouldn't mind…."

In answer, Ms. Godea nodded.

"Oh." Vampire sex. "There's your excuse after sleeping around. An accidental vampire bun in the oven."

Someone sitting behind Ecaterina spouted a viperish stream of words, causing the girl's face to fall.

Camille leaned to the side to get a better look at the interloper's profile. A guy, college aged, garbed in a smart button-down and Levi's, finished a glass of wine and turned around. He had bloodshot green eyes, mussy brown hair that reminded Camille of the students back at Texas A&M who constantly pulled all-nighters.

"Excuse me," he said, his English clipped and heavy. "I think she is full of crap."

Camille leaned on her elbows, willing to hear more, but a swarthy old woman sitting at a table next to them spoke first.

As she chided him in a flurry of Romanian, the room quieted. Ms. Godea translated, even though Camille was catching a good deal of the content herself.

"'Petar Vladislav'—our innkeeper's son, I believe— 'do not encourage the Westerner,'" Ms. Godea said.

Oh, great. Camille's presence was about to start a turf war. From across the room, she could see Griff tensing, easing to the edge of his chair. Camille sent him a reassuring glance.

The old woman, who wore a black shawl over her gray head and frail body, crossed herself. As she moved, a silver crucifix sparkled under her timeworn coverings. Her skin was crinkled, like ancient parchment bearing lines and marks, spells written in the old hand.

God, if Camille could only talk to *her,* there was no telling what she'd find out.

As the old woman continued, so did Ms. Godea. "'We should not allow strangers to ask questions. We should send her home with her charming tourist stories instead. See how even now she is destroying the peace we have worked so hard to cultivate?'"

A curiosity and a menace. That's what Camille was to these people.

Petar refused to speak in Romanian, forcing Ms. Godea to work double time for the old woman's benefit. "And how much peace will there be when your *strigoiaca* come?"

"They will not," the elder answered. "Not if we defend against them as we have for years. A fall from faith is all the invitation they need."

Camille scribbled furiously as voices overlapped, languages mingled.

"We will see," Petar said. "It *is* that time of year. The time they supposedly attack. I am willing to take a holiday from university to wait for them here."

The woman's voice grew ragged, harsh. "Quiet, boy. Your arrogance and disrespect will cripple Juni, just like the other villages when they lost their way. When they let go of their morals to outside influences. When they forgot tradition and history."

By now, everyone in the room was perched on the edges of their seats.

But the college student—young, know-it-all, cocky—leaned back in *his* chair. "Those other villages you speak of? The vampires you blame? Please. Vampirism is another word for sickness and death. And as for the men who disappeared from the villages? There are many reasons for a husband to leave his wife, yes?"

The men in the room chuckled, but mirth was in short supply. There was a nervous strain connecting everyone together. Camille could feel it.

Petar continued. "I have learned much at university. I have learned about tuberculosis. I have learned how our glorious local Communist police forces used vampirism to explain the disappearance of husbands and sons."

"Perhaps you also learned that the vampires have benefited from these excuses most of all. But you have not learned of how the *strigoiaca* can sense a so-called educated fool and spirit him away. Lack of fear does not make us stronger, Petar Vladislav, only weaker."

"Bah. Here is what I think of your vampires." Petar stood, held open his hands and stared straight at the woman. "Hello, *strigoiaca?* Do you hear me?"

"Sit!" the old woman snarled.

Petar merely grinned. "Mighty *strigoiaca,* we in Juni invite you over for dinner. We are expecting you now, so do not disappoint."

Mumbling under her breath, the shawl-covered woman began rocking back and forth, squeezing her eyes shut. The room sat in silence, and when they slowly returned to their chatting and drinking, there was a noticeable change—mutters instead of laughter, whispers instead of shouts. Even Petar's mother came over to slap him upside the head.

Petar made a dismissive gesture toward all of them, then moved to Camille's side. From the corner of her eye, she saw Griff rise from his own seat, making his way over to her.

Her heart clenched, anticipating his arrival.

As Petar formally introduced himself and Griff slid to a seat on her other side, the old woman raised her voice.

"'Unbelievers will pay,'" Ms. Godea translated.

A chill nipped down Camille's spine, followed by the jarring brush of something much more solid and real. She whipped around to see what it was.

A huge black dog panted over to the woman, who claimed him with a loving touch to the ear. When the animal spun around, Camille blinked, hardly believing it.

Someone had painted an extra set of white eyes on the animal's forehead.

Protection against vampires, she thought, remembering a local superstition.

But Camille also felt another pair of eyes on her.

Slowly, she looked up, meeting the gaze of the ancient lady. The ageless, deep-set eyes. The nightmarish accusations and fear she thought she'd left back in London.

Unbelievers will pay.

"Hey." It was Griff, rubbing her back, chasing the

shivers out of her skin. "You've definitely got them riled up, Sherlock."

She swallowed her doubts, regaining her confidence.

"The better to glean information, my dear Griff."

She did her best to smile, but when he answered, she didn't hear a thing. She could only focus on the old woman as she turned her back on Camille.

Even though she couldn't see her face anymore, Camille felt the warning. The danger.

The eyes—as unblinking as the center of two dead flowers—that were always upon her.

Chapter 7

Present

A tang of fear settled in the back of Camille's throat as her driver cut the engine.

Hopping out of the Humvee, she lifted her gaze to the jagged castle that sat on top of a hundred-foot rise. It was the location Ashe had "felt," the home of the *strigoiaca* and their captives.

They would soon see.

Black-winged birds circled the ancient battlements against a graying sky, and a thick mist shrouded all the halting vehicles, lending a sense of doom. From here, the castle resembled a face sneering down on them— spiked hair culled from the bared branches of dead trees; empty, malicious eyes and a grimace where some of the stone had fallen away; the crooked nose shaped from a leaning keep.

She could actually be near Griff. Near darkness.

Just remember, she thought. These weren't magical, fairy-dust creatures. Vampirism could be cured, just like many other ailments.

Ashe came to stand next to her. She smelled the herbs wafting off his skin, the ground and dried pine needles that had mixed with something in the air that was more ominous.

Death.

"I feel that one vamp has been searching for Ecaterina," he said, staring at the castle, too. "When she returns to the castle, they'll be thinking of taking a new tribe member."

Early this morning, after Camille and her team had woken up from a restless sleep and taken ritual baths in a nearby stream as instructed by Ashe, Camille had emphasized how the *strigoiaca* would not only go after the men, but would likely also want one of them.

She'd even given the women the option of using Sarge's extra military-issue knives. The Humvee drivers—three women who would stay with the vehicles and coffins during the hunt—had snapped up two of his semiautomatic Browning Hi-Power .40-caliber pistols loaded with custom-made silver bullets.

Much to her chagrin, the rest of the Vasile women had accepted Sarge's offerings and training, too.

She'd seen him model hand communication signals. Had watched him teach the art of back slashes, thrusts, lethal cuts, while pantomiming the motions in her mind, but refusing to take part.

Camille herself had then reiterated the earlier lessons she'd given the women about clearing a room and using their defense devices to the greatest effect. But the ladies seemed far more comfortable with their new toys.

Violence versus peaceful resolution. Why did it seem that Sarge's way was the most convincing to them?

"He's not such a bad guy," Ashe said, smiling.

Camille took a step away from the Wiccan. As if that would keep him out of her head or feelings or…whatever.

"Listen," Ashe said. "I'm going to tell you something no one really knows about my business partner because you're a sympathetic soul. I feel you'll help him in the long run."

"Actually, I don't care to know much about the guy."

"Oh, I think he likes you. He hasn't shot you yet."

Uncomfortable, she laughed, but Ashe didn't.

"Well," she said, "then go ahead and tell me. Might as well go with the cosmic flow, as you people say."

Ashe placed a hand on her shoulder. "What you see on the outside of Sarge isn't the whole story. Sure, he seems a little merciless, coldhearted—"

"A little?"

"Okay, a lot. There's a reason he's riding you so hard about betraying him last night."

She wouldn't have appreciated being used as bait, either, but there'd been real hatred in Sarge's reaction. Real hurt. Real shame, on her part.

Ashe went on. "You've probably noticed that scar."

"I've been too polite to mention it."

"It's from another woman. Hana, our first vampire."

Ah, Camille thought. The rumors. Sarge's initial kill. Her eyes widened in interest as she turned to face Ashe, wanting to receive the full story in spite of herself.

"I'm not at liberty to disclose details, but—" Ashe shrugged "—it happened in a Third World hot spot. We were on a classified mission, going after hijacked nuclear weapons a warlord had gotten his hands on. We were to take him and his lieutenants into custody and secure those weapons on the quiet. Hana was his youngest daughter, a lowly member of the family, and we thought she'd turned informant against her father."

Because of Flora, Camille already knew about Sarge's Special Forces status. It was his "vampire hunter" selling point, not that it explained his obsession with the undead. "Hana lied to you?"

"Right. She was a real seductress, and she got to Sarge. He was smitten, but Sarge never acted on his feelings for her. He was too devoted to the mission. Par for the course, though. Ladies generally think Sarge is too intense for romance anyway."

For some reason, these personal details were making Camille blush. She tried to play off the telling heat by cracking a joke.

"Maybe he should start by not grabbing his dates' throats like he did at our first meeting," she said.

"That's foreplay for him." Ashe's grin was fleeting. "Hana lured us into a trap. Instead of leading us to a meeting where her father and his advisers would be, we walked into a nest of waiting vampires. They took almost everyone down—a whole team of highly trained operatives."

"Except for you and Sarge."

"I was lucky because, when I was called on to save lives, Sarge covered me. That's when Hana finally got to him. She tore out half his neck with those fangs, and Sarge had to take her out. It was the first military kill he ever took personally. To make things worse, we found out that our intelligence was bad. Hana had died two years ago. She'd been a vamp for that long, and we had no idea."

It was starting to make a little sense. Sarge's bad attitude, his distrust.

"After the massacre," Ashe said, "he quit the Special Forces, started polluting his body with smoking and drinking, didn't care about much of anything except revenge. He'd never been a guy to believe in ghoulies, but this attack convinced him. He almost became religious about ridding the world of vamps, since Hana had shown him how evil they could be, without a care for life. The guy's always had zealots' blood in him—his mom was a real Sunday schooler and his dad… Let's just say his instrument of belief was a leather belt with studs on it."

Camille drew back, horrified. "That's awful."

"It's a motivating force. His parents have crossed over to a better place now, but Sarge keeps hunting. In fact, if he ever stops, it'll be because he's caught Nicolae, a father figure if I've ever heard of one."

Nicolae. She'd read the name a thousand times in her studies. A Romanian master vampire who roamed the world, killing, spreading his own blood religion. So this was why Sarge knew the local language.

"Now, there's a scary vamp," Ashe said. "He selects minions and trains them to seduce people into his cult. They practice sacrifice in his name. This creature is a megalomaniac, but luckily he's gone underground for the moment. Yet that's what worries us the most. No one knows what he's up to."

"Are you saying Nicolae has designs on world domination?" she asked, half-kidding.

"He's smart enough to." Ashe raised a pale eyebrow. "Nicolae is Sarge's obsession. They came face-to-face once, and the vamp gave him a big paternal whooping."

"That's why this hunting is so personal for him. Hana."

And Nicolae. An object of revenge for the childhood beatings?

"He's not all bad, Ms. Howard," Ashe said. "If the time comes for mercy, he'll show some. He's spared lives to get to Nicolae, worked deals, but...I digress."

Camille hadn't seen any mercy so far, but the Wiccan showed such conviction that she wondered if it was true.

Would Sarge show these vampires—possible cures for the virus—mercy?

While the Wiccan smiled and ambled away a few steps to bow his head and chant over an oil vial he'd extracted from his robes, Camille didn't move.

Did Sarge's past change how she felt about him?

Well, at least it provided some insight. Maybe she could grow to understand him, even if she didn't like him.

When she looked up again, the castle loomed in her sight. Damn, she'd put it to the back of her head. Maybe that's why Ashe had told her Sarge's story. To get her mind off the imminent danger. To relax her.

Then the first wolf howl sounded from the windy dirt road leading up the rise and to the castle. A road too narrow for the Humvees to travel.

She shivered, the goat carcasses that littered the rocky entrance taunting her. It was as if the animals had been delivered to the vampires and summarily flung out a castle window after their life force had been used up.

Is that what the captives ate before the *strigoiaca*, in turn, dined on them? Is that why Ecaterina had been hunting? To keep their victims healthy enough to produce blood?

"I can't wait till we get those wolves to shut up," Sarge said, stepping in front of her, blocking out the threat of the castle.

Instead of giving him her usual oh-would-you-just-scram stare, Camille looked at him in a new light. Underneath his skin, this man was a warrior fighting demons. She didn't know all the names of them, but she knew them all the same.

Maybe they really were more alike than she'd first cared to admit.

As two wolves cried in harmony, Sarge cleaned the dirt from under his nails with the tip of his bowie.

And that's when she went back to the old way of looking at him.

"I'll bet they're shape-shifters," he said. "I've sparred with plenty. Hard as hell to kill. Strong."

More delusions from the world of Sarge? "The *strigoiaca* don't turn into wolves or bats. They're still somewhat human beneath it all."

"Still—" Sarge scratched his head with the knife blade "—if we're in the right place, those could be our evil ladies in disguise. I hope so. Come on down, and let's get this crap done right here, I say. I don't need to tour another decrepit castle."

Camille busied herself by opening the Humvee door, donning her equipment: her UV wand, adrenaline gun, knockout dart gun, restraints and mouth sealers, plus a rope and a medical pouch. Comparatively, all Sarge's weapons made her feel a little naked. A little naive.

But she knew what she was doing. She'd studied these creatures and knew what it took.

Ashe approached Sarge, anointing the hunter's forehead with oil. When the Wiccan was done, Sarge gestured toward Camille, sending Ashe to her with his concoction.

His protective concern covered her in another one of those blushes. She hated when that happened.

Tucking an errant strand of hair away from her forehead, she accepted Ashe's magickal treatment. Couldn't hurt to go through it, even if all this "magick" was a feel-good placebo.

"I'll tell you," Sarge said, "this oil really helped last time, when I got a dart in the throat."

Patient as always, Ashe grinned as he dipped a finger in the oil and prepared to anoint her. "Think about it. Camille turned out to be your protector."

"I told you, Sarge," she added, "it wasn't meant to be lethal."

"You just kept me alive to use as bait again."

Camille tried not to act surprised. Had he found out that she and Bea had been discussing that exact option?

Sargent patted his friend on the back. "But Ashe told me to watch out for flying darts this time."

The Wiccan sent Camille a look that said "So much for your grand plans," and drew a shape on her forehead.

"Ashe," she asked, "is that a pentagram?"

"Yes, but don't worry—it's not inverted." He touched each of the five points. "These represent the Spirit— which is on the top, not the bottom—water, fire, earth and air. This symbol has been used through the ages for protection. Only relatively recently has the upside-down version become a sign of evil."

"No sweat," Sarge added. "Sweet Boy Ashe wouldn't hurt a fly unless it bit him first. Then, watch out."

With an encouraging pat on Camille's upper arm, the Wiccan left, wandering over to the other women, oil readied for more action.

One quick glance told Camille that the villagers were ready to go. Nervous as hell, too. Camille had hoped to avoid the wolves by striking the castle by daylight; after all, the vampires would be somewhere dark, where it was always night. A dungeon, maybe. Schedules prob- ably didn't matter with the *strigoiaca*. It's not as if they were fictional vampires who slept in coffins by day.

However, in spite of her sunlight hopes, her team had spent hours training with the knives and guns, eating up the minutes.

As they stood waiting for Ashe to anoint the women, Camille suddenly felt Sarge's gaze on her.

"Question, Howard," he said. "Is there something more than scientific discoveries in that castle for you? Maybe it's one of those captives you're so protective of…."

A muscle twitched near her eye. Heart beating double time at the thought of Griff's loving smile, she covered it by strapping on her headset and light gear.

"That's it, isn't it?" he said. "I've hit the jackpot. So who was this *friend* Flora Vladislav told me about? Were you and the captive—?"

"Just get ready, Sarge."

"Ah. So you're rescuing the princess in the tower?"

"I really don't want to talk about this." It hurt too much. It made her more nervous, realizing that Griff's life was in her hands—if he was even still alive.

The wolf pack—maybe five, six of them?—keened together. They were on that path somewhere.

Camille stepped past Sarge, toward them. "My future might be up there."

Her salvation.

Because if she didn't save Griff, there'd be nothing left. Nothing to have faith in.

Besides, *she* was the one who had brought him to Juni. She would be the one to bring him back, too.

Camille touched her baby ring for luck. For reassurance.

When Sarge spoke again, his voice was low, touched with something she couldn't identify.

"Whoever's there, Howard, he ain't the same anymore. It's been a year, and those things have had their teeth in him. They've probably sucked out his soul, too."

"Bull. They've taken blood, but that's it."

"You can't imagine…" he began, then stopped.

His demeanor had changed. There was a split in his armored skin, a wound in the center of his eyes, a slump to his normally rough-and-ready stance.

His tortured gaze told her he was somewhere else, somewhere in the splatter of a crimson-soaked memory.

"The minute these things take their first bite, they lose their souls. They become true monsters, warped, living by rules that regular people can't understand." He gripped the handle of his machete. "To be a killer, you have to be a little in love with death. Know what I mean?"

No. She hated death. Hated the dark. Hated…that she *did* understand.

"Listen, Sarge." Her voice quavered. "You think I'm going to abandon every code I've created during my life? You think I'm going to snap and enjoy chopping off heads and ripping out hearts as much as you do? Not going to happen, cowboy. Know why?"

"Enlighten me."

Bottled rage boiled, struggling to find an outlet. "Believe it or not, I respect the *strigoiaca.* I hate it, but I do. The more I study them, the more I admire their ability to exist for hundreds of years. Their physical adaptations are astounding, Darwinian theory at its best—like great white sharks. Their bodies are pure machines, streamlined for survival." Her head filled with phrases from all the books she'd read, all the fascinated repulsion she'd fed herself on.

"I respect their great desire to live," she added, "because we humans feel the same way. You don't go around *annihilating* this evolutionary wonder just because something pissed you off. There's a world order and we're not its royalty."

Sargent's face had reddened by now, the scarlet anger creeping down his neck. But it avoided that white-hot scar, branching around it, making the network of raised, dead skin flash like a warning beacon.

"You feel this way, even after what you saw in Juni?"

Did she really? Or was she making a mad grab at staying sane? Of keeping order in her world?

"Your pristine faith ain't gonna be so lily-white after some blood has been splashed over it," Sarge added.

"I was never lily-white in the first place." Damn him. What did he know about her?

His face fell, as if recalling something. "God, Howard. God, I'm sorry. I shouldn't have said that."

That Howard Girl. When they had first met, he'd mentioned her reputation. He'd even confessed to feeling sorry for her parents' murders. She felt as if he'd reached into her chest and yanked out a living, beating piece of her heart.

His eyes held a genuine apology. "I forget who you are without those news cameras on you. The Howard Girl."

Not anymore, she thought. That person died a year ago in Juni.

They faced off, pulses of tension separating them. Drawing a thick black line between both of their worlds.

Ashe had been listening, standing quietly to the side. "Hate to interrupt, but we're all ready now."

Ready to travel up the short yet never ending castle road. Ready to see if Griff was there.

Please, God, have him be there.

"Let's go," she said, controlling the dormant anger. She touched her hand to her headset. "Bea? We're on."

"My darling girl," Doc answered, filling Camille with the calm she'd been lacking. Aunt Bea was her lucky star, her anointed protector. With her watching over Camille, there was nothing to worry about.

At least, that's what she tried to tell herself.

Switching on her head-mounted light, she marched toward the slender castle road.

Ready to capture some *strigoiaca*.

Ready—and, in fact, terrified—to see whether or not Griff had survived.

As twilight set, they'd left Ashe to put up another magick circle around him and the three drivers, including Irina and her broken arm. Two out of three women were armed with their own semiautomatics. All of them had dart guns and UV wands. They were prepared and trained to fend off wolves or anything even more dangerous.

Ashe intended to wage his own battle back at the Humvees, using binding spells to protect their enemies, as well as the team. Like Camille, he believed everything had souls and could make good choices. If he could help the wolves and vampires stay in the light, he would.

The Vasile villagers had been impressed with his talents, especially Lucia, a woman who'd initially been recruited as a driver but had taken the hapless Irina's hunting spot.

Even now, as the six vampire hunters wound up the rising road, the blond, lanky Lucia wore a goofy grin. Her infatuated expression clashed with the rest of their game faces.

Excellent. This hormonal new girl would get them all in trouble if she was thinking of Ashe and not the hunt.

"That is not where your mind belongs," Camille whispered to her in Romanian.

Lucia blushed from her high, rounded cheekbones to the collar of the long-sleeved black Lycra bodysuit with gloves that Camille had provided for the crew and herself.

"Lucia," Camille said, trying to inject some optimism into their mission. "You can dream about boys later, when we are out of the castle."

Reveka's guttural voice blasted into her ear. "It is useless, Miss Howard. Lucia, she lives to make boys into men. That is the way of it."

The rest of the women—Delia, Ana and Lucia— laughed. Sarge, who was walking next to Camille at the point of their group, made a fed-up face and shook his head. He didn't have a headset and, with the way he'd been walking around last night with his eyes closed, he really needed it. Camille hadn't packed any extra communications devices, though she could've sent for some from the university. But, right now, he was out of luck.

She swept her gaze over him. He had a new weapon tonight—a 12-gauge pump-action shotgun. Otherwise, the flamethrower, stake, crossbow, machete and bowie were all waiting patiently for use. He'd also donned a pair of leather vambraces on his forearms, giving him a modern, yet medieval, appearance.

As the crew climbed upward and rounded a corner, Camille tensed. The back of the rise dropped clear off a precipice, and the path was so narrow that only one person could go at a time. And, even then, they'd have to suck in their guts and scrape the cliff face with their backs.

They stopped, assessed the road. It widened again after about one hundred feet.

Camille touched her headset three times. "Bea?"

"Right here."

"Could you have those choppers on standby in case we need to airlift the specimens down from the castle?"

"Yes. Done."

They'd had two Hueys waiting at Vasile, just in case the Humvees weren't sufficient transportation. For a second, she wondered if they should wait for the choppers to take this crew up to the castle, too, but that would be another waste of precious minutes because, by the time the Hueys arrived to pick them up, they could've already arrived at the castle.

Surely they could deal with a little bad road.

"How did carriages ever get through here?" Camille asked, using Romanian to include the women.

"This place is ancient." Sarge moved to the edge and peered into the chasm, fearless. "Fourteenth century, maybe? I imagine the road crumbled after the place was deserted."

Delia, who seemed so much like a china doll dressed in commando clothing, spoke up. "The legends keep the people away from Castle Bethlen."

"The ghosts," Ana added. Under her headset, she still wore her red scarf. She was a married woman who said she'd die before she'd see her husband taken, and that had impressed—and saddened—Camille. She'd felt all too much in common with her.

Lucia chimed in, too. "No one but *strigoiaca* would dare live here."

"If they are here," Reveka said.

"They are." Sarge turned his back to the fog rising out of the gorge. "Ashe isn't wrong. Too often."

He directed a pointed glare at Camille, then motioned her ahead on the path. Nodding, she stepped onto the three-foot-wide ledge.

Without looking down, she crept along, feeling the shift of rock under her boot. Good God.

Behind her, someone slipped. Sarge's arm whipped out to catch Reveka before she plunged over the precipice.

After she recovered, they all held their breath, inching along, the light waning as their headlamps cut through a patch of mist. Wind whispered in their ears.

Griff, said her own personal ghosts.

I'm coming, she thought. *Coming for you.*

With renewed purpose, she felt her way along the rock. Soon, the path widened considerably, allowing them to gather together and help each other to safety. Good. All accounted for.

Something stirred behind her, rattling the leaves of a bush.

Camille spun around, finding nothing. She checked her wrist tracker. Silent.

Turning back around, she saw Sarge scanning the area, still weighed down with his weapons, his shotgun primed.

Quiet steps, shuffling over rock. A snuff. A growl.

No one moved. All eyes were trained on something behind her. Slowly, she started to take out her dart gun. Started to turn around.

Eyes. Six pairs of preternaturally shining orbs glowing from the skulls of wolves.

A huge gray one slunk forward. The alpha female. It flashed teeth. Fangs.

Inching her hand toward her belt, Camille grabbed her guns—both dart and adrenaline. "Aunt Bea? We're about to go Red Riding Hood."

Behind her, she heard Sarge cock his shotgun.

In front of her, the alpha wolf licked its lips.

Chapter 8

Juni, approximately nine months ago
The night before the strigoiaca *came*

"**P**rofessor Bragg?" Camille asked, addressing her squawking, good-for-nothing cell phone.

Just seconds ago, ensconced in her spare, fire-warmed upstairs room at the Juni inn, she'd been talking to her adviser about her dissertation. Now she'd lost the connection.

"Great," she said to Griff, who was lounging on her bed with his cellular modem computer on his lap. "Crummy provider. Are you still online?"

"Not anymore." He shrugged, shut down and closed the laptop. "I wasn't working on anything important anyway. I thought the rainstorm might complicate reception."

Nodding toward the window, he indicated the gray skies and restless tree branches stirring behind the embroidered curtains.

Camille's heart squeezed at his tousled, bed-head hair. Ruffled, boyish, carefree. Could he be any more lovable?

"So much for work," she said, turning off her phone and tossing it onto a chair with faded blue upholstery.

Due to yesterday's enlightening confrontation between the old woman and Petar Vladislav, she'd wanted to get Bragg's opinion about the legend of the male vampire tribe. Wanted to know if she should focus her questions on them or if she should continue with the old angle. She trusted her adviser implicitly; he had a vested interest in her success since he was a family friend. That's why she'd chosen Texas A&M over Yale—her alma mater—or any other graduate school. Because of Bragg's unheralded expertise and the personal attention he offered.

Like Camille, Griff got rid of his workload, too, placing it on the nightstand next to a wreath of wild roses and a clunky light with tassels hanging from the cover. He motioned to her.

Come here.

She did, lazily crawling to his side. With a hint of kittenish delight, she swept her bare foot over his jeans-clad calf, resting her toes between his legs.

He bundled her into his arms, tugging at a handful of her pink long johns. "I think we've both labored enough."

Since chatting with Ecaterina yesterday, Camille had interviewed six more Juni villagers, but the feisty old woman had quietly left after the afternoon's showdown. Bummer, because there was no telling what Camille could've learned from her.

Griff leaned over to douse the light. The fire snapped in its grate, casting lopsided shadows over the wood walls and sepia-tinged paintings of saints.

"So," Camille said, running an index finger down the front of his shirt, "you getting bored yet?"

He laughed in answer, then said, "How could I possibly tire of watching you in action? You're a veritable poem in motion, with the way you collect pieces of this cultural puzzle. And I enjoy seeing Ms. Godea warming up to you."

"Sure. A trip to the center of the sun couldn't thaw our translator." Camille drew her finger downward, over his rib cage, his stomach. Under his shirt.

When she brushed the soft down leading into Griff's jeans, he buried his face into her hair, groaned.

She paused before asking her next question, almost afraid of the answer. "You're not ready to go back home?"

Her finger sketched back and forth on his belly, and he gripped her long johns. His breathing quickened, tickling her ear with sensuous warmth.

"Do you want me to leave?" he labored to ask.

All her emotional baggage, all her short-term fumblings for love, had taught her that men deserted when they'd gotten what they wanted. Oddly enough, Griff was still around, even after finding out that she wasn't exactly the most normal girlfriend he could've hoped for. Half of her needed to give him an easy way out, just in case he was secretly searching for one. The other half cried for him to stay.

"No," she said. "I don't want you to leave. It's just…this research could go on for a long time. Depending on what I find, I might even decide to stay in Juni, collecting anecdotal evidence of this male tribe."

"Hey." When he looked into her eyes, she could see the fire there. The hunger, raw and passionate. "When will you stop running?"

"I'm not."

"Then we'll call it hiding, Camille. You're still hiding from life—this time using vampire folklore as a temporary shelter. Are you ever going to go home?"

"Home." She leaned into the hand he was using to play with her hair, kissed his palm. "Home's a pretty abstract word."

He didn't say anything, no doubt knowing that her past made nesting kind of tough.

"The closest thing I have to home is—" she peeked at him from under her eyelashes "—well, you."

As the words hung in the firewood-tinged air, something pooled in the depths of his brown eyes. A tidal shift, covering desire with deep emotion.

Had she really said what she'd said? Jeez, talk about putting your heart up for grabs. She waited, wondering what he'd do.

After a tense second that seemed more like a year, Griff closed his eyes, rested his forehead against hers.

Oh. The bad-news pose. The grandiose *but* in the you're-a-great-girl-but scenario.

"Griff." She pulled away slightly, grasping his hands in hers. "I shouldn't have opened my big mouth. Sometimes it's good to have patience. Maybe not blurting out every feeling as it registers would be more prudent, you know? I'm just not used to a guy who'd wait two weeks to sleep with me and—"

"I would have waited longer, if that's what it took to win your heart."

Her trail of excuses came to an abrupt end. "You…you would have?"

He touched the ring around her neck, and that seemed to explain everything for him.

What was he saying?

Griff's smile was sad, weighted down slightly at the tips. She wondered if it was because she was dancing around this next step in their commitment. Fear held her back.

He kissed her, his lips soft and warm against her mouth. "I can't imagine life without you."

The blood melted to a buzz in her veins.

Tentatively, she touched her mouth to his, echoing his sweet gesture. God, he felt right to her: the way he fit into places that needed filling. The way he warmed her, body to body, when nothing else would work—not fires or blankets or thoughts of academic success.

They sipped at each other, testing, enjoying the taste of lingering wine from the evening meal, of basking in this new awareness.

With every tender caress, every kiss, he branded her

with growing realization. Griff was more than just a fleeting neediness, more than a longing to be adored or finally thought of as beautiful by a man.

He was scary territory, unexplored.

Could she give everything to him? Not only her body, but also her soul?

Griff pressed his lips to her neck, her ear.

"I love you, Lady Tex."

The elusive words triggered an implosion, years in the building. The edge of a sob caught at her chest.

Weakened, strengthened, Camille collapsed against him. "Me, too." A racking breath tore through her. "Me, too."

He chuckled, almost sounding relieved. He petted her cheek, then her hair, while rain tapped at their window.

"Well," he finally said. "There it is."

"Admitting it wasn't so terrifying."

"Not at all."

They stared at each other for a moment, the fire popping, raindrops increasing in strength, tumbling on the roof now. A rogue shadow stole over Griff, darkening half his face, lending him a slant of danger.

Spurred by a jolt of intense desire, Camille rose to her knees, leaned forward, skimming her hands under his shirt, lifting it off his body. Unable to wait for the material to clear his head, she dived underneath the cotton, capturing his mouth with hers.

His arms were raised, caught by the shirt.

"This means you're mine." She laughed. "All mine."

He jerked when she pattered her fingertips upward,

echoing the rainfall. Over his chest, under his arms. She raked through the hair there, tickling him.

"Bloody hell," he said, trying to tug the shirt off his head. "Could you give a bloke a little help?"

She caught one of his nipples in her mouth, swirling her tongue over it, feeling it harden.

"Uh-uh," she moaned.

Still, he managed to free himself, whipping the shirt away, then driving her into the bed's down quilt.

He loomed over her. "I've got you now."

"Yes, you do."

A beat passed, one in which his expression turned from teasing to serious. "No more running?"

She swallowed, her pulse speeding up. She'd been found in her hiding place, revealed.

What would come next?

"No more running," she said, pulling him down to kiss her again.

He lengthened his body over hers, cradling the back of her head with one hand. Camille went liquid at his gentleness, at the way he moved over her, shifting his hips, making her ache.

She shucked off her long john top, then molded her bare chest to his. Her distended nipples grazed the toned smoothness of his skin, and she arched, pressing closer.

When he slid a knee between her thighs, she opened for him, wrapping one leg around his, gliding her hands downward, cupping his rear, urging him to fit against her.

He did, nudging the slick center of her with his erection. She wiggled against him, wanting more.

"Let's see some of that patience," he whispered, his voice strained and breathless as he took her earlobe into his mouth.

In response, she undid his fly, stroking him, urging him out.

"That's not very patient." His lips traveled down to her neck, where he nipped at her.

Camille shivered, digging her nails into his back.

He made a low, guttural sound, then bit a little harder, but not enough to wound. Never to wound.

Camille rocked against him, and their rhythm picked up. He rammed against her, and she cried out, needing him inside.

"Come on," she panted, sitting up, working off his jeans and her long john bottoms. "You're killing me."

Then they were both exposed, the slickness between her legs heating her, making her blood pound and thrash there in readiness.

"Camille…" Sweat and firelight burnished his skin as he settled on top of her, guiding her to lie on her back. He pushed the hair away from her damp face, then, with one easy thrust, entered her.

"That's it," she said, gasping.

She was home. No more running. She'd stop in her tracks for Griff. Would always be where he was.

She anchored her hands against the iron headboard as he pounded into her, their skin moist, sliding.

Thunk. Thunk. Thunk, went the headboard against the wall.

Or maybe it was her heartbeat, accelerating now, near to bursting with the love she felt for this man.

Thunk...thunk...thunk...

On the backs of her eyelids, red, swollen circles throbbed, pumped, raced for what seemed like hours, then bumped against each other, faster and faster.

Thunk, thunk, thunk...

It was almost as if the scarlet cells were living, pulsing into vivid bursts, stretching until they almost exploded.

Thunkthunkthunk...

With a thunderous boom, her world crashed, then expanded, shuddering into crimson drops that settled just under her skin.

Still beating. Needing.

Camille opened her eyes, watching Griff work to his own climax. She stimulated him until he strained to the breaking point, loved him as he spilled into her.

Afterward, when they held each other, Camille stroked his face, his high cheekbones. The dimple of his satiated smile.

"We've really done it," she whispered. "Now I'm never going to let you go."

She'd never said truer words, and their intensity scared her. Exhilarated her.

"You'd better not," said Griff, gathering her closer.

She had no way of knowing how much her promise would mean when the *strigoiaca* did finally come.

The very next night.

Chapter 9

Present

Camille aimed her dart gun at the approaching alpha wolf, surreptitiously giving herself an adrenaline shot at the same time. Four muted pops behind her indicated that the Vasile women had done the same.

"Sound ready for monitoring," Beatrix commented through the headset.

The beast's eyes glowed vampire-red as it stalked toward the team. The rest of its pack—five other very big grays—snarled in back of their leader, shifting nearer.

One of the four village women behind Camille uttered a quick prayer.

"God be with you, dear girl," Bea said. "Come back to me." Her transmission fuzzed to an end.

I will, Camille thought. *With Griff.*

Taking a stance next to Camille, Sarge pumped his shotgun, pointed it toward the alpha.

"Please!" Camille said to him, adrenaline fluttering through her. "Let's see if we can knock them out first."

"This ain't *Wild Kingdom,* Howard."

"Ashe would want you to keep them alive, too, unless there's no other choice."

Sarge cursed but didn't put down his weapon. "Usually I get to hear his scolding after my work's done but, lucky me, I've got you here instead."

Reveka's voice, low and calm, filled Camille's earpiece. "There is another one behind us."

"Super," Camille said to Sarge. "We've got seven of them."

Then, to the women, she said, "We cannot let them circle us. Take the nearest wolf. Fire when ready."

A volley of mechanical spitting sounds cut through the mist, thunking when the darts hit the wolves. During the responding yelps of surprise, Camille reached into her utility belt for another dart from her supply, then popped one into place, targeting and firing again at a smaller wolf hanging near the back of the pack.

Her team had kick-ass aim, but it wasn't good enough. Only three of the weakest wolves crashed to the ground, dust kicking up around their heavy bodies.

But four of the animals, who were roughly the size of tiny horses, stayed standing, nipping at the darts embedded in their fur.

"Maybe," Sarge said, "nobody told them they're supposed to pass out."

The next thing Camille knew, the roar of a gunshot split the air, taking out one conscious wolf while the other stutter-stepped backward.

Camille whipped around to find Delia, revolver in hand. Ana, Reveka and Lucia had gotten theirs out, as well.

She should've known they'd be packing.

"See," Sarge muttered. "Your women know that bullets might be useless on these vampires, but they're great for bringing down howlers."

One-handed, he produced a pistol he'd hidden in another ankle holster, then tossed it to her while still aiming his shotgun.

She made a move for it, but with speed that scrambled the eye, the wolf sprang at the gun, batted it over the cliff with its snout and rocketed toward Sarge.

Firing, he caught the wolf in midair with a screeching yelp. Undaunted, it landed on him, teeth gleaming, paw knocking the shotgun aside with a powerful swipe.

The weapon twirled through the air, flashing around like the blades of a chopper, then shattered against the trunk of a pine tree.

She'd never seen anything so fast before. A blur. A smudge ripping into Sarge's leather vambraces.

"Dammit!" That gun would've come in handy about now.

Instead, Camille reloaded her own device, hoping two darts would do the trick.

What the hell were these things anyway? Superwolves?

Trying to keep her cool amid the chaos of the other two beasts going after the women, Camille targeted.

Zing!

A second dart lodged into the alpha wolf.

Two doses of tranquilizer and a shotgun gouge to its chest. It should've brought down an elephant.

As the animal sank its teeth into Sarge's protected arm, Camille holstered her—yes, she admitted it now—*worthless* dart gun and glanced around, gaze lighting on a thick tree branch. She grabbed it, ran over to Sarge, lifted the makeshift club above her head and brought it down with a bang against the wolf's skull.

It ignored her and kept right on digging into Sarge. But the mercenary was holding his own, throttling the beast with one hand as he reached for his machete with the other.

A round of shots sounded in back of her, then a death yelp. The women had got one. Two wolves left.

The alpha's jaws worked, teeth mangling Sarge's left vambrace to shreds. It slashed, bit, inflicted fang-tear damage on the mercenary.

He couldn't get to his machete. "Howard! My knife!"

He angled out his leg, clearly wanting her to use his bowie.

With a rough yell of pain, Sarge threw back his head as the wolf clamped his bare arm in its mouth, chomping.

His pain tore into her, too.

Driven by fear for him, Camille dropped her tree branch and dived for his ankle sheath, yanked out the knife. Then she grasped the handle in the ice-pick grip she'd seen Sarge demonstrate this morning and put all her strength into stabbing the wolf in its neck.

The blade slipped into fur and skin all too easily.

Blood spurted out of the wound, and the wolf instantly snapped at her, beat at her with a paw.

That gave Sarge the opportunity to maneuver, to roll out from under the wolf enough to access his machete. Then he knelt, brandished the weapon, ready for more.

In the meantime, Camille used her free hand to shove the alpha away while pulling out the bowie. When the wolf came at her again, she delivered a roundhouse kick to its snout.

It winced, caught her boot in its teeth, yanked, flipped her to the ground.

Slam. The air jarred out of Camille's lungs, and the world went lopsided. Fur…teeth…red eyes reflecting the emerging moon…

She had to get to her feet. Now.

Launching herself up to her knees, she saw that Sarge, his left arm shredded crimson with hanging skin, was playing machete chicken with the wolf. It'd snap at him; Sarge would strike. They were both so fast Camille could barely keep track of what was happening.

There was a scream behind her, near the narrow path.

When she turned around, Reveka was wrestling on the ground with the other remaining wolf while Lucia, Delia and Ana madly slashed at it with their own new knives.

A particularly vicious growl from Sargent reclaimed Camille's attention. The alpha was attacking his bloody left arm again, vising onto it, tugging.

Was it trying to dismember him?

Sarge arced his machete downward, burying the blade in the fur of its back. Still, it hung on, determined.

He reached for his flamethrower, couldn't grab it.

Camille wiped the blood-slippery bowie handle on her bodysuit, then sheathed it in her belt, intending to use something more lethal.

Save Sarge, she thought, the words speeding through her head. *Nothing else is as important as defending his life.*

Sarge would help her get to Griff. That was why she needed to go after those wolves now.

With all the courage she could muster, she flew forward, planted her boot on the wolf's back and pulled at the machete.

Resistance from wounded muscle. A wet sucking sound.

"Oh, God," she said, fighting to get the blade out.

One more tug, one more shove of her boot and...

Sluuuurrrrp.

It was out.

She took a batter's stance, then swung the machete around, embedding it in the wolf's neck.

Immediately, she backstepped, unsheathed her knife and picked up the tree branch, ready to defend herself.

The animal glanced over its shoulder, choked out a bubble of blood. A saliva-thick thread of scarlet crept out of its mouth as the beast fell down from Sarge to its feet, weakly crouching in preparation for another attack.

Both Camille and Sarge exchanged miffed glares, then backed away.

With quicksilver speed, the alpha leaped at her. All Camille saw was fang, dimmed red by Sarge's blood.

She had enough presence of mind to swing the branch first, catching the wolf at the head, but that didn't stop its momentum. Yet it *did* allow her to use the leverage to push herself away.

No time to think. Just move.

Blindly, she swung her other arm backward, upward, spinning around, ice-picking the wolf's soft belly.

It fell, wheezed, eyes fixed on her, tongue lolling out.

Why? it seemed to be asking. *This is my function in life. You didn't have to kill me for it.*

When it banged to the dirt, Camille actually felt the thump of its weight through the soles of her boots.

Her breath felt like sharp ice in her lungs, spiking each attempt to draw in air, the chill rushing to her head.

Slowly, she bent down, withdrew the knife with a final tug, grasped a handful of the wolf's fur and squeezed.

You were keeping me from Griff, she thought.

Wasting no time, Sarge moved to them with his flamethrower, pulled Camille away from the wolf, tore the machete out of its skin, then torched the beast with one long burst of flame.

She watched for just a moment, absently tucking the knife into her belt.

They hadn't been shape-shifters, she thought, taking in the carnage around her, the wolves who were only that.

Wolves.

But they hadn't been your garden-variety howlers, either. She had to admit *that* much.

A scream and a burst of more gunfire shook her back to the moment.

Reveka and Lucia were on their stomachs, reaching over the edge of the narrow path they'd recently conquered. Ana was aiming her revolver over the side. She took a shot.

Where was that last wolf? Where was Delia?

Camille ran to them, skidded to a stop. Saw Delia's gloved hands gripping the ledge.

Good God.

Dropping to her belly, Camille reached out, too, joining the other women in gripping Delia's wrists, trying to pull her to safety.

Delia's china-doll eyes were wide, her mouth opened in a soft mewl of terror. Her body seemed much too heavy for her size, and she was thrashing from side to side. As Camille scanned lower, she saw why.

The last wolf was dangling also, jaws latched on to Delia's torn leg, its fur matted with blood from Ana's gunshots.

The taste of bile burned the back of Camille's mouth. "Hold on, Delia."

The woman groaned, gnashing her teeth together. Her body jerked as she lost her grip on the ledge. Reveka and Lucia strained, tightened their holds on her wrists.

Dammit, this wasn't working.

Camille got up and sprinted to Sarge, who was setting flame to all the wolves. His left arm hung at his side, but he didn't seem to mind the ribboned skin or the pain.

"Machete," she said with no further explanation.

He merely shot her a look that said it all.

Welcome. Glad you've arrived, Howard. Glad you've decided that killing ain't such an immoral thing after all.

Yeah. She'd deal with her conscience later, when there was time.

He handed over the weapon. Nodding, she acknowledged the loan, not his judgment.

Then she took off for Delia, undoing a rope strapped to her utility belt, securing it around her waist.

"Ana," she said, summoning the villager whose gunshots weren't helping the situation.

Camille wrapped the other end of the rope around the other woman. "Hold on to me."

She could see the surprise in Ana's eyes, the respect for Camille's willingness to go over the edge for them.

But Camille felt guilty accepting the admiration. She wanted Delia back. Even with a bum leg, she could fight the vampires with the UV wand's stunning powers, and she could use a dart gun.

The mercenaries who'd come before them had failed, not only because they didn't have the proper weapons, but also because they didn't have *women*. Women would even things out in a battle for Griff with the *strigoiaca*. And the more women Camille had with her, the better.

When Ana finished with the rope, Camille patted the

woman on the shoulder. Without further ado, the red-scarved peasant anchored herself, calling over Sarge for support. Good. Camille hadn't been forced to ask him.

Machete clutched in one hand, she eased herself over the ledge.

As Camille braced her boots against the rock to walk down the face of the cliff, Delia watched her pass, and Camille forced a smile, trying to calm her.

When she got to the wolf, it was biting almost all the way through Delia's leg in its bid to stay alive. It looked at Camille sidelong, exposing the panicked whites of its eyes. The woman's gnawed boot hung off her shattered ankle. Tendons fluttered away from bone.

Camille had seen body parts before, but her stomach still turned.

"Sorry about this." She grabbed a hank of the wolf's head hair and positioned the machete at its throat.

Don't think about it.

With an efficient heave, she sliced from left to right. But even though the beast's body went limp, its jaws wouldn't let go of Delia's ankle.

As its blood dripped down, down into the mist, Camille cursed, then hacked the rest of its head off. Then, after an endless second of skin being ripped from muscle, the body fell into the chasm, too, pawing the air.

Delia, probably feeling the sudden lack of weight, also glanced down, saw that the head was still attached.

"Ayyyy!" she screamed, shaking her leg to get it off.

"No, stop!" Camille tried to hold her motionless.

Reveka and Lucia pulled at Delia, but the woman had already let go with one hand, swatting at the head.

"Delia!" Camille reached for her swinging arm.

Both Reveka and Lucia cried out at the same time, and Camille looked up.

In what seemed to be slow motion, Delia's glove peeled off, and she slid out of their grips.

The next thing she knew, Camille was reaching for her, grasping air, watching the pretty, porcelain-skinned woman plunging into the mist. Her face was upturned in confused terror, her mouth gaping, her hands—one gloveless—waving.

They could hear her screaming even after she disappeared. And then the sound jarred to a stop.

Shocked, Camille couldn't look up from where Delia had disappeared into the swirl of gray.

Part of her felt as if she'd fallen into the abyss, too.

When they got up to the main structure, the blaring moon revealed black, winged gargoyles perched on the roofs of Castle Bethlen. Eagles' nests decorated the ramparts, but they were empty, devoid of life.

The only evidence of that were the bones. Rabbits, rats, sheep, foxes. Humans. Her hired mercenaries?

They littered the packed dirt like morbid cobblestones.

As the team members paused in their numb exploration of one of many courtyards they'd found, Camille said, "They won't be up here. No protection from the sun."

Besides, she thought, the stench of vampire was

missing. That notable lack of humanity, that faint mustiness of things left abandoned.

Drained of energy, she glanced around. A chapel, moss covered, studded with shards of faded, colored rock resembling the fragments of broken stained glass, squatted in one corner. In the middle of the courtyard, half of a well waited, its stones scattered by the hand of time.

Sarge stood next to her, left arm bound with bandages from her first-aid pouch. He seemed unaffected, but then again, she'd seen him pop a lot of Motrin pills earlier.

All of them were weak, their adrenaline spent. Grief. But they just didn't have time to wallow.

After Delia had died, Camille had updated Bea and used the doctor's own coagulating gel to stop Sarge's bleeding. There'd never been any question about his turning back or having one of the drivers replace Delia. It was almost as if the reminder of mortality had doubled the team's inner strength, their rage to succeed.

So, instead of waiting for backup, Sarge had asked Lucia to contact one of the Humvee drivers about having Ashe stir up the magickal big guns—a Dragon, he'd said.

Camille had almost reminded him that Delia had died, unprotected by any of Ashe's spells or magick. But she didn't have the energy. Not after watching Delia fall.

Besides, their team had ended up beating those wolves—those preternaturally fast guardians.

She thought of their speed, their size. *Was* there something besides Mother Nature at work in this part of the world? Or was the stress driving her batty?

Either way, she had confidence in her team. They could do this, even with their numbers decreased by one.

She watched Sarge as he closed his eyes, moved toward the well.

"You're right about them not being up here, Howard, but they're somewhere real close."

A shiver ripped down her spine, almost as if someone—something—was watching.

She glanced over her shoulder, but all she saw was one of those gargoyles, its massive wings spanning the face of the moon.

Creepy.

She tapped on her watch tracker. If the vampires were around, shouldn't it be thumping by now?

Sarge took a few steps toward the chapel. "Listen."

Following him, she tried to tune into what he was picking up.

"I don't hear anything," she whispered.

"It's not so much hearing, it's…" Sarge shrugged, his weapons clanking as they both moved away.

"Do you have sonar?" she asked. "How is it you know what to do without tracking devices?"

"Part of it's trusting yourself, I guess."

His face went stony, chiseled out of hard knocks. She knew Hana had crossed his mind.

"And," he added, "I've got a sort of touch with the vamps, and with predators in general. When Ashe told you about Hana, he didn't tell you about how *I* found *her.* I was just too green to realize she was a vampire."

"Okay, first, how do you know Ashe told me?" There

hadn't been a moment for the men to chat between her conversation with the Wiccan and the start of their trek.

"I asked him to." Sarge shot her a cocky glance. "Ashe doesn't like to deceive, but we thought a little of your sympathy aimed in my direction wouldn't come amiss. And seeing as how we both know you'll have no use for me when we get to those bloodsuckers, I wanted you to think twice about turning on me, Miss Bleeding Heart."

"Play on my better instincts, why don't you. How do you know that I don't think you're a complete ass now, even after the stories?"

"Hey, your opinion of me couldn't get any worse than when we started."

Argh. And the worst part? He was right. Ashe's story about Hana and dear old Dad had gotten to Camille, all right. Even now, as she stood next to him, there was a hum of awareness separating them. An unsettling need to glance at him just to see if he was watching *her.*

"You have another question?" he asked. "We need to go silent in a second here."

She heaved in a huge breath, head swimming at the thought of being so close to her mingled hopes…and fears.

"Sarge, are you some kind of chosen one, then? A Buffy without the fashion sense?"

He laughed softly. "I don't know what I am, but I figure the good Lord gave me a leg up on vamps for a reason. That's why me and Ashe hang around together—two birds of a feather. Back in the day, the other operatives trusted him, but thought he was kind of strange. I didn't. I sort of understood his *feelings* and all that. Not that I'm an empath, too. I'm just…"

"Adapted to your surroundings. Like a good survivor."

She wondered if he'd developed his talents while avoiding his father's belts. If he'd chosen hiding places as a little boy, adjusting his senses so he'd always know where the predator was.

But that was a kooky theory. True, humans didn't use a fraction of their brains' potential, but that didn't mean they were all walking psychics.

Speaking of which…

She felt it again. That very reasonable niggling. The knowledge of being watched.

A shadow rolled over in front of Camille, and she switched her focus to the roofs.

There should've been a gargoyle where she was glancing. There'd been one there just minutes before. Now it was five feet to the left.

Or maybe the moon had just moved.

"Crossbow?" she whispered to Sarge.

Again, without question, he handed it to her. Camille took aim at the monstrous winged guardian, then fired.

The arrow zinged straight toward the gargoyle, veered to the right just as it was about to embed itself in its skin or scales or….

Why had the arrow deviated so sharply?

"Your crossbow sucks," she said.

"You just can't shoot the big boy," Sarge said, taking the weapon back. "And don't waste good ammunition on decorations."

All of the women were watching her as if she were bonkers. And maybe she was. Their watch trackers weren't thumping, and Sarge wasn't "sensing" anything about that gargoyle.

"Little jumpy there," Camille said, adjusting her utility belt. "I just want to find these things."

Sarge cast her an amused gaze, then froze and turned toward the well. With a hand gesture, then a raised palm—which she took to mean "Stay here"—he stalked toward the fixture.

She could hear her quickened breathing. Her loud-as-thunder pulse.

Then he motioned her forward, signaling for the women to come, too.

Blump. Blump.

It was her watch starting up. Faint. Reliable.

Her heart stuttered.

They all bent over the well, looking into pure darkness. Even their headlamps didn't lend illumination.

The smell. Blood. Near death.

Vampire.

Her common sense told her to run, but that would be a betrayal of everything she cared about. This time, the darkness held life for her, and she wouldn't turn her back on it. Never again.

She stood, untied her rope, then secured it to an iron stake poking out of the ground. Without a word, Sarge tested it, seeing if it'd hold her weight.

Thumbs up.

Positioning herself at the edge of the well, she pointed to Sarge, then Reveka, Ana and Lucia.

She didn't look down, just grabbed the rope in one gloved hand with her UV wand in the other. Here it went.

With a what-the-hell breath, she jumped in, balanced her feet against the wall, sprinted downward, her head-lamp shining a lone ring of light on the stones in front of her.

Fifteen seconds later, she hit bottom in an attack-ready crouch, tracker telling her that she was safe for now.

Blump. Blump.

The tunnel was clear. She jerked the rope as a signal for Sarge to follow.

A fetid wind rushed over her, but Camille stood her ground, just inviting one of those harpies to take her on.

Let's go, she thought. I'm so ready.

When something brushed her shoulder, she proved her mettle by swinging back her elbow in a dedicated punch while flicking on her UV light.

Crash! Something got it right in the jaw.

On guard, she turned to find Sarge with his good hand still on the rope. Since his bad arm was hanging by his side, she guessed he'd rested it during the descent.

But his pain showed in his gaped mouth.

Impulsively, she jumped up, hugged him to relay her remorse. Uh-huh. Hugged. Him.

A surprised, or maybe agonized, grunt answered her, but she couldn't let go. For a crazy moment, it felt too good, too natural.

Two halves of a whole strengthening themselves by clinging together in the dark.

His body was honed, hard, comforting in the way a handle would be if you'd fallen down and had to grab on to something. When his healthy arm slid up her back, Camille stiffened, realized she had crossed a line. Had enjoyed the fleeting reassurance way too much.

Immediately, she backed up, reached out to slap his good shoulder, stressing to him that she still thought he was a sexless side of beef.

Her lamp revealed his responding gaze. It burned over her, almost as if he hadn't wanted her to let go of him.

Which, truth be told, she almost hadn't.

Weirded out, she busied herself by turning off her UV wand to conserve its energy—they'd need every second of juice—and adjusting her scientific armory as the rest of the women came down. They left the rope hanging since there was no way to undo it.

All around them darkness hovered, cold and threatening. She couldn't breathe…oh, God, she couldn't…

Griff. Dammit, the dark wasn't going to stop her.

Clawing for oxygen, she fortified herself. With a burst of courage, she forged ahead into the darkness, ignoring the painful blaze of her pulse, the terror of the unknown.

Griff. The name pulled her through the blackness.

Using the increasingly agitated beat of her tracker, she led them down a passageway, probably a secret one, she thought, from days gone by. A place where a royal family could hide during a revolution or siege.

It seemed to go on forever, this trip into the cold void. She wanted to start running, blindly chasing the yearning, the hunger to find Griff.

Blumpblumpblump…

Closer. She couldn't stand this.

Stealthily, the team gripped their UV wands, while Sarge readied what looked like an explosive device or two. They gathered by a gap in a stone wall that led to a chamber with half the ceiling torn off.

Inside, lit by a shaft of moonlight, two men were crumpled in the corner. Their clothes were nothing more than strips of material, their skin washed out, their hair long, their sky-tilted faces hidden by beards.

With a barely restrained cry of fright, relief, curiosity, joy, horror—she wasn't sure what—Camille surged forward, moving to flick on her UV wand while shooting herself up with adrenaline.

But not before she saw the bestial red eyes of the *strigoiaca* streaking toward them.

Chapter 10

Juni, approximately nine months ago
The night the strigoiaca *came*

Camille cuddled against Griff as yesterday's rain continued. Clouds covered the moon, casting the room into pure darkness, spreading a chill due to the spent fire.

Today, she'd interviewed five more villagers—men who tried to act like Petar Vladislav's rash words hadn't mattered. She should've been excited to witness the effects of folklore in action, to see how the tales were coloring village dynamics and relationships.

Instead, she felt on edge.

Maybe it was because she could imagine Flora Vladislav bursting into their room to punish her and Griff for sleeping in the same bed. Maybe she felt protective of Griff in light of how the *strigoiaca*—even if they didn't really exist—preyed exclusively on men. Or maybe it was all these tales of the undead, seeping into her bones like water into earth.

Death can come back to life.

She wanted to believe it, wanted to pull her parents back from the grave, tell them how much she missed them. How much she wanted them to meet Griff.

The thought was attractive, but impossible. Silly.

Vampires and resurrection existed only in fiction.

So why was she more willing to embrace the concept with each passing day?

In his slumber, Griff clutched her tighter against him, and Camille melted into his arms. Time to rest. Time to feel safe and warm, forgetting all of her questions.

She must've slept, because when she heard the night's first scream, she bolted, caging Griff with her arms.

"What…?" he mumbled.

Camille fumbled for the light. It wouldn't turn on. "Did you hear that?"

Her heartbeat was like a card stuck in the spokes of a bike wheel, fluttering. Caught.

Blinking away the sleep from her gaze, she froze, listening.

Nothing.

But hadn't both of them heard it?

They'd packed miniflashlights in their backpacks, so Camille tumbled out of bed in her long johns, felt her way around the room, intent on finding one. "Go back to sleep, okay? It was a bird or…" What?

Another scream. Closer this time.

A male?

Come on, she thought. Imagination working over-
time.

"I heard *that*," Griff said.

While she battled the fear creeping over her skin, Camille finally found her backpack where she'd left it, by
the foot of the bed. Digging into the front pocket, she
groped for the small light device.

She heard Griff sit up. "Bloody dark. Tex?"

"Griff, stay in bed. I'm going to knock on Mrs. Vladislav's door down the hall to see what's happening."

But it'd be nothing. She was sure about that.

Outside, the wind howled, slapping rain against the
window. Then it calmed to an eerie whistle.

She found her cell phone first, turned it on, lighting
the space around her with a blue glow. "No signal."

The covers rustled as Griff tossed them away.

"Where're you going?"

"Down the hall, as you said." There was the swish
of denim rubbing against itself. He'd found his jeans
and had thumped back onto the bed to put them on.

She almost told him to bag his testosterone and get
back under the covers. But why bother? What protection were covers?

And why was she worried about it? What did she
think was happening? One of the fabled vampire attacks?

She tried to laugh at the thought, but couldn't. Not
after hearing that old woman a couple of days ago.

There, the flashlight. She prepared to turn it on.

The door hinges squeaked, the opened barrier ushering in colder air.

"Griff, just stay in bed, okay?"

He paused.

"I am in bed."

Time stopped, blood pounding in her head. Camille dragged her gaze to the doorway.

A pair of eyes was watching them. Red, glowing. Bobbing as a slight buzzing sound filled the darkness, mingling with the moaning wind.

Sweet Jesus, she couldn't move.

Another male scream rent the air, but it was closer this time. It came from down the hall. A female yelled the name "Mihas!"

Mr. Vladislav?

Then a shatter, glass breaking. An inhuman screech that yanked Camille to her feet, trapping her breath in her chest.

More from a jerk of terror than anything else, she flicked the flashlight switch.

The same monstrous yowl filled their own room as the thing in their doorway was revealed.

Moon-white skin. Shredded nightdress. Long, wild dark hair. Claws. Fangs.

And the eyes.

Camille dived toward Griff, covering him, sending them both crashing against the wall. The useless lamp smashed against the rug-covered floor planks. She wanted to get him out of here…to do something…anything.

"The hell?" Griff said in her ear.

But he barely had the words out when the thing zipped forward, bare feet never touching the ground as it winged to him.

Drawing on instinct, Camille thrust out her leg, kickboxing style. Once. Again. Each time, the thing darted away.

Too fast. While Camille helplessly stood in front of her boyfriend, unarmed except for her balled fists, the vampire hovered two feet away. Then something long and slimy—her tongue?—shot out of her mouth and past Camille so quickly that she doubted she'd seen anything at all.

Behind her, Griff's body crumpled into hers with a pained cry.

Crying out in terror and rage, Camille launched toward the vampire, nails bared.

Get away from him.

But with one swoop of her arm, the female casually knocked Camille over the bed and into the opposite wall.

Her shoulder slammed against wood, numbing skin and muscle. The world swam and she throbbed all over. Still, she struggled to sit up.

This isn't really happening.

There were no such things as vampires.

From down the hall, Camille heard more screams, more crashes and devastation. But all that existed for her right now was this horror.

As the vampire floated before Griff, her body seemingly suspended in water, the moon turned its face away from the clouds. Light filtered through the window, shining on him.

Confused, he was leaning on the nightstand, looking toward Camille, eyes bleary. Dimming.

Have to get to him, have to...

She swayed to her feet, and he reached out to her.

"No..." She scrambled over the bed, not knowing exactly what she was going to do, but she was going to save him, make the life come back into his gaze.

The vampire flashed her fangs at Camille, hissing.

"No, *you* back off," Camille said, her voice unrecognizable, low and garbled. Even though her body was wailing in agony, she crawled toward Griff, holding her hand out to him.

Their fingers brushed.

They're real, his gaze was saying.

Then he hunched forward, eyes rolling back in his head as he fell into the waiting arms of the vampire.

Camille's mouth opened, but no sound came out. Instead, the victorious screech of the creature shattered her heart. In a blur, the vampire bundled Griff over her shoulder, shooting out the doorway.

Leaving Camille grasping air.

Motionless, she thought. Can't move.

Griff...?

Had it really happened? Maybe she was going to wake up any second to find him next to her. That was it.

Numb with shock and the sharp anguish of her pulsing shoulder, she ran her hand over the warm indentation where he'd been sleeping only minutes ago.

A woman's agitated voice shook her to reality. "Ms. Howard?"

Camille startled back to all the screeches, all the downstairs chaos. Flora Vladislav and Ms. Godea were standing in her doorway with lanterns. The older woman's light was shaking, making the tin of the cover rattle. Even the usually unruffled Ms. Godea was wide-eyed.

"They have Mr. Vladislav," his wife said, voice wavering. "It's taken him outside already."

"They are waiting for the rest of the tribe to choose their males," Ms. Godea added.

A refusal to interfere? It almost seemed ritualistic, thought Camille. The realization came from the one single brain cell that was still functioning.

But... Ritual. Tradition. If the creatures weren't helping each other, that was to Camille's advantage.

Her hope kicked into high gear. According to the legends she'd heard, the *strigoiaca* didn't kill the men immediately.

So Griff was still alive.

She'd be *damned* if she let him die like her parents.

Without another wasted second, Camille sprang off the bed, darted toward the window, threw it open. Wind and a mist of rain blasted against her, but she didn't care.

Never looking back, she hopped onto the porch roof, running to the edge, surveying the landscape.

There, by the edge of a neighboring forest, three vampires were holding their quarry and waiting for the other two. She recognized Griff instantly, crumpled over the shoulder of the vampire with the long black hair. Mihas Vladislav and Andrei Bartha were the other victims.

She knew what she had to do. Spying a drainpipe, she leaped, grabbed on to it, ignoring the slicing pain of her shoulder wound. She slid downward, splashing into the mud with a jarring thump.

Even though the breath got knocked out of her, she was on her feet in the next instant, mud soaked and breathless, seeing nothing but Griff in that creature's grasp.

But that's when someone ran out of the inn, bowling her over. She went face first into the mud, sputtering as a pair of hands encased her ankles.

She kicked, trying to free herself.

Got to get Griff.

Her captor wailed, and Camille flipped to her back, still kicking at hands that wouldn't let go.

"Stop!" It was Petar Vladislav, lying on his stomach, blood caked on one side of his head. "Ms. Camille!"

Petar, the guy who'd summoned the vampires.

"Let go," she yelled.

He gaped at her and shook his head frantically.

Camille was about to jerk one of her legs out of his grip and kick him in the face when they were both whipped toward the inn, sliding through the mud, banging up the stairs, their heads and bodies getting hammered, bruised, on every step. At some point, Petar let go of her, and they slid on the floorboards, parallel to each other.

When she finally skidded to a stop, Camille opened her eyes. Lantern light flooded her new location. Liquor bottles, glass cases and a mahogany bar rose above her.

Using that bar, Camille levered herself to her feet, gasping at her stinging, pulsating wounds.

But before she could steady her nerves, another vampire zoomed in front of her, on the other side of the bar, hovering in midair, keeping a quaking Camille from running back outside to Griff. This creature had short brown hair and was garbed in what was once a colorful wool dress.

She flashed her fangs at Camille as Petar fumbled under the bar for matches, then lit fire to one.

Wasting no time, Camille grasped a whiskey bottle and smashed it against the wood. Then she took up a boxing stance and brandished her own jagged weapon.

Just zap out that tongue, she thought.

But the vampire was busy watching Petar, who'd set fire to a bouquet of napkins he'd scrounged from under the bar. The flames kept the creature at a temporary distance.

Why wasn't it using that stinger on Camille?

Behind the vampire, across the room, a large group of village women was attacking another beast with torches and the sharp legs of broken chairs. In a split second of consciousness, Camilla noticed they weren't getting the tongue treatment, either. But the vampire was still stronger than a Texas tornado.

As a matter of fact, one woman went spinning through the air as the creature tossed her out of the way to get access to a male cowering against the wall. As the rest of the women threatened the beast with fire, Camille ducked, avoiding the flying victim. The villager crash-landed next to Camille, shattering the glass casings, her arm breaking off from the impact, her neck snapping to a grotesque angle.

A horrified gasp racked Camille as she shielded herself from flying debris and blasting blood. But she recovered quickly, standing, waving the broken bottle at her own menacing vampire. The one who only wanted to take Petar and be on her way.

Part of her wanted to leave the mouthy student to his own devices because he deserved it. Griff didn't. But part of her couldn't do that. It wasn't in her to kill, even indirectly.

At her feet, Petar whimpered as his napkins were consumed, burning down to his stubborn fingertips.

As she looked up from him, something sharp caught her eye. A blade.

One of Mihas Vladislav's medieval weapons.

Forget a sharp whiskey bottle.

Yet…God. She couldn't be like the person who'd murdered her mom and dad.

But could you actually "kill" a vampire if she was undead?

As the beast jetted about, keeping Petar in her sights, Camille grabbed a small handheld ax, dropped the bottle, then gripped a larger, heavy battle-ax.

"Petar," she said, her pained shoulder causing her to scoot the heftier weapon to the floor near him with her foot, "use this."

She hoped he could do the killing for them both.

Now. Time to attract this thing's attention, if they were going to get out of this alive. She made a sudden movement, and the vampire locked on to her. Wordlessly, Petar grabbed the ax, just as his napkin fire burned out.

The vampire saw Petar's flame disappear. Now that the fire was gone, she darted her tongue at him.

But Camille was swinging her ax before the vampire had even started.

As the stinger emerged, whip quick, Camille cried out in fury, in utter fear, using all her strength to cut into the creature's tongue, nailing it to the bar.

The disembodied pink appendage wiggled through the air, landing on the floor squirming.

Immediately, the vampire turned toward Camille, red eyes wide, blood gushing from her mouth. She didn't seem to understand what had just happened.

But after a lightbulb moment, she hunched, face shriveled in a frantic hiss.

Oh, God, oh, God, oh…

Camille fought the urge to run, but she couldn't. Wouldn't.

Flying forward, the beast bared those fangs. Gasping, Camille ducked, avoiding most of the spraying blood, taking extra care not to allow any into her mouth just in case it carried toxins or something even more damaging. The tales said that only the exchange of blood would create another vampire, and she had to beware of that.

"Petar!" she yelled, voice choked. "Do it!"

Nothing was happening from his end.

Damn it!

Wanting to scare it off without actually killing it, Camille swung her small ax, desperate to defend herself. Then, as the vampire struck forward in a death blow, aiming her claws at her foe's throat, Camille finally let go of her fear.

There was no other choice.

In a mindless explosion of adrenaline, she drew the weapon way back, holding her breath. Swung it forward. The blade cut into the vampire's throat and stayed embedded there, spurting more blood, bathing the mud from Camille's skin.

"Dammit, Petar! Do it! Now!"

The vampire flailed, gurgling, swiping at a panting Camille with her claws while holding her own neck with the other hand. Camille struggled to evade the creature, but it was too strong and quick, even wounded.

Phu-whump. She slapped a palm against Camille's forehead, pinning her to the wall, liquor bottles falling from the shelf, breaking.

Fangs gleamed as the vampire opened her mouth.

Death, thought Camille, heart exploding in her chest. This is death.

She felt to her right, hand closing around the grip of another weapon. It might've been a knife.

Whatever it was, she flailed forward, instinct ruling her actions, defending herself so she could stay alive.

In reaction, the vampire blindly rushed straight at the blade.

And found herself impaled on Camille's weapon.

Panicked, Camille grunted, pushing the vampire away from her, back onto the bar. With a shock, she saw that the long blade had speared through her body, stapling the female to the wood.

A fountain of blood burbled from her chest, and she sighed, clutching the knife. A bitter sting closed Camille's throat, as she stood there, quaking.

The vampire jerked twice, then moaned pitifully, blinking up at her opponent.

Unchecked, an angry tear slipped down Camille's cheek, slicing through mud. Blood.

As they stared at each other, the vampire took one last breath, then started screeching, the varied tenor growing in volume and desperation. A death alarm.

Screeeeeee—

The whoosh of a blade blurred past her sight. Petar and his battle-ax, chopping off the wail. The head.

It rolled over the mahogany, stopping to face Camille, mouth locked in that death scream, eyes sightless, but still watching her.

Always watching.

"Thank you," Camille said through clenched teeth. Petar seemed so proud of himself.

That didn't last long. There was a long screech across the room as the other vampire, still battling the village women, turned toward her fallen comrade.

The creature threw back her head. *Screeeeeeech!* The same death alarm, uninterrupted this time.

The sound tore Camille apart, releasing more terror into her bloodstream. Bullet-like, the vampire zipped over to one of the fighting women—Ecaterina, the girl Camille had interviewed. But instead of trying to get to the man again, she captured the girl, flew away from the other women to a lone corner, then bit into Ecaterina's neck. The teen dropped her stake, jaw slack as she passed out. The vampire lifted her head, mouth ringed with crimson, then deposited the slumped teen on her shoulder.

No! Camille thought. They couldn't get away with taking Ecaterina, too.

The fighting villagers, including Flora Vladislav and Ms. Godea, were exhausted, but they did their best to recapture their neighbor. They threw plates, rushed forward with their torches as Camille ran around the bar, toward the chaos.

Since the villagers hadn't expected the attack on Ecaterina, they scattered, going after the limp teenager, leaving their male exposed. Ecaterina's vampire took advantage of this, zinged over, stunned the man, then cradled him over the other shoulder while flying toward the door.

Hovering there—God help them—was the rest of the tribe. The three who'd been waiting near the woods.

Camille froze in her tracks, chilled by the sight. Then, still carrying their own males, they swarmed Petar, stunning him, spiriting him away, before Camille could even gather her energy and get back to that side of the room.

As they whizzed out the door, their prey carried like limp sacks of grain, Camille caught sight of Griff, his arms flapping against his vampire's back.

"No... No!"

She chased them outside, where the moon shone over wood houses and mud-swirled streets. Tripping down the steps, she tried to keep him in view, but they'd already disappeared into the woods.

Dammit, she could still catch them if she tried.

The sobs came, hard and fast, as she stumbled, not giving up. So tired, so wounded. Exhausted, Camille's bare foot caught in the mud, and she pitched forward, face first in a thick puddle.

"I'm coming," she said, choking on wet dirt.

Then she began to crawl.

There was still a chance.

A hand grasped the back of her long john shirt, the soaked material slurping off her back.

"They are gone," said Ms. Godea's weary voice. "Even if you were fast enough, you would die."

Camille glanced up to see the translator, blood spattered, hair spiking out of its chignon.

"Not such fiction, after all." Ms. Godea helped Camille up, fear still painting her gaze.

Impossible to stand, knees just now starting to give out, wounded shoulder and spent adrenaline clouding vision…

This couldn't have really happened, she thought.

"They took him," Camille whispered. The words echoed, dreamlike, trapped in another dimension.

Quietly, Ms. Godea started sobbing. "The tales—the ones you and I did not believe—say that they will feed on him, but he will not die. Not yet."

Camille was still too stunned to feel anything. "So how can I find him?" Her words quavered, ran together.

Shouts from the inn interrupted them. Families and wives were tearing at their clothes, weeping. Already they were arguing about hiring a rescuer by pooling their meager funds. But some villagers—no doubt the ones who hadn't lost a son or husband—pointed out that these males were sacrifices. Going after them would only bring further destruction to the village.

Leave the *strigoiaca* to their tradition, they said.

Never, Camille thought.

"Ms. Godea, tell them I'll pay for their hunters. Weapons. Tools. Anything."

"I will." The woman's tears waned. "I would also introduce you to a woman, if you please. Dr. Grasu at the university."

"I don't need another therapist."

"No. She is…" Ms. Godea paused. "Knowledgeable about *nosferatu.* She has studied vampirism for years and will be able to recommend solutions. Offer explanations."

"Like…?" Camille still couldn't think straight. Her heartbeat was confusing her.

"Something more than the brute force that failed us tonight. Something more useful than superstition."

God. She was right. They needed more than the weapons Camille had accidentally stumbled over. So much more.

Vampires. Even though she'd seen them, she couldn't believe it. Didn't want to believe it.

"What are you saying?" Her body was cold.

So cold.

"Dr. Grasu will help you. We can bring the dead vampire's body for study and…who knows after that?"

"But they have him *now.* I need to get to him."

"Then you are as good as dead."

Camille couldn't stop shaking. The fear, the aftermath, brought her to her knees. Her body couldn't even take the stress, so what made her think she could save Griff herself? The only way she'd ever be able to attempt a rescue would be to train. To make herself into a being that couldn't feel pain.

An unstoppable machine.

"I want to meet her," Camille said. "This Dr. Grasu. Tomorrow, five minutes ago, whenever you can arrange it."

Ms. Godea nodded, started to tear up again, then ran away, leaving Camille alone.

Really, truly alone.

And that's when the tears came. The all-consuming, rage-washed sorrow and promises of vengeance.

For almost a year, she sent out her mercenary teams. As they failed, one by one, Camille grew stronger.

Eventually, their deaths bought her enough time to become a huntress.

The woman who was now facing two captives.

One who might even be the man she loved.

Chapter 11

Griff stared at the same moon that greeted him night after night. His hair, which had grown long and scraggly, curled over half his sight. Not that seeing was important.

He didn't depend on watching the moon's patterns to keep track of time. Didn't while away the endless hours by worshiping the moon with his gaze. Didn't even much care about the moon itself, as a matter of fact.

But he needed to watch it just the same. It was the same moon the rest of the world saw. The same moon that sang Camille to sleep in whatever bed she rested in now.

Back at the beginning, when all the Juni men had

been alive and daft enough to give fight to the Girls, as he called them, they'd won a small battle. No, they hadn't gotten to keep their blood, their pride, or even the strength all men were born with.

They'd won the moonlight.

After sleeping all day in a lower chamber, chained to the damp stone walls until they were awakened by a vampire for a dinner of goat tartare or rat surprise, the males used to make demands of the *strigoiaca*. They would yell for air, activity, anything to keep them from going stir-crazy.

Anything that would give them enough freedom to encourage their dreams of escape in those days.

The Girls would merely cock their heads at them, dumb to human language, except for Ecaterina. She'd taken a few weeks to shed all of her humanity. To turn vampire after the one Griff called Drusilla had bitten her and forced her to exchange blood in a demented kiss. A kiss that had turned Ecaterina from girl to bloodsucker once and for all.

Yes, Griff had paid close attention to the way the *strigoiaca* worked, even back then. Lady Tex would be proud of the mental anthropological notes he'd taken while living among this foreign tribe.

To make another vampire, blood and saliva were needed, he'd realized after seeing Ecaterina's initiation.

As if it were yesterday, he still remembered her rite of passage on that first night. Remembered the pungent terror of waking up in the arms of Mina—his very own nightgowned vampire, so named for a character from *Dracula*. She'd been feeding off of him, slow slurps of greedy pleasure, and he'd lashed out, so bloody afraid.

But, like every other time he or the other males had tried to rebel, the *strigoiaca* would retain that blank expression and tilt their heads, quelling their captives with a throttling claw around the neck.

It quieted "dinner," but never killed it.

Being a new vampire in those days, Ecaterina had still been half-human, had understood their feisty demands. With some sort of screeching permission from Drusilla, Ecaterina had soon led the males to this Moon Chamber. Every time they visited here, the vampires would stay in the dark and the males would soak up the wan light. Griff couldn't help thinking that he and the guys were a little like tots being taken to the park for playtime.

After all, the vampires needed to keep their food healthy, if not happy.

But in spite of many playtimes in the Moon Chamber, Griff's blood supply had dwindled, and his body had weakened. Ultimately, days—weeks? months?—ago, Griff had finally admitted that he was dying.

That he'd never see his Camille again.

Unlike the first days, when all the males had been alive, he and Petar Vladislav were the only meals left for all five of the female vampires. Their energy was disappearing exponentially because the other male pets had died off, one by one, their bodies piled in a corner of the sleeping room, leaving a sickening, hollow stench as a reminder of what would happen to all of them.

That's when Griff had made the big decision. Had sold his soul in order to be with Camille—the one passion who'd kept him alive all this time.

He tried to picture her face in the light of the moon. Her strong cheekbones, the cheetah-like shape of her light blue eyes, the shoulder-length red hair that reminded him of volcanic lava and its soft flow.

But it was getting harder to think straight now. Lately, pieces of his mind were falling away like dead autumn leaves baring a tree to the sky.

Yes. The sky. The moon.

Griff glanced away from it and tested his legs by inching one out in a poor excuse for a kick. Still so weak. But he'd been a little stronger lately because of what he'd done to stay alive.

The sacrifice he'd made to see Camille someday.

A moan sounded next to Griff. Petar. Dying.

"Buck up," Griff said.

He inspected Petar: his dirt-crusted, shoeless feet, his island-castaway jeans, his emaciated bare chest with bite marks piercing the skin. The *strigoiaca* didn't limit themselves to merely feeding on the neck. When they wanted a snack, they also amused themselves with other locations, other means of pleasure.

But Griff blocked out thoughts of their games. He tried to, at least. If he ever did come face-to-face with Camille again, he might not even be able to look her in the eyes after this nightmare.

Petar hadn't answered Griff. Not even an "I am fine. And you?" That would've been more like the old days, when they'd had the will to talk while the *strigoiaca* lounged like cats in a parlor, wasting away the hours until feeding time presented itself.

Griff groped over, felt Petar's pulse. Barely there.

"So sorry…" Petar's voice was a whisper.

Not again. Ever since Griff could remember, Petar had been apologizing for inadvertently calling down the vampires that day in Vasile.

"Rest," Griff said, the word an effort to get out.

Petar's eyes rolled back, as if asking *Why? Why do I need strength now?*

Griff didn't have an answer.

The buzz of vampire movement caught his attention. Tentatively, he rolled a bit to the left, using his adapted dark vision.

The female he called Star had entered. He called her this because her timeworn Gypsy skirt and blouse reminded him of a lovely vampire from *The Lost Boys*. This more hideous version of Star had been Mihas Vladislav's mistress, but had taken a liking to Petar's neck since her pet's death so long—or maybe just days—ago.

She floated near the other three females, who were lazily draped over stone slabs. Mina's nightdress billowed in the slight wind, caressing Drusilla's decayed seventeenth-century ball gown as she stroked blond Claudia's bare leg. The last vampire was garbed in khaki backpacking gear, and Griff had always thought she might've been an unfortunate hiker caught by the *strigoiaca*.

All of their clothing—what there was of it—split open down the spine, accommodating those tiny, agitated wings.

Odd, he thought, watching Star screech to the others and bob up and down with the help of those wings.

The *strigoiaca* used them when they were afraid, worked up or on the hunt. In their castle, they walked freely. Griff wasn't sure of the last time he'd seen the wings flutter.

Maybe this had something to do with Ecaterina, who hadn't been around for—how long had it been? She'd gone hunting for the males' food and had never come back.

Griff held a hand to his head, temples pounding. Lately, there'd been aching spells. Black spaces in his memories. And now it was happening again….

Bits and pieces of his past, his present, his—he wasn't sure—mashed through his mind: Camille smiling up at him while they took tea in Leicester Square. A jack-in-the-box popping out to scare him with its hideous clown's grimace. His parents' stoic faces as their little boy watched from the back window of an auto, their forms getting smaller and smaller as the strangers took him away from home. The revolving red sphere of a Web site he'd designed. A long tongue darting out of Mina's mouth, shading his world to darkness.

The pieces rubbed together like two edges of stained glass that didn't fit, leaving gaps in his perception. Leaving him confused.

What had he allowed himself to become?

Soon his sight cleared, and he squeezed his eyes together, opened them again, his gaze blurring.

He saw that the vampires were lined up, their red eyes beaming through the darkness at the broken wall to the left. At the rings of white light hovering there.

Light?

At the *pows* of four muted shots, like staple guns thrashing into a slab of wood, the Girls speared through the hole in the wall, their eyes streaks of red lightning. Something—a body?—came flying into the room, crashed against the opposite stairway. It moaned as Drusilla, the strongest and brassiest vampire, zinged over to it. With animalistic glee, she batted the object—yes, a body—back and forth, a feline with a yarn ball and claws.

Then a second body spun into the room, cartwheeling through the air until Claudia caught up to it, catching it midspin, then twirling it the other way.

This was all good fun for the Girls, but so surreal that Griff didn't even know if it was actually happening.

Blurs, flashing pieces of vision…this was his world now.

Suddenly, there was a flash and a bang in the air, then a shower of flares sparking into the room, flaming it to light. Claudia jerked her head up, and her catnip revolved to the floor, kicking up dirt. Even Drusilla halted her vicious taunting, leaving her unwilling playmate alone.

The vampires scattered, zipping to different ends of the room, and Griff crept a hand over his eyes because they stung. He wasn't used to daylight. Hadn't seen the sun in…

A woman lunged into the room, gracefully clearing the stone wall. In front of her face, she held a sword of pale energy, its beams blocking her features and suffusing the area, making the *strigoiaca* scream with fury. Making them freeze.

Only now did Griff become aware of Petar, whose breath was jagging out in taut wheezes.

Even Griff was entranced by the woman.

Then a man, dressed in camouflage, his left arm swathed in bandages, stormed in next to the warrior woman. He was bracing a crossbow against his good shoulder, aiming with one arm, but not firing. Then another woman, stocky and mean, charged in, carrying that strange sword.

The other two bodies—the test versions—struggled to their feet, wobbling, offering their light-wands, too.

The room looked like a lobby from Heaven. White light played over walls, making the unmoving *strigoi-aca* seem like macabre decorations. Drusilla, with her divine dress, was hanging from the ceiling like a chandelier. Star was flattened against a wall like an empty torch holder. Claudia, the hiker girl, was perched like a lone vase on a dilapidated staircase that led to the sky.

Mina was gone.

All the intruders headed for a vampire, but the leader, the woman with the light-wand blocking her features, grabbed the man by his good arm.

"Not so hard to take 'em alive," she said in a tough voice. "Remember, if you kill any of them, they'll be after two, three, four of us women. And then you'll be on your own to fight the new vampires. *Us.*"

He gave her a long stare, unreadable, then went back to covering the vampires with his crossbow while the rest of the women charged forward with what looked like restraints. Griff wondered when he and Petar would be discovered. If these fighters were actually worse enemies than the ones they already knew.

After watching the man retreat, the leader woman moved over to Griff and Petar, the restraints in one hand, the wand causing Griff to cringe. A circle of light from her headset glared at them.

When she lowered her wand, it shadowed her from underneath, casting hollows beneath her cheekbones, giving her eyes an awful glow.

"Griff?" The foreign name cracked out of her throat.

Good Lord. This had to be an illusion. Now someone was talking to him with Camille's voice, her face. Or maybe this was one of his many visions, where she told him everything would be okay if he hung in there, that he needed to find a way out to get back to her.

The soldier dropped the light to her side, making her less nefarious, and Griff a little stronger. Her lips parted; her eyes pooled with moisture.

Camille? Not this steel-tough commando in a black bodysuit with weapons and devices hanging from belts. With a headset and microphone and a severe braid that had lost a few misguided strands of red hair.

When he still didn't answer, the hopeful lift of her brows crumbled. Her body practically slumped forward.

"Okay." She swallowed, struggled to talk. "Can you tell me your names, then?"

"Lady Tex?" Griff croaked, chancing that his words wouldn't chase this dream away.

For a second, she didn't react. Then the light came back into her eyes. "Griff?"

He just drank her in, hoping she wouldn't disappear.

She leaned forward, brushing the hair back from his face. God, he'd repulse her if she looked too hard.

"Griff!" A sob tore out of her. "Oh, dear God! Look at you. It's you! It's you!"

Heart contracting, expanding, he reached up for her. Camille. Real? Really here?

Springing to him, she dropped her light-sword and loaned some darkness to their corner, extending her arms to embrace him.

He made a mad grab for her. *Camille.*

But they weren't fast enough.

A streak of bedraggled white nightgown slammed into Camille, knocking her over. The restraints jangled to the ground.

Mina.

The vampire was on top of his girlfriend, nipping at Camille's throat for the bite. In turn, Lady Tex held Mina by the neck, her arm like a strong column, fending her off.

Griff slid forward, kicking out at his vampire, but too weak to lift his leg. He collapsed to the ground, spent with the effort.

Bloody hell. Bloody, bloody hell. He couldn't just sit here and watch his world be destroyed.

While Griff panted on the ground, he gathered all his strength so he could be with the woman he'd loved through every skin-prickling minute of the life he'd been living.

Whatever it took to be with her, he'd do it.

The sacrifice couldn't be any bigger than what he'd already done.

* * *

Sobbing, laughing and reeling with terror at the same time, Camille reached for a mouth sealer with one hand, holding off the bitch who'd captured Griff with the other.

Oh, yeah, she thought, staring into those flaming, bottomless eyes. I recognize you. And you don't know just how long I've dreamed of revenge.

Her arm shook with the labor of holding the gnashing creature back. The adrenaline shot she'd taken just before diving into the room helped, but it only evened the odds.

Yet Camille wasn't going to lose. Not when she'd finally found Griff again. *Hell,* no.

She caught a glimpse of him out of the watery corner of her eye. He was laid flat on the floor, probably from all the blood loss. He was as pale as a hospital sheet, but alive.

Alive.

With a burst of sublime energy, she finally grasped a mouth sealer on her belt, then cried out, switching it on and slapping it upward.

Just in time, the vampire hissed, averted her face. Her long dark hair trailed over Camille's arm as the mouth sealer missed its mark. It sucked against the female's cheek, making the creature pick at it, miffed.

Camille didn't hesitate. She kicked up with one leg, found purchase against the vampire's belly, then shoved.

The vampire went flying a few feet away, but she swooped back to attack position. While she fixed Camille with the evil eye, she yanked at the mouth sealer. The device only pulled at her skin, stretching it like taffy.

While the creature experimented with the deterrent, Camille had enough time to snatch her UV wand off the ground. The creature went still as soon as the light hit it.

"Nu!"

It was Reveka across the room. Her own UV light had gone out, but she'd already shot a dart into that vampire in the seventeenth-century *Pirates of the Caribbean* dress. Oddly enough, the creature was still hissing and clinging to the ceiling.

The tranquilizer wasn't working on this one? Why? Was it because the ball-gown beast was a lot older than Ecaterina had been? Did she need a bigger dose than the younger vampire?

"I have got you covered, Reveka," Sarge said in Romanian. "Use your restraints. If she moves, I will shoot."

Camille thought she detected a mocking note in that last phrase. He was dying to spill some vampire blood.

"How will I get her down?" Reveka asked.

Good question.

"I can shoot her," Sarge said.

Oh, huge surprise.

"Sarge!" Quickly Camille grabbed her dart gun, then tagged her vampire in the neck. Watched as she plopped to the floor. Thank God, this one was susceptible. But she still bound her with the steel-alloy restraints for good measure.

At the same time, she cast a glance at Griff, just to check on him. Just to reassure herself that he was really here.

Still resting on the ground, hair wild around his face, covering it.

Her heart warmed, still thudding with adrenaline. Thank God. He was safe.

Lightning fast, she bolted another dart into her gun. As her UV wand flittered to darkness, she aimed, shot the chandelier vampire.

Hit for a second time, it stiffened, then went limp. Unfortunately, the intricate dress had snagged on an iron ceiling beam, so her body hung in space, upside down.

A strange bell, swinging back and forth.

Camille pointed at Reveka's waist-bound rope. "Maybe," she said to Reveka, "we can loop that over her head and give a big tug?"

"Don't you know how to lasso?" Sarge asked, crossbow still targeted at the dingdong vampire.

Camille shrugged. "Living in Texas didn't make me a rodeo queen or anything."

Reveka started to play rope-a-dope with the dangling creature, leaving Camille free to help Lucia, who had a bum shoulder because of a vampire's rough play, then Ana, who had an ugly leg gash visible under the rip in her bodysuit. All of them restrained and drugged each creature in turn. Soon, they had three in captivity.

Three live vampires who could lead to a cure for the disease.

"Griff?" she asked, bounding down the stairs from

Ana's restrained vampire, wanting to reassure herself that he was there while things were mellow and looking good.

For an insane second, she wondered if the UV wand had posed any threat to him. Sarge had planted all that doubt in her mind about the captives being as bad as the vampires.

Well, Sarge could kiss her grits.

She found her boyfriend craning his neck to catch a glimpse of her. He seemed mystified, and even though it broke her heart, she couldn't blame him.

This wasn't his Lady Tex with her Bugs Bunny scarves, her hair flying free in the London breezes.

But Camille could be that girl again. Just as soon as—

A deafening buzz shattered the near silence.

When Camille looked over, Reveka was in mid-rope throw. However, the hanging vampire had either awakened or stopped fooling them with her lack of movement.

Damned clever monster. It zoomed off the ceiling, making a beeline for Ana.

"Watch—!" Camille yelled, her breath running out as she started forward.

Unfortunately, the woman hunter had relaxed now that her vampire was contained. Big mistake. Ana, the only married Vasile peasant, had been in a daze staring at Griff and the other man—God, Camille hadn't even checked to see who it was—with a fearful glaze covering her eyes.

Almost as if Ana's own husband, who was safely

back in their wooden Vasile home, could've been one of these men.

At the sound of Camille's shout, Ana jerked back to reality.

But Sarge had already fired at the attacking vampire.

In the time it took for his arrow to travel, the ball-gown vampire zapped down and yanked Ana upward by the leg, attaching her mouth to Ana's wound. In a second of blurred motion and screams, she slurped blood, then fluidly cut her own lips with a fierce claw as she spun Ana upward, seeking the villager's mouth. With a frenzied kiss, she forced Ana to drink her blood.

From her spot, Camille shuddered as Sarge's arrow found a target in the vampire's arm. The creature lifted her mouth away from Ana's lips, screeching in that death wail.

Damn him! Now that the other females were under sedation, Sarge was feeling free to murder. After all, the drugged *strigoiaca* couldn't turn the female team members into vampires while knocked out.

He was clear to kill without immediate consequences.

At one point, Sarge had told Camille that his arrows were tipped with holy water, and it was evident from the way the vampire was writhing and caterwauling. Her scream tore at the insides of Camille's ears.

The vampire dropped Ana's limp form down the stairs.

First, her arrow-spiked arm began steaming, disappearing. In seconds, her entire body smoked, wilted. Evaporated.

For a divine moment, the ball gown floated in the air by itself, as if a body still held it up. Then it collapsed onto the stairway, hollowed into nothing.

Before Camille could process the fleeting sight, she was on Sarge, thrashing aside his gun and pushing at him with all her might.

The adrenaline was still in her system, so her shove was aggressive, sending him crashing against the side wall.

"You son of a bitch," she yelled.

He nodded toward Griff and the other male. "You're just lucky I didn't aim for your boyfriend first. I told you, Howard, all of these things are—or will be—beyond help."

This time Camille flew at him, slapped him soundly across the face.

Smack!

The force of it stunned both of them.

For a man who'd almost had his arm torn off today, Sarge looked truly wounded. His scruffy cheek reddened with the imprint of her hand. She wanted so badly to take the slap back, to make him see how important it was for her to hold on to Griff.

"You don't get it, Howard."

Tears pulled at her throat. "And I never will."

He didn't say it out loud, but she knew he could've.

You understood pretty well when it came to slicing up wolves today.

"Believe it or not," Sarge said, stepping away from the wall, his gaze a hard plea, "I've kept a vampire or two alive in my day—if they could help exterminate the worst of them."

"I *don't* believe you."

He sighed, defeated.

"Let me put your friend out of his misery before the nightmare really happens. Because it always does with vamps."

Frustrated, Camille drew his bowie from her belt and pounced forward, touching the tip to his throat, willing to do anything to stop him.

He didn't seem to care. "You never gave the knife back to me. Shouldn't that tell you something?"

"Now's not a good time to irk me, Sarge."

"Ah. So, now you'll knock me out? Are you and Dr. Grasu through with me?"

A pitiful cry from the other side of the room answered for her heart. And it took her a second to realize that it wasn't her body responding at all.

It was Ana.

As they both fixed their gazes on the new vampire, Camille kept the knife to Sarge's throat.

Ana was sitting at the bottom of the stairs, staring at her hands, looking just as human as can be, but with blood running from her mouth, her leg.

Clutching her chest, she said, "I am burning inside."

Please, no, Camille thought. This isn't happening.

Reveka and Lucia, who'd been gathering the three unconscious vampires, watched, just as helpless as their boss.

"She's turning," whispered Sarge.

He moved away from the wall, and Camille knew exactly what he wanted to do.

"Hell, no," she said, horrified, putting more pressure

on the blade at his throat. "We've got them under control. Ana won't be a problem."

That didn't stop him. He shrugged his crossbow to its resting place on his back and took the stake out of its holster. "I'll be decent about it and drug her first so she doesn't feel a thing. Lucia?"

The woman jumped, then let her hand fall to her side.

"Sedate Ana," Sarge said.

"No," she said to Lucia. Then, to Sarge, "We're winning. We don't have to paint the room with their guts. Let her stay alive so I can take her back with the others."

Lucia still didn't fire her dart gun.

Clutching the stake, Sarge started walking away. "Who said we're going to keep the others alive?"

Desperate, Camille mirrored his stride, increasing the pressure of the knife again until blood trickled down his throat from the broken skin.

"Dammit, Camille." He dropped the stake, grabbed her wrist with that good arm, spun her around in a lock, jamming her arm between her shoulder blades and squeezing until she dropped the knife.

He couldn't use his bad arm. That'd cost him.

Dropping to her knees, she held back a wince and twisted out of the lock to catch him off balance, spinning, kicking, sweeping his legs out from under him.

He crashed to the ground, rolling to his back, hindered by his shredded arm.

In one smooth, adrenalized motion, she got him in a *kasagatame* hold, slipping her arm under his neck, drawing her knees close to his shoulder, grasping her inner thigh with her hand, whisking his arm under her armpit.

Continuing the flowing hold, she slicked her hand down his arm until the blade of her wrist bone met his trachea, then drove downward, choking him.

"I will *not* let you do this," she said.

He strained against her, driving to his side, trying to escape the hold. But he was coughing, face reddening.

Bastard. He wasn't going to stop.

Someone else must've known it, too. A hand grabbed her dart gun, loaded it, then pressed it to Sarge's neck.

Thunk.

Out of breath, dizzied, Camille turned to find Griff, who'd crawled to her rescue. Holding back her sadness, she pushed Sarge down, waiting until he passed out, meeting the accusation in his gaze.

I warned you, she thought.

By the time he'd relaxed, Griff had crumpled to the ground again, breath heaving, eyes narrowed. They watched her as she reached out and hesitantly brushed a lock of his dark hair away from that beautiful face.

Side by side with the sleeping Sarge.

There couldn't have been more of a difference between the two. One was a killer.

The other was her savior.

Chapter 12

Inside one of the two Huey helicopters that Camille's fortune had secured for the mission, she finally gave in to months of exhaustion.

They were just about to take off from the dawn-soaked Humvee site, where the four captive vampire bodies had been loaded into UV coffins after being air-lifted from the castle with the rest of them. From here, the Humvees would drive the coffins to Bucharest while her team flew to different destinations.

On the floor next to Griff, Camille sank against the wall, dropping a rucksack filled with hunting devices.

It was done.

She slid a gaze to her boyfriend. He was huddled in a lightweight Gore-Tex jacket, refusing to touch her.

Why?

It was almost as if they'd just met, personal-space bubbles intact. Strange, but it made sense somehow. He'd been traumatized. She needed to be patient, to nurse him back to the way things had been before that night.

Her heart clenched. Still, she'd expected more emotion from him. Had he fallen out of love with her during the year they'd been apart?

The thought hurt, because *her* love had only gotten stronger.

She touched his jacket, imagined his arm underneath the material. His painfully thin arm.

"I'm taking you to Bucharest," she said.

He nodded, went back to hunching and watching her with that hesitant disbelief she'd noticed back at the castle.

After Sarge had been knocked out, Camille had radioed Bea to send Hueys to help transport the five unconscious bodies: Sarge, Ana, the three other vampires. Their fighting area hadn't been far from a decent spot for the choppers to land, thank goodness, so they hadn't needed to drag the bodies a great distance. And, since the Hueys' doors had been removed in anticipation of a speedy evacuation, load-up had been mercifully simple.

Petar Vladislav, the other captive, had needed to be carried, and Reveka had taken him under her wing as if he were a lost child, promising to get him back to his family in Juni. Of course, he'd be examined by Beatrix first, when the other chopper reached Vasile.

As of a minute ago, when Camille had checked the other Huey, Reveka had been rocking Petar against her ample chest, cooing to him. Lucia had been holding her arm, favoring the shoulder Ashe had already healed while she stared into space.

Grieving for Ana and Delia.

Right now, back in Vasile, Bea was breaking the bad news about the two woman hunters. But there was hope for Ana in Bucharest at the lab, Doc would tell the villagers. She and Camille would cure Ana and the other *strigoiaca* using their scientific theories and the captured vampires.

But doubt was beginning to seed in Camille's mind: the superanimal wolves. Sarge's holy-water arrows. The vampire disappearing into the air like steam from a teakettle.

How could she explain these with logic? The science and order she'd always embraced? The excuses she'd clung to so she wouldn't have to face the unknown?

Griff lifted his head again, dark curls covering most of his gaze. He hadn't talked much. Hadn't smiled. Camille yearned to see those slightly messed-up British teeth.

"You remind me of a dog that's been kicked around," she said.

He paused. Slowly held out one arm.

Elated, she took a cleansing breath. "Griff, I've missed you so much."

Throat tight, she snuggled against him and his Gore-Tex jacket, wrapping her arms around his painfully thin torso.

This was where she belonged now.

Home.

He squeezed her to his chest, rested shaking fingertips on her upper stomach. If Camille hadn't known better, she would've said he was going to push her away.

But he didn't. They just sat in silence, breathing against each other.

Then he bent close to her ear. "Bath," he murmured, voice hoarse.

"Shh. Don't talk." She couldn't care less about his eau de dungeon as long as she had him against her again.

He plucked at her bodysuit, and she knew what he was asking. How had she gotten this way?

Still holding on to him, Camille sat up. Griff tried to back off, but when she pulled him closer, he looked away.

Take it slow, she thought. Let go a bit.

Reluctantly, she relaxed her hold, gave him some room. "After you were taken I wanted to run after you. Ms. Godea stopped me. She convinced me that it'd be useless, that having a plan would be smarter, seeing as we'd just been beaten soundly by the *strigoiaca*. She introduced me to a professor in Bucharest, Dr. Beatrix Grasu."

Griff was closing his eyes, his throat working. What was he battling? Emotion?

As she continued, she held his hand, and he clamped on to the grip.

"You'll adore Bea as much as I do. She's really a scrapper. She came from a small, superstitious village and educated herself right out of poverty. Her whole life, she's been fascinated by vampires, researching the lore. But she's also studied animals, diseases, anything that could explain all the tales. When I came to her, she believed my stories about the *strigoiaca,* offered to teach me everything she knew. I learned. I trained. I hired teams of men, hunters, to find you, to bring you and the *strigoiaca* back alive so we could put an end to their sickness. But when the others didn't succeed, I took over."

"You wanted the Girls alive?"

She couldn't see his face. "We wanted a cure. Without specimens, we thought we wouldn't be able to help any survivors or overcome the disease so future generations wouldn't have to deal with more attacks."

Throwing caution out the window, she skimmed her hand behind his head, guided him to her shoulder. His mouth settled in the crook of her neck, and she shivered at the touch of his lips against her skin. His warm breath rasped against her, tickling her with overwhelming need.

He parted his lips, blessing her with a soft kiss.

She groaned, then spoke into his ear. "The *strigoiaca* even have a chance of getting better. It'll take a little time to experiment, but—"

He pulled her closer to him, his mouth opening against her neck.

"Griff." She made a soft sound of pure need.

His body stiffened. Pushing away, he fled to the back of the chopper, hand over his face, trembling.

His primal reaction tore at her. "What the hell did they do to you?"

His head reared back, and he looked ready to howl with anguish. Then he fisted his hands, recovering, rested his head against the wall.

"I thought I'd never see you again if I didn't…" His voice twisted to a stop.

In the back of her mind, she heard the chopper engines warming up, then the blades, slapping her with every thrash of movement.

She *wasn't* letting him go again.

Determined, she crawled over to him, but he held out an arm, halting her.

And this was how Sarge found them—with the man she loved pushing her away.

As Sarge and Ashe stood in the Huey's entrance with one of the UV coffins, he saw the captive cowering in his corner. Saw Camille on her hands and knees, a stricken look on her face.

A few days ago, he'd have loved to see Juni's "huntress" humbled. But now…

Not so much.

"Checked for fangs?" he bellowed over the engines, wind from the wash of the rotors blowing his hair on end.

Not waiting for an answer, he and Ashe quickly maneuvered the cargo into the chopper. She leveled a half-hearted glare at him, sank against the wall, then checked out the coffin.

It was for her boyfriend. Just in case.

Instead of commenting on his symbolic slam against Griff, Camille yelled, "Good morning."

He could've ripped into her for disabling him for the second time in two days. But Sarge knew he didn't have to. There were splinters of guilt in her irises.

Ashe gave Sarge a shove into the chopper, then followed him in. They both pushed the coffin next to Camille, then sat opposite—what had Ashe said his name was? Pretty Boy? Oh, no. It was Griff. That's right.

The comforting smell of metal, canvas and oil greeted Sarge, and he relaxed. Hueys. This vanilla ride was no technologically superior Pave Low chopper—the kind that used to shuttle him to and from Delta missions—but it was in his comfort zone anyway.

He settled into his seat, glad he wouldn't have to drive his Jeep today. Ashe had hired a Vasile man to get the vehicle back to Bucharest. There Sarge was supposed to get medical treatment for his arm, something more than Ashe could provide at the moment.

Sure, his friend had performed some healing spells and used his special herbs and crystals on the torn skin, but that hadn't done any good for what was really ailing Sarge.

As the chopper lifted off, he watched Camille and her boy toy. It wasn't the homecoming she'd expected, was it?

Good.

Yeah, he was a bastard for thinking it, but Sarge couldn't help himself. Somewhere along the line, he'd gotten a little attached to Howard—just a sexual thing, of course. She was spirited, would be amusing for a short time before he went on to his next job.

If he could get over this one.

He wasn't exactly happy about leaving these particular vampires intact, but if Dr. Grasu could cure them...

Nah. He still wouldn't be satisfied. He'd just have to visit the lab himself, make sure the vamps were under control, maybe see how Howard was doing. Maybe.

The Huey was catching air now, speeding away from Castle Bethlen. As the vampire nest became a speck on the ground, Sarge asked the copilot for two headsets. He tossed one to Camille, gestured for her to wear it.

With a put-upon expression, she did.

"I was serious. Did you check loverboy for fangs?"

The captive fixed a lowered glare on him.

"Why would he have fangs, Sarge?" she asked. "If he'd been turned, he would've attacked already, right? And he wouldn't be walking around in the sun. Besides, I sort of wanted a more tender hello."

"You clearly got it."

"Eat me, you jerk."

"That's something you wouldn't regret."

Apparently at her wit's end, she doffed the headset and stared straight ahead, out the open door at the passing morning-lit countryside.

So this was what he got for trying to be helpful. Cut off from communicating with her. The cold shoulder.

He supposed it was better than a dart in the neck.

Next to him, Ashe was shaking his head, the gesture louder than the scolding he might've deserved.

Don't do it again, Ashe was probably thinking. Don't let the adrenaline and danger of a mission fool you into thinking you've got the hots for a woman.

It wasn't serious. Not even close. There was definite

lust, though. Camille Howard might not be the Victoria's Secret definition of beauty, but she had something that attracted Sarge with its burning light.

Passion? Dedication?

Imagine having someone feel about him the way she obviously felt about this Griff guy.

The thought scarred Sarge a little because no one had ever cherished him in that way.

Images scored him: The intensity in her eyes as she'd restrained him from going after Ana and the revenants. The sharp glint of moon on Hana's fangs as she dived for his neck, ripping his flesh.

As with Hana, Sarge had blinded his instincts with Camille. He'd trusted her, if only briefly. He'd honored her beliefs, her need to keep those vamps alive, because he knew it meant so much to her.

Hell. Around Camille, he even thought he could go back to being the type of guy who thought a little more about sending a creature to the great hereafter.

Damned idiot.

Across the chopper, Pretty Boy stirred. Sarge tensed, ready to pin him against the wall with a stake if he made a wrong move.

His hand crept to his side, seeking reassurance from the aspen wood.

As if provoking Sarge, the captive grabbed for Camille's hand, engulfed it in the clasp of his. While the two lovebirds locked gazes, shutting everyone else out of their world, Sarge sensed apologies, promises.

Sighing and smiling, Camille nestled against her boyfriend, closing her eyes.

Interesting. Even though Griffie was holding her close, he kept a distance. It was in the way he angled his mouth away from her, the way he stared into space.

Ashe, the empath, the one who could read feelings, didn't even try to remove Sarge's hand from his stake.

And that was all Sarge needed to know.

She'd collapsed into sleep. Not a very soothing one, but enough to shut down her systems and erase all worry.

The dark numbness of a snooze. The calming spin of patterns on the backs of her eyelids. The ecstatic contentment of using Griff as a human pillow again. His embrace seemed stronger in her dreams, and she wished it was because her love had made him that way.

But then he was ripped away from her, making the nightmares come back.

Startled, she jerked awake, discombobulated. Alone.

Swaying to her knees, she instinctively felt her hips for the utility belt, her devices. Nothing there.

Instead, she found herself in a helicopter with Sarge using one arm to drive Griff to the wall.

"Sarge!" Her voice crackled with rage as she stumbled to her feet.

"Stay back," he said, snarling at Griff, who was gazing down at him with a stony expression.

His eyes…

No. There wasn't anything wrong. They didn't have a tinge of heat or of…wildness.

"Let him go," she yelled, forcing herself awake and pulling at Sarge's straining arm.

Ashe had gotten to his feet also. He leaned over to speak in her ear. "Sit down, Camille."

"What's with you two?"

Sarge tossed his words over a shoulder. "He's a vamp."

Something—her nightmares—plunged into her heart, and she stumbled backward.

Ashe was talking again. "While you were asleep, he grew more and more restless. Then he flashed fangs. He wants your blood."

"What, did you *feel* this, Ashe?" Her voice mocked him. "Did one of your Dragons tell you? Well, maybe it could tell Ana, too, or... Oh, no. Too late for that. Ana's already been bitten."

The Wiccan's peaceful facade crumbled. Dammit, she'd crushed him with her words, with her own pain.

But just as she reached out a hand to touch his arm, Griff struck.

He pushed off the wall, mouth aimed at Sarge's neck.

In turn, Sarge whipped him around, throwing him to the floor of the chopper near the open door. The tops of forest trees wheeled by in the background.

Ashe dived toward the front of the Huey.

At the same time, Camille tried to pry the men apart. "Sarge, get the hell off him!"

"Look!" He slid a thumb into Griff's mouth, lifting the upper lip.

The sight of two tiny canine fangs sent a blast of shock through her, rocked her back onto her heels.

She hadn't wanted to admit it. Goddammit. She hadn't even looked for fear of what she'd find. He'd hidden them so well.

And she'd been so sure. He'd walked in the dawn light, hadn't he? So how...?

This couldn't be happening. Not after all the hope, the training, the rescue...

As she cradled her arms over her head, shutting out her legacy of death, Griff turned his face toward her.

But it wasn't really Griff. Those weren't his reddened night eyes. That wasn't his mouth fixed in a razor-sharp grimace.

"He drank from one of the *strigoiaca*," Sarge said.

She needed an excuse. Any excuse to make this go away or seem less cataclysmic. "He can't be that far along."

"He will be."

Ashe returned, obviously having shuffled through his rucksack. He returned to them with a silver crucifix. The sight of it took Camille aback.

"For real serious situations," Sarge said, noting her surprise. "Wiccans don't believe in the devil, but they believe in good."

She knew that symbols, crosses, garlic wouldn't literally affect the *strigoiaca* or...whatever her boyfriend was now. She needed the wands, the mouth sealers, the—

Griff was staring at the cross in wonder.

"Got him," Sarge said, still levering him to the floor.

Scientific fascination mixed with relief that Sarge wasn't killing him, and Camille knelt next to Griff, noting his responses to the cross, wondering if this was anything like charming a snake. Maybe he was attracted to the silver shine, the shape...

"I think you set him off, Howard," Sarge said. "He got a little excited from the scent of you."

"Are you talking about something like psychic vampirism?"

"They don't always live off blood. Sometimes they don't have to touch you to draw out your strength. When you were nookying all close to Griffie, he was probably sucking out your energy. That's what I meant by vampires feeding off souls."

"Even though the *strigoiaca* got him, he's not their kind."

Something like guilt flashed in his eyes, and Sarge abruptly jerked his chin toward the back of the Huey.

As Camille wondered why Sarge would feel any remorse, the chopper took a dip downward, skimming lower over the forest.

The movement caused Ashe to lose his balance, taking the cross out of Griff's line of vision. In that split second, the Wiccan lost control of his vampire.

Griff bared his fangs, went for Sarge's bad arm, tore through the bandages.

"Griff!" she yelled.

"Just get away from him!" Sarge's voice was steeped in pain.

Helpless, Camille jumped back as far as she could.

But Griff took advantage of the distraction to heave Sarge to his back. However, the soldier didn't allow the younger man to get the upper hand. He rolled Griff over, too, positioning her boyfriend's head over the ledge of the open door.

"Don't hurt him," she said, knowing Sarge was beyond hearing.

Ashe joined them there, crucifix at the ready.

Had her scent really been the reason for bringing this out in Griff? If so, the smartest thing would be to stay away, not to ride to his rescue again.

But she needed to protect him.

Determined to do so, she glanced around the chopper's belly for her rucksack. The UV wand was dead, but maybe she could use a mouth sealer?

She thought of how the vampires had torn at the vacuum device, maiming themselves. She couldn't do that to Griff.

How about a knockout dart? Were there any left?

She scrambled to her rucksack, took out the gun and one final tranquilizer while looking over her shoulder.

Ashe was pressing the cross against Griff's neck, where it steamed into his skin.

As her boyfriend roared in agony, Camille felt it, too. It tore at her, making her want to cry for him. She clutched a dart in her fist.

In his frenzy to get away from the crucifix, Griff pushed backward, over the chopper's door ledge.

Oh, God...

Sarge braced himself, holding on to the door sides, but Griff wasn't letting go. He twisted, tore at Sarge.

And they both plunged out of the chopper.

Heart in her throat, Camille scuttled to the door, a scream in her throat, dart still in hand.

The Wiccan pointed to the nearby treetops, and she

calmed herself, understanding his gesture. Had their fall been broken?

Ashe rushed over to the pilots, and they circled back.

It didn't take them long to land, and as soon as they hit ground, Camille and Ashe were out the door, her dart gun armed with one projectile. He had the crucifix ready.

Follow the empath then overtake him, she thought, dogging his heels as they wove through the trees. She needed to get to Griff before Ashe did, dammit.

The witch's skills were sharp this morning, because he led her right to them.

As they approached, Griff was holding on to Sarge's bad arm and beating his full body against a tree. One of the mercenary's legs snapped backward and, as Sarge disengaged from Griff, his body collapsed to the ground.

She skidded to a stop on pine needles and dried leaves, cringing for Sarge, horrified. Had her blood scent made Griff so brutal? Damn her, why hadn't she just stayed away from him?

Because she couldn't.

And getting close again would give Griff even more strength.

As Ashe forged ahead, Griff picked Sarge up by the scruff of his T-shirt, wrenching his head with the other hand, seeking access to the neck. His mouth opened, preparing to strike.

"Stop, Griffin!"

Her voice rang through the forest as Ashe hovered nearby, waiting with the crucifix.

Griffin froze, cocked his head, glanced over his shoulder with that familiar voided look of the vampire.

Seeing her, he dropped Sarge. At first, the mercenary stayed on his knees, catching his breath. Either Griff had been throwing him around quite a bit or he'd taken a nasty spill from the tree that had slowed his fall from the chopper. Blood gushed from a head wound, coating half his stony face with red.

With that broken leg, Sarge couldn't stand.

This slow, excruciating death match crushed Camille, cutting her in half. She didn't want either of these men hurt.

Arm quaking, Sarge pointed to Ashe, calling him off. Then he groped for the stake that was sheathed by his side.

She could barely look at him reaching for the last threads of life, of dignity.

By now, Griff had turned all the way around. He sniffed the air, took a step toward her.

Sarge withdrew the stake. "Get out of here, Camille."

As sorry as she felt for the mercenary, he was going to kill Griff. The man she'd fought so damned hard to get back.

Taking a risk, she walked nearer to her boyfriend, raising her dart gun. She'd take him down and put him in the UV coffin, keeping all of them safe until they got to Bucharest. They could cure him there.

She could make this work.

"Come here, Griff," she said softly. "I'll keep you safe."

Her gaze caught Sarge's, and the connection felt like a kick to the stomach.

Her betrayal. His hurt.

Obviously, he couldn't understand why she needed to keep Griff alive. Why she'd allow Sarge to suffer while doing it.

Damn this decision she had to make.

When he opened his mouth to say something, she shook her head, telling him that she'd choose Griff every time.

His gaze went hollow.

Please don't continue, Sarge. Because if you try to kill Griff, you know I'll stop you.

He hesitated, just as if he'd understood her desperation. Camille exhaled, relieved beyond measure.

Finally, the clod had gotten it.

Beaten, Sarge smiled weakly. But then, with a warrior's cry, he gave a savage leap, using his good leg to spring forward, cocking the stake backward, thrusting it toward Griff's back, where he'd pierce the heart straight through.

Camille's hopes dropped. As Sarge speared toward Griff, she thought about hitting him with the last dart. But what about Griff? How would she contain *that* danger?

Left with no other choice, she lowered her gun, permitting Griff to stay alive.

To take Sarge out.

It was the only way to keep Griff.

As her boyfriend ducked, Sarge's body arched over Griff while trying to spike him. Right away, the fledgling vampire flew upward. Fangs flashing, he reached out, screwing Sarge's good arm as if it were a jar lid, flipping the soldier overhead and to the forest floor.

The stake tumbled away as Griff tore into Sarge's belly.

Ensnared by an empathic moment, Ashe watched her, read her, possibly too stunned by her sacrificial thoughts to move.

With panicked speed, she pointed her tranquilizer at Griff. "Don't kill him. Stop, Griff."

He didn't.

Why can't you do this for me? she thought.

Now Ashe plunged forward with the crucifix. But, in a flash, Griff took off, escaping through the trees.

With a last glance at Sarge—one that would haunt her—she gave chase, tracking Griff. He hadn't gotten much of a head start, so when he was in range, she shot him, bringing him crashing to the ground.

As she walked over to him, dazed, she couldn't forget Sarge. Couldn't forget the lacerations in his stomach, in his throat. His broken bones. His fading gaze, so much like the alpha wolf.

Why? it asked.

She hadn't meant for this to happen.

Numb, she took care of the prone Griff, bringing him back to the chopper, resting him in his coffin, turning on the UV bulbs and tenderly brushing the hair back from his face.

Then she went back to see to Sarge, finding Ashe kneeling over his friend's still body.

"What can I do to help?" she asked, stomach churning at what she had done to him.

"You can get out of here, Camille," the Wiccan said, not even deigning to glance at her. "Call for some transportation in Bucharest. But just leave."

"Is he…?"

"Go!" He roared the word at her, still avoiding her gaze.

Guilt-ridden, she left, feeling like the murderer who'd shown up at a victim's funeral because she'd wanted to get caught.

Chapter 13

One month ago, Camille had chosen Griff over Sarge.

Now she stood on the other side of Griff's security-glass cell in the lab near the university, watching a male assistant garbed in an *Outbreak*-type hot-zone suit while he prepped Griff's arm for an injection.

Her boyfriend's hair and beard had been trimmed long ago, and he was bare chested, revealing the slight amount of weight he'd added with a change in diet. Revealing the cross burn on his neck and a hint of the once emerging vampire wings that had already devolved into faint gray ruffles along his spine.

Seeing Griff's progress, she felt validated in having kept him alive—no matter what it'd cost.

Overcome by guilt once again, Camille's stomach

roiled at the blood-soaked image of Sarge lying on the forest floor. Then she popped an antacid tablet, listened to Bea's voice as she explained Griff's condition to a touring group. Today was dog-and-pony-show time for visiting doctors who were also studying vampirism worldwide.

Dressed in her own spaceman garb, Bea was speaking to them with grandiose flourishes of motion. She wasn't wearing headgear—it was needed only when she visited the vampires, since the suit kept her scent contained.

As Sarge had said, scent had been a trigger for Griff's attack and Bea had confirmed this in the lab. But right now, Camille had forgone the required suit and was wearing regular clothing: red cowboy boots, jeans, a pink T-shirt with the baby ring necklace.

Today would be the big test for Griff.

Camille would finally get to stand—suitless—next to him for the first time since Griff had returned.

Inside her boyfriend's sterile cage—for lack of a better word—a team of suited-up males waited with their defensive devices: mouth sealers, restraints, stun darts.

Protection from just-in-case scenarios.

But for now, Bea was still speaking to the guests. "I would like to introduce you to our male vampire, Griffin Montfort. He is a success story for us.

"You have seen how our daily UV treatments, initial blood transfusions and the withholding of human blood have caused the female vampires to shed most vampiric characteristics. Our process has made them think more like humans and act this way, as well. For Griffin, we are also using a strict diet of animal blood that has been cleansed of all hormones. At the same time, we are gradually introducing human foods—grains, meats, vegetables and fruits. Administering serum shots, the first of which you are about to witness, will be the next phase in their healing. We have examined our subjects and come up with a formula of proteins and antibodies that will hopefully be the final cure. I will be taking you to the lab proper to discuss the composition in more detail."

Bea signaled to the male assistant, who in turn injected Griff with his first serum dose. Griff lowered his head, hands grasping the padded table he sat on.

Camille couldn't bear it, so she glanced behind her, at the row of captive *strigoiaca*.

At the moment, Tina, a cute graduate student, was feeding Ana. Camille's fellow hunter was doing well, almost fully healed since she hadn't been infected for long. She'd be going back to Vasile within days—under observation, of course. And the one Griff called Claudia, the backpacker girl, wasn't very old, either. Her wings had shrunk to nubs and she had a quasihuman disposition and pallor. However, Mina and Star were old—over two hundred years, Doc had estimated. They hadn't shown as much improvement yet, and were being kept in cells at the end of the hall, isolated until more progress was made.

"Good morning, Griffin." Bea's voice was amplified by the cell's two-way speaker.

The sound of his name hooked Camille's attention. She touched the glass, wanting to feel *him* instead.

But the cold, hard material was nothing like the skin she remembered. The body she hadn't laid hands on for so long.

His own greeting was a polite nod, a glance of those serious brown eyes before he closed them and clenched his jaw.

Camille watched closely. Was he having a reaction to the serum?

"You already know that Griffin and Petar Vladislav were the remaining captives," Bea said, studying Griff, too. "Mr. Vladislav, who is living safely under surveillance with his mother in Juni, survived without exchanging blood with the *strigoiaca*. But our Griffin kept himself alive by doing just this. As he described it to us, he used a stone to open his vampire's palm one night. He drank of her blood while she was feasting on him. Then he used the last of his strength to put his mouth on hers. To exchange saliva and complete the process. After that, she would allow him to drink from her, sustaining him. He was her pet, and it was to her benefit to keep her food healthy."

There went Camille's stomach again. A tearing ache.

Though Griff hadn't talked much since his rescue, he'd told Camille and Bea about his experiences. But the reserved black centers of his eyes made her wonder if he was revealing everything.

"I remembered the stories about male vampires," he'd said on that first day, after being extracted from the Huey in his UV coffin. "It was clear that I could be a vampire—alive—as well. I drank Mina's blood just to be with Camille. I would've done anything."

Just as she had for him.

Now her stomach rebelled again. Was she too young for ulcers? Thinking about Sarge, the blood, the tragedy, she couldn't help punishing herself with contained guilt.

What'd happened to him? What'd Ashe done with his body? Buried him? Done useless magick on him?

And did Griff even remember laying fangs into Sargent?

Sometimes she wondered if the UV treatment had scrambled the kill out of his memory. He never talked about it. But both she and Bea had agreed that broaching the subject could wait. The truth might be detrimental to his healing, they reasoned.

All Camille knew was that her conscience weighed heavily with Sarge's downfall every morning. Every night.

Griff relaxed his white-knuckle grip on the table, and she sighed, averted her gaze to the soothing sight of their guests and their white coats.

Bea was still talking, bless her exuberance.

"It is interesting to note that the *strigoiaca* sought male victims because they were addicted to the testosterone derived from the blood."

Scanning the crowd, Camille took in the clipboards, the handheld recorders. Academics. Her old milieu.

"Yet Griffin seems to work differently. Among other things, he craved the estrogen from healthy human women. When he was rescued, the scent of my assistant, Ms. Howard, excited the need for this addictive hormone in him. It brought out the monster, triggering superhuman strength and capabilities."

As Bea went on about how the vampires' fangs hadn't disappeared yet, even though the rest of their symptoms were in the process of doing so, Camille stared at the intellectuals, missing the safe structure of their world.

One man toward the back of the crowd caught her attention. Tall, light brown hair.

A flicker of panicked hope shook her. Sarge?

Drawn, she moved away from Griff's cell.

"Ms. Howard?" Doc was watching her as if she'd called Camille's name a few times already.

Rattled, Camille glanced back to Sarge, only to find empty air where the specter had been.

But it wasn't the first time her brain had created his image, had flashed that neon reminder of her victim.

In a daze, Camille stepped back up to the front of the group, next to her mentor.

"You are here to witness a momentous step for Griffin," Doc said. "We have kept him in this sensory-deprivation chamber. He has not caught the scent of humanity until now."

Bea tucked on her headgear and ushered Camille toward the reinforced-steel door. But Camille couldn't help glancing to the back of the crowd, just one more time.

No Sargent.

Hell, her conscience wanted him back. That's all.

She shook it off, steadied herself. An assistant unbolted the door.

"You fine?" asked Bea. "I worry about you."

"Thanks. But there's no reason to." Camille winked,

just to keep Bea happy, then she strode through with Doc trailing her.

The room lacked scent since the air system kept the atmosphere sterile. As she approached, every lean muscle in Griff's arms bunched, letting her know that he was just as apprehensive about this as she was.

The armed male assistants shuffled, ready to strike if Griff made a move.

She came to stand next to him, the need to touch him overwhelming her. Conversations via the window hadn't done the trick.

"Hey," she said softly. Shyly.

"Hey."

Well, this was first-date awkward. "How're you feeling so far?"

He breathed in, crept his fingers to his forehead and squeezed his eyes shut again. "Headache."

Bea stuck a stethoscope on his back. Through her suit's speaker, she said, "A reaction to the serum. We will monitor that."

"Your body's under a lot of stress," Camille said. "Migraines could be normal for what you've been through."

Doc grabbed her student's hand, squeezed it. "Now you touch him?"

She knew how much this meant to Camille, yet it was Aunt Bea's big moment.

Still feeling the observers' cold, assessing stares on her, she hesitated. Her loving touch, the moment she'd been hungering for since...forever...would be reduced to scrawls on clipboard paper.

She inhaled, held her breath, skimmed her fingertips over Griff's upper arm. He shuddered, watched her with that foreign who-are-you? curiosity.

Bea gave a tiny, thrilled hop and walked toward the window. "Look, they are applauding."

When Camille glanced over, she saw doctors nodding, beaming, bringing their hands together in a pantomime of approval.

So why did she still feel so alone? So beaten?

"Tomorrow," Bea said, coming to put an arm around her and Griff each, "we move on to more contact. Maybe even a hug this week, yes?"

Yes, Camille thought, wanting so damn much more.

Maybe she'd even get a hug from him this week.

Over the next two months, Camille ventured into Griff's cell for more time each day. They progressed to holding hands, then that long sought hug.

Under constant observation, they cautiously talked about general things: The summer weather outside the lab. Camille's lunches with their old friend, Ms. Godea. Camille's record of having avoided the paparazzi for over a year now. How Camille had put off her doctoral work and how Griff wanted her to continue. She'd still been researching the male tribe in the Carpathian Mountains, but her heart wasn't in using it to further her lot in life.

And there were things they didn't talk about: How the *strigoiaca* were acting more human each day. How Camille had started a weapon collection.

She tried not to think about why, or how each added

machete or stake amounted to the sum of her fears. An arsenal had replaced her faith in logic, and she couldn't admit it.

Couldn't let go of what had been keeping her together all these years.

Though the conversations flowed and looked good on lab reports, they were definitely lacking in intimacy. After all, having a team of vampire restrainers in the room wasn't the most romantic of settings.

In the meantime, she contented herself with knowing he was alive and getting better. Knowing that he was starting to watch her with something less dangerous than vampire hunger, or less disheartening than his distant gaze.

So on the night when Griff was finally released from his cage, Camille was beside herself with excitement.

Bea had seen to it that he would move into an apartment in the laboratory until she was convinced he was in full remission. Their confidence in Griff's recovery had been spurred by Ana's moving out of the lab three weeks ago, definitely recovered, though Camille had hired an assistant to monitor the woman in Vasile for the next year. Also, as a precaution, more guards armed with sedatives had been added to the around-the-clock shifts.

Meanwhile, the rest of the *strigoiaca* were still in their cells, receiving more treatment.

To celebrate his return, Camille had gone out and bought ingredients to make a prescription-friendly chicken curry, one of Griff's favorite dishes.

Regular food, she thought with a smile. Maybe

thrifty, home-cooked meals would make her uncle Phillip feel better about the fortune she was spending "out there in Europe." She could just imagine him back in New York, steam coming out of his ears as her accountants blabbed to him about her secretive investments. Well, too bad. She didn't take his phone calls anyway, so she didn't really care what he thought.

With a liberating sigh, she cheered up. Chicken curry would be her and Griff's return to normalcy, the beginning of forgetting.

So why did she still feel as if Sarge was following her?

It was crazy, she knew, to think he was behind her when she walked the city streets to shop or run errands. It was nuts to feel him stalking her while she researched male Carpathian tribe lore in the university library.

"You must put Sargent behind you," Bea had told her several times, deep mother-hen concern etched into her wrinkled skin. "If you had not brought Griff back to us, the world would have suffered. Sacrifice needs to be made for science, sweet girl. Remember this."

She'd try, Camille thought, opening the door to the apartment she'd furnished for Griff: sleek steel furniture with black accents, computer equipment, a kitchen stocked with nutrients for Doc's specially prescribed diet.

And there he was—the most valuable furnishing of all, sprawled on the lone couch. He was watching a grainy detective movie on a plasma TV, waiting for her.

Dropping the market bags on the ground, Camille rushed over to him, and he stood to meet her. They embraced, laughing like kids who'd gotten surprise presents.

He crushed her to him, hands buried in her loose hair.

They were a little more comfortable with each other now, after three months of lab courtship. But when they pulled away to grin at each other, there was still that chasm. A gulf filled with things they now knew about themselves but were too afraid to share.

"Finally away from prying eyes," she said, breaking the ice.

"Not a sneeze without Dr. Grasu penning a lab report."

Now that they were out of the glass cage, his sheepish gaze had been replaced by something more mysterious—that chemical need of a man wanting a woman.

He had his urges under control with the help of continued treatments, Camille thought. So it seemed safer to experiment with emotion now. Besides, he'd been desensitized to her scent. There was no need to worry.

She held back a smile as he realized she wasn't wearing a bra under her thin white tank top. The dark centers of her breasts were visible, stimulated just from the intensity of his gaze.

"It's so different," she said, "not being watched."

She didn't add that there was a definite element of danger. The knowledge that he'd killed and she'd allowed him to do it.

Before she could catch her next breath, his mouth was on hers, sipping, lulling her into a swaying dizziness. He slipped one hand down her spine, shaping her to his lean body, then resting his palm at the small of her back. With the other hand, he held her head, pressing her closer. Devouring her.

Then, what started as a fierce hunger slowed. Their kisses stretched into lazy tastes of possibility.

He was here, thought Camille. She'd done it. Gotten him back. Risked everything for these kisses.

She rubbed against him, and he moaned, fisting her hair. He was getting aroused, stiff with wanting her.

As she stroked his mouth with her lower lip, she talked. Her kisses doubled as words.

"How do you feel?"

"Don't become officious, Tex. Just keep snogging me."

A smile claimed her, and he snuggled against her neck, planting tiny kisses along the center of it until he reached her lips again.

She playfully grabbed a handful of hair, taking control, forgetting her inhibitions and giving in to her painful longing for him. Under the pressure of his kiss, she opened for him, meeting his tongue with hers, then sweeping inside his mouth. Between her legs, she grew damp, slippery with eagerness.

Then her tongue scraped against his teeth.

The still present fangs.

They both stopped. Griff put a hand up to his lips, as if hiding what was there.

The background noise of the TV became much too loud. Two people arguing. A gun exploding.

"I…" She didn't know what to say, only knew that she ached for him.

Making a casually frustrated gesture, Griff spread out his fingers, let his hand drop to his side. "Maybe I can get these bloody things filed down now?"

The fangs had grown over his human canines, forcing them out during the first phase of vampirism. Camille and the doc had wanted to see when they'd be replaced by human teeth again, but maybe they could observe Claudia instead.

"Forget it," she said, forcing a smile and backtracking to pick up her dropped market bags. "I've waited for you a long time. I can wait a little longer."

"I'm okay, otherwise." He paused, and the missing words echoed between them.

I think I'm okay, at least.

He was right. Besides the fangs, Bea and she hadn't seen remainders of the disease in him. No fins, no claws, no red eyes… He was cured, for heaven's sake. They'd even fed him human blood last week, just to mark his reaction.

No reaction. Except for some understandable gagging.

While she unloaded the groceries, she heard him turn off the TV, move to stand behind her. Ignoring the urge to turn around—good God, she could keep her back to her own boyfriend, couldn't she?—Camille washed the vegetables, arranged to cut them.

He cleared his throat. "I couldn't talk about this in front of all those people, but since we're alone…"

She started chopping the celery. *Please don't bring it up. Don't—*

"I killed your friend. Mr. Sargent."

The knife jarred out of her hand, nicking her index finger. But she didn't register the prick. Instead, she turned around, searched his face. His shadowed eyes, the cross Ashe had burned into his neck just below his jaw.

"Sarge wasn't a friend," she said, hiding her light cut from Griff. "Never a friend. Besides, you didn't kill him. I did. It's all on me."

"No." He moved to the sink, facing her. "I don't recall much of that day, just bits, really. My head is like a broken film spliced with scenes from another life, but...I killed him. And I remember enjoying it."

There was an odd shine to his eyes. Camille groped for the water faucet, wanting to wash away the blood on her finger. As she did, the pressure hissed against porcelain, and she thrust the injury under the cleansing stream of it.

Closer. He was inches away now. "Sometimes I wonder if my head's all together, Tex. I wonder what that serum has done to my body. My mind. Maybe I should be back in that cage. Maybe my innards have been muddled so much that I've become something you never planned to create."

"We know your fears." With a forced smile, she purposefully shut off the water. She'd give her right arm to make him feel better. "You're living in the aftermath of trauma, and you're still under observation so we can keep an eye on any fallout. There're guards posted around the lab. Don't worry."

"Then why do I feel somewhat insane now?"

She wanted to cover his mouth, to stop these words.

"Stress. Really. This all has a rational explanation."

You still believe that, Howard?

The echo of Sarge's voice shook her.

Get out of my head, she thought. You knew what my choice would be if it came down to you and Griff.

Her boyfriend paused, took her wounded finger in his hand. Her heart clutched.

Stupid to be afraid. They'd gotten every ounce of vampire out of him.

Yet the others—Claudia, Star and Mina—were a different story, their bodies having embraced the disease for years and years. Their progress was understandably slower. *They'd* be the dangerous ones to release.

There was no reason to be threatened by Griff.

Still, she drew back her hand from him. It wasn't bleeding much—only a slight bead remained. But what if it was enough to…?

"Camille." He pressed his lips against her temple. "You're the only one who understands. We're both alone now. Removed because of the shame of what we've done."

Please don't remind me. I want to forget.

He'd started to toy with their baby ring, testing it between his fingers. "I want you."

And so did she. Already, she was heating up again, that pulse beating steadily between her legs, making her wet with the thought of having him.

And what was stopping her? She was a big girl who'd done a damned good job of taking care of herself this past year. Besides, Griff was okay now. He really was.

She told this to herself over and over, even as he sniffed, closed his eyes, pressed a palm against a temple—something he hadn't done for a while now.

Camille covered that hand with hers.

Griff tensed. Another sniff. A low, strangled sound. Then he wrapped her in a shuddering embrace.

He needed Camille just as much as she needed him, and she wasn't about to turn him away. He was everything—her soul, her savior. Her every thought.

"Let me take care of you," she said.

"My head."

"Would ice help?" She made a move toward the fridge. "Or maybe we should go back to the lab—"

Flash quick, he backed her against the kitchen wall, cuffing both her wrists over her head with his fingers.

A sharp breath tore out of her.

Even though he had her caged, she forced herself to relax. When she'd furnished the apartment, she'd stored defensive supplies in cabinets, under the bed. Everywhere.

Not that she didn't believe he was better, but...

"Tex?" His voice was snarling rough.

"Did my blood get to you?" How could she sound so calm when her heart was thrashing around?

"No. It's..." He scented the air again.

Slowly, he drew her to him, glided his mouth down her body. Friction heated her breasts, her belly, as his hands stroked down her spine, her rear. He parted her legs from the back, and she gasped, fingers threading his dark hair.

"I love you so much." His breath heated the slick area between her thighs, even through her faded jeans.

Blood rushed there, making her wetter. Swollen.

He loved her. It was a human sentiment, not animal.

Her fingers released his hair as he nuzzled her, nudged her, brought her to utter weakness.

It'd been so long, too long, and...oh.

He was gnawing at her jeans, between her legs, making her squirm.

Losing all strength, her knees buckled, sending her in a perilous slide down the wall. She braced a hand against the nearby cabinets, barely noticing that he was undoing the buttons of her fly, then easing off her boots, jeans, underwear. Her heartbeat filled her ears, her skin.

When he guided one of her bare legs over his shoulder, Camille grabbed at the cabinet door for something to hold on to, swinging it toward her. Griff pushed back one knee, spreading her wide, and she bucked forward, slamming the wood closed again.

"Camille." He'd formed her name on her inner thigh with his mouth, trailing it upward. Closer.

When he parted her with his fingers, Camille reached out with her other hand, knocking down a standing Big Ben clock. It crashed to the tile, and she faintly saw the cogs and springs spill out.

She'd spent so much time hunting that thing down, she thought. She'd hoped it would remind him of ho-oo-ome....

She rose up in response to his tongue circling back to the center of her. Then, with maddening strokes, he kissed her thoroughly, lapping at her juices, feeding on her heat.

Mewing, she moved with the motion of his mouth.

More fluid pumped out of her, bathing her inner thighs, his face.

He coaxed one hand up her belly, under her tank top, seeking her bare breast. While he used a finger to tease her nipple, Camille ground against every suck, every pull, greedy with want.

When he plunged his tongue into her, he growled. In a way, it was almost as if her fluids had taken the place of mere blood. He was being strengthened, primed.

Maybe I'm something you never planned to create, he'd said.

Her head whirled, shot through with pleasure and confusion.

Transudate.

Secretions from blood vessels mixed with humanity's most powerful life force.

Passion.

Her pulse raced around her body, charging every cell, every nerve ending. Making her skin prickle. Build. Heat to a searing flare.

Explode.

Something. Never. Planned.

The pieces of his doubting words spiked into her, abrading, tearing, stinging.

This wasn't a thank-goodness-we're-together-again Griff making love to her. This was…

Panting, she threw open the kitchen cabinet, tried to dive inside for what she'd stored there.

But a forceful yank brought her back to Griff, and she lay there, gaping up at him.

She stared at the new creation that had maneuvered

himself between her legs again. He hovered, then stalked upward, skimming his palms over her thighs, hipbones, belly.

She gasped at the touch to her sensitive tummy, instinctively opened her legs wider. Air blew over the most vulnerable part of her. Eyes a blaze of gold, he peeled up her tank top, lowering his mouth to her ribs, sliding upward to the underside of her breast.

Golden eyes, she thought, holding her breath, almost afraid to move.

Had the serum changed their color from *strigoiaca*-red to this?

Had he become a new kind of monster?

The breath sliced out of her as he bared his fangs, flashing a lethal smile.

She'd been around him for months, but never in this state of arousal. Was her intense stimulation his latest trigger?

She crept her hand farther into the cabinet.

"Quiet now." He petted her inner thigh, fangs still lingering over her chest. His fingers crept into her tender folds again, but she was too on guard to respond.

Her hand wrapped around a mouth sealer in the cabinet.

"Don't move," she whispered. The quicker she got him back to the lab, the better.

With split-second speed, she grabbed the restraining device, flicked it on, reared up to slap it over his mouth.

But he beat her to the punch, grabbing her wrist, latching his mouth under the swell of her breast and piercing her with fangs.

Crying out, she jerked at the sting, the flow of blood draining out of her.

Then, while grinding her teeth, Camille pushed at him, but he was too powerful.

He kept sipping. She kept getting weaker.

Using her palms, she shoved at his forehead, intent on getting that sealer on his mouth, on saving them *both* from tragedy this time.

Desperate, she levered her leg against his chest, pushing with all her might. "You'll kill me, Griff!"

Startled, he bounded upward, her blood coating his lips, his chin. A drop shivered from a fang. Dripped to her stomach.

Like an abandoned plaything, she rag-dolled against the wall, spent.

Head swimming with fright, she saw Griff cock his head, draw closer to her. Sniff.

Then he froze, glowing golden eyes focused on her chest.

On the baby ring.

A look of pure devastation wracked his face.

But Camille had listened to her heart enough to turn away from it this time. With her last burst of energy, she surged forward and smacked the sealer over his mouth.

He reared backward, hand to the device.

"No choice," she whispered, reaching back into the cabinet for the dart gun now.

At the same time, she smoothed her hand under her breast, applied as much pressure as she could to stop the bleeding. He hadn't taken much, but it was enough.

With the stain of feeding, the flush of shame suffusing his skin, he tilted his head at her, his eyebrows lifting in question. Then, he reached for her jeans, covered her with them.

Don't let him fool you, she thought, even though the gesture wrung out her heart. *He sucked your blood.*

Dart gun in hand, she loaded it.

He was shaking his head, getting to his feet. The old Griff.

"Let me sedate you. Please."

Now he stiffened, eyes heating. The monster was back.

"No!"

Too late. He'd bulleted to the locked door.

She took a trembling shot at him. Missed.

The sound of hinges being torn from the wall urged her to reload. But dizziness slowed her down, made her clumsy.

Pressing a hand to her wound, she realized that she couldn't stand. Needed to rest for a second, just like after a blood donation. It gave her time to put on her jeans, dial the cell phone in her back pocket.

First, a call to the guard station. Then one to the lab, alerting Bea and securing first aid for herself.

But it needed to be done damned quickly. She had another monster to hunt.

And, this time, Camille Howard had no idea what she should do when she caught him.

Chapter 14

Blood.

His body screamed for it, quaked because it craved more.

More.

The creature that had once been Griffin had sped out of the apartment, away from its appetizer—Camille. Lady Tex. Whatever he used to call her.

Now he was crouching in a supply closet just inside the lab, working at the mouth sealer, having arrived before the scientists and the two guards who'd just been posted at the door. They were armed with the dart guns that had worked so well during Camille's castle rescue.

Too bad for them that UV wands weren't an option anymore, Griffin thought. The vampires had been ex-

posed to too many treatments for the rays to be effective now.

But that was brilliant for him and the *strigoiaca*. The
less defense, the better.

The sealer sucked at him, numbed his lips with a
quiet mechanical hiss. Since, for the past three months,
Camille had shared all her science projects with him
during their touchy-feely conversations, Griff knew exactly what the sealer was about. How the device lasted
for fifteen minutes. Consequently, he'd learned to
breathe through his nose, to wait out its short, battery-
operated life.

After that, he could carry on.

Saliva flooded his mouth as he anticipated the blood,
the rush. The snap of sublime energy he'd tasted from
Camille already.

Today's sudden hunger was as much a surprise to
him as it'd been to her. He'd become conditioned to her
scent with her daily visits, had convinced everyone—
even himself—that she was no longer a stimulant for his
wild side. But today, the intensity of her body had gotten to him. The arousal. The resulting animal lust and
thirst.

And that blood he'd sipped from her hadn't done
anything but make him long for more.

Just outside the closet, the doctor, Grasu, paced in
her Ugg boots, skirt and lab coat, plucking at her latex
gloves. Because of the crack between the door and wall,
he'd been able to watch her flitting all over the place
since she'd gotten here.

Minutes before, the doctor had sent her assistant,

Ike, out of the lab with a first-aid kit. Probably for Camille and her little fang wound.

As Griffin visually stalked Grasu, jagged pain shot through his forehead. He lurched, almost knocking over a broom, then pressing his hands against the wall for balance. His mind separated into pieces, images, like sand in a whirlwind.

He reached out to grab a grain of memory. Camille's face, her pale-blue eyes shiny and soft with wanting him. Warm, comforting, uplifting.

Then another vision whipped into its place. Mina, waking him up during the dead of night, her white skin and red gaze making him instinctively smack her away. Dark, freezing, horrifying.

Blade sharp, another image sliced over the other one: a little boy staring in a mirror that reflected his new bedroom. He wanted to grab all the playthings, the quilt, the clothing in the closet and hold them to his chest, never letting them go. He was doing what he couldn't do with his parents: keeping what belonged to him.

Another memory.

Mina hissing, laughing in her own demented version of mirth.

Another.

The curves of Camille's chest as she held him to her, keeping him. Valuing him.

Ano—

Mina opening her mouth, preparing to strike. To feed.

Blankness. Sand settling, reshuffled in different patterns.

His mind resting. A moment of peace. Until he realized he needed help. So much help. Yet…

With a restrained groan, Griffin tried to grab on to something that would stop him from going into the lab. From showing Dr. Grasu how far he'd regressed in so short a time.

But maybe… Should he reveal himself? Should he tell the doctor how he thought the UV treatment and serum had turned him inside out? That the chemical combination of Camille's aroused scent and his new composition was tearing him apart?

Could she explain why letting go of his morals and taking what he needed felt so right? So good?

Yes, he would go in to see the doctor. She'd know what to do.

He struggled to rise, face dragging over the wall, his braced hands. They were still perfumed with Camille's erotic scent, the heady memory of her juices.

Without thinking, he took in the smell of his fingers, imagined tasting her again. He shuddered, yearning.

Remembering what he'd done back in that apartment.

God, he'd bitten Camille, sank his teeth into her.

Sickened, Griffin stumbled into the laboratory. The suck-hiss of his mouth sealer whined over the hum of electronics, computers, Dr. Grasu's anxious footsteps.

As he moved closer, she spun around, horn-rimmed glasses low on her prominent nose.

"Guards," she yelled, then changed gears and nodded at him as if this were just another daily appointment. "Camille phoned to inform me of the setback. Ike is seeing to her. And as for you, please come with me to the cell."

Back to his cage.

He heard the two guards enter, come up behind him.

"If you please, Griffin," Dr. Grasu said, "let us make you comfortable."

They were going to shoot him up with sedatives.

An explosion of fighting anger rippled through his every cell. Survival. As the vampire-animal took over, Griff spun, gripped the throats of both guards, then squeezed, thumbs on their windpipes.

Then the old Griff came to, panicked by what he was doing. Without hesitation, he loosened his grip, and the guards passed out on the floor.

Meanwhile, Dr. Grasu was fumbling with her dart gun.

Griff's mouth sealer whirred, jerked, fell away from his mouth. Dropped to the tiles with a clatter.

Saliva coated his lips, and he used his tongue to catch some of it.

He tasted Camille.

Hunger clenched his belly, his mind.

Again, his head scattered into a million fragments, and he swallowed, wishing blood were coating his throat instead of this bland spittle.

"Griffin," she said, raising the gun, "we will take care of you."

Hadn't Camille promised to do that?

His vampire voice came out in a rasp. "You never looked into my soul with your microscopes. Even your psychologists couldn't predict this."

Judging by the rise of her eyebrows, the wheels were turning in her mind. "Your results showed no aberrations. This will need further study."

"Actually, no. Camille and I…" He cocked his head. "How can I politely say this?"

Not understanding, she just waited. Then, "Ah. Aah. So you were not so sensitized to her. Well, this is why we did not allow you out of the lab building. Let us get back to work. We will fetch Camille for a set of very discreet experiments now."

He thought of the huntress's blood, how sweet it'd tasted. Then, in a crash of conscience, he thought about how wrong it was to want more.

Sod off, he said to *that* Griffin. The dead Griffin who had some humanity left.

"Can you imagine what it's like to feel your teeth cutting into a person's skin?" he asked. "It's terrible. Beautiful. Knives through butter. Then the blood…"

He covered his face with his hands, inhaled. The scent of sex filled him, buried him in shaking need.

Dr. Grasu's gun clicked, but nothing happened. She scrambled, trying to fix it.

He licked a finger, wanting more than just this hint of promise. Wanting something thick, coppery, invigorating.

Sound pounded at the back of his brain, but it had nothing to do with his body. Rhythmic thumps channeled through the floor, the walls.

His preternatural hearing was picking up the far frenzy of music. A mass of heated bodies.

Camille had told him about the disco down the street.

How she wanted to take him there as soon as they were able to dance together again.

His body keened at the thought of all those young bodies in heat. All the boiling blood in their veins.

Dr. Grasu raised her gun again.

Irritated, he darted over, knocked it away.

Backing up, she leaned against a steel table, eyes wide and magnified by her glasses. As Griffin came closer, her short gray hair moved with the beat of his breathing.

"I'm departing your lab," he said, leaning closer, lips against the withered skin of her throat now.

Blood, thumping in her veins. Need. Drink. Thick. "Don't stop me, Doctor. Just…"

See that Camille is okay.

He shook the thought away, allowing a coat of red to slide over his vision, overcoming his senses.

"The posted guards will not allow you to leave." She pushed away from the table, her chest knocking against his, her gaze searching for the dart gun he'd knocked from her grasp earlier.

"Really, you should've given the guards actual bullets," he said. "Though I doubt even those would work on me now."

Need. Blood.

She hesitated, staring at him. Maybe even regretting trying to cure him.

Then she threw herself downward, thunking to the floor, reaching, thrashing her body in order to get to a gun he'd only toss away again.

The vampire sighed, bent over, tugged her up by the lab coat and firmly seated her on the steel table.

"I'm trying to make this easy for the both of us," he said. "Help me by staying still."

Her arms flailed, and he easily restrained her, grabbing both her wrists. With his other hand, he stroked her soft, gray hair back from her forehead.

"I won't make you one of me, Dr. Grasu. I only want a drink to sustain me before I leave. Please."

She kicked, railed. The vampire stopped trying to calm her and pressed his hand over her mouth. His very own version of a mouth sealer. Not very scientific, but effective.

While she bit at his palm, he leaned over, gently pierced her neck with his fangs. Like knives through butter. Sucking, taking her into him, tasting the tang of life and energy. The sustenance made him giddy with power.

Whimpering, she stopped moving. He went back to stroking her hair, calming her, slowly working his mouth at her throat.

Flash floods of memory washed over him: slipping inside Camille, fitting into the places only he could fill, her slick muscles clamping around him, throbbing, pulsing as they moved together.

This drinking was personal, too, something he could keep for himself. Something he could hold on to, unlike his parents. Unlike his old life with Camille.

Dr. Grasu's blood was *his* now. No one could take that away because he'd internalized it. Owned it fully.

And that only made him hungrier.

When he drew back, moisture soaking his lips, she was limp, eyes fixed on the ceiling, her fingers twitching as her palms lay upward on the table.

The old Griffin's conscience clicked into the vampire's mind. *Did I drain her?*

But the vampire seized control again. *Who cares?*

The musical tattoo of a techno song invaded his perception again, washing away his guilt.

Dancing. Sweat. Lust. Blood.

His veins thrummed, wanting it all.

Time to leave. Time to open the door to a new world where he had the control.

Filled with the surging power of someone else's life, the vampire laid Beatrix Grasu down and headed for the *strigoiaca's* cells. On the way, he ripped out the throats of three dart-gun-bearing guards, all the while thinking about how his Girls could use a good drink, as well.

When Camille and Ike ran into the lab, she screamed at the sight on the steel table.

"Bea!" She stumbled forward, spying Doc's punctured throat.

Remembering her own struggle with Griff, Camille clutched at the bandage under her breast. The male assistant had secured it over Griff's bite, the gauze coated with coagulating gel that'd stopped her bleeding.

A sob heaved through her.

As Camille took Bea in her arms and cuddled her limp body off the table to the floor, Ike cursed, rushed away, yelled, "The *strigoiaca* are gone! Guards are—"

She could hear him gag to a stop.

"Ike, contact the entrance guards, see if they've encountered Griff and the Girls." Camille ran a loving gaze over her mentor, saw the fang marks in her neck.

"Talk to me, Doc. Come on. And, Ike, get the coagulator."

He rushed around the lab, contacting the guard station, collecting medical supplies and setting up for Bea's blood transfusion.

"They're not answering," he said, cell phone to his ear as he passed in a blur, arms full of jars and tubes.

No. They had to be there. If they weren't, that would mean...

Glancing down at the doc, Camille contained her rage, her sorrow. Tried not to break down and spill how much Bea had come to mean to her. How much fortitude she'd taught her. How much she'd been like another parent.

"Did Griffin...?"

"Yes." Her voice wasn't even louder than a scratch.

Ike heaped the same coagulating gel he'd used for Camille on the old woman's neck. She caught his grave expression, and translated for herself.

Too much blood lost already.

Please no, not Bea, too...

With a burst of energy, Doc grabbed Camille's hand, moved her mouth as if to talk. Camille leaned over so she could hear better. Unbidden, a tear landed on Bea's neck, mingling with the blood.

"He...is not *strigoiaca*," she said. "More evolved. Methodical. Perhaps introduction of female blood acts exponentially as steroid on male system..."

Camille wanted to tell her to rest, to be at peace, to stop this grueling torture of a body that only needed stillness. But she had to know more before she went after Griff and the *strigoiaca*.

Before she stopped them from doing *this* to any-one else.

Bea's lips were moving again, and Camille cradled her head, listening, the tears pooling in her eyes.

"This is his response to stimulation…."

Ashamed of her part in this, Camille took it out on Ike. "Are you ready to transfuse yet?"

"I am trying."

The old woman exhaled, her body seeming to shrink right in Camille's own arms.

"Should have tested sexual reaction…" Bea wheezed, and a blood bubble popped at the side of her mouth, spiking Camille's cheek with moisture. "Sci-ence. Fickle thing."

"We're not perfect. We'll get it right next time."

"Next time."

Bea choked, and Camille strengthened her hold on her.

"Transfusion!" she shouted, voice breaking, but this time Ike was too busy to answer.

"Hey, Aunt Bea," Camille said, throat tight. "Just hold on until Ike gets the equipment ready."

The old scientist tried to smile, forcing Camille to lose control, inviting the angry tears to spill.

Ike shouted from his transfusion station, "Ready!"

Grasping the collar of Camille's tank top, Bea des-perately tried to tell her something.

"Don't talk, okay?" Camille tried to calm the agi-tated old woman.

"Can save him." She pulled Camille down closer, fire in her eyes. "You and Ike adjust serum formula."

"But it didn't work in the first place."

"It will work, darling girl."

The doc seemed so confident that Camille couldn't doubt her.

But they should've known better. Try to fool with nature, and science would come out the loser. Damn their arrogance.

As the life bled from the doctor's body, Camille held tighter. "Stay. Come on, Bea, don't give up, here. You've got lots of work to do."

"No." She made a quiet rasping sound. "Is your work now."

And the woman who'd devoted her life to science made the ultimate sacrifice for it. Her body lost form in Camille's arms, drained of too much blood.

But Camille wouldn't believe it. Couldn't grasp the truth.

"Stop it, Aunt Bea." She gave her a gentle shake. "I want to see you jump up and down when I bring those vampires back. I want to see you all cute and excited."

"She will not jump, Ms. Camille."

It was Ike, standing above them. He was still pretty young, in his thirties, his winged black hair giving him a mad-doctor look. Camille had always been amused with his clichéd appearance, but not now.

Not when she needed to get her ass over to the guard station to see why they weren't answering the phone.

She tenderly picked Bea up, laid her on the steel table as if it were a comfortable bed. Then she cradled the old woman's fragile, liver-spotted hand. Held it to her cheek, feeling the coldness. The lack of blood.

With all the care in the world, she positioned Doc's hands over her chest, leaving her at peace.

Then, to the sound of Ike's sobbing, Camille collapsed to the floor, body heaving with sickness. Shock.

Just a minute, she thought. A minute to regroup.

But, as with the death of her parents, it took much longer than a minute for her to get back on her feet.

The guard station looked like a slaughterhouse.

White tile steeped in blood, necks and bellies torn, eyes sightless, dart guns and mouth sealers scattered all over the floor. Door torn off its hinges and mangled to steel curlicues on the ground.

As a tearstained Camille marched out of the lab building and into the night, she tried not to fear this change in the *strigoiaca*. They clearly weren't just stinging a potential pet with their tongues, then whisking him off to a private place for some feeding.

They were frenzied. Indiscriminate.

And judging from the clawed-open stomachs of three guards, wanton in their appetites.

Dressed in her jeans, tank top, cowboy boots, watch tracker and the baby ring, the talisman that had thus far always protected her, Camille took a dimly lit side street, following the *blump* of the tracker and the trail of bodies.

All male victims, so far—beggars by the look of it. But the big question was: were the *strigoiaca* exchanging blood and saliva with women to replenish their tribe?

She'd soon see.

While she passed a stone church oddly located in the center of an apartment's concrete courtyard, a pack of dogs barked from one street over. Camille kept the minor threat of them in the back of her mind, one hand on her aspen-wood stake, the other on her machete.

The weapons felt so cold to her, foreign, as if a part of her had died and she'd woken up to find herself changed.

But science had failed her.

It was time to get real.

The guardhouse massacre only validated the gathering of her weapons. Three months ago, with the images of the disappearing vampire and the castle wolves still fresh, she'd purchased an arsenal that rivaled Sarge's. Though she'd stored them in her apartment closet, their presence had given her harsh comfort. A just-in-case balm. A safety net for her inevitable fall from scientific grace.

Dammit, she was getting such a late start. Obviously, the vampires had taken their time feasting on the guards. The carnage indicated that they'd made slow work of killing them. There were even claw marks on the men's thighs.

Playtime for the *strigoiaca?*

And what about Griff? Had he hung back, enjoying the sight of their carnal frolicking or…

Stomach churning, she pressed on, resolute.

It was time to fight death with death, no matter what her mentor had taught her.

Still, what would she do when she saw Griff? Was there a chance he could be saved?

Bea, pale and still in her arms.

Shaken, she concentrated on her tracker, which was going crazy with the *blumps* of vampire recognition, mingling with the hammering music from a disco.

She recognized the place. Chill, it was named. She'd wanted to dance there with Griff some day. To forget all their worries in the primal humidity of dance-floor catharsis.

Stopping outside the door, she noticed there was a line to get in. People were chatting, laughing, staring at the whacked-out girl dressed in red cowboy boots and wearing everything from blades to a crossbow with a quiver of holy-watered arrows.

As she strolled right past the bouncer while staring at her ever *blumping* tracker, he tugged at her bare arm. The yank reminded her that Griff had bitten her under the breast, and the wound thudded with bruised agony. It was more mental pain than physical, but sharp all the same.

Ignoring the injury—she'd popped a few Motrin before leaving the lab—Camille grasped the wrist of her captured arm with her left hand, violently levering her right arm out from his brawny grip.

"You'll thank me in a second," she said in Romanian, hand on the machete hilt.

The bald brute's mouth gaped, and he didn't have much to say in return. Satisfied, Camille sauntered into the club, through the red-velvet lobby. After that, she was enveloped by the cloying mist of pheromones and the pounding blast of ear-shattering music.

Immediately, she lost herself in a sea of undulating

bodies, sweat coating her arms, moistening her tank in the gathered steam of a summer night. She glanced around the huge, smoky room—the balcony where patrons leaned over the railing, the private alcoves where women in their short skirts and stilettos straddled men, the endless dance floor, the colorfully drab flickers of a light show.

But her tracker told her something was in here. It flashed red, pounding out big bangs of proximity.

Then she saw it. The vampire Claudia.

Good Lord. The science-lab treatments made her blend with the crowd.

She was no longer dressed in tattered hiking gear, but wearing blue pajamas, compliments of the lab. Her blond hair had been washed daily, making her seem as groomed as a normal barfly while she danced with an unsuspecting male. He was grinding into her, and she was returning the favor. What that poor meat substitute didn't realize was that she was stroking his neck, baring fangs.

So this was the *strigoiaca's* new game. Quiet attacks, now that they'd gotten over the initial hunger by snacking on the guards.

As if that weren't enough, Camille's spine came alive with icy shivers. She turned around to find Mina and Star dressed in the guards' bloodied tan uniforms and hats. They stared at her from a private table in the corner.

The UV treatments and serum hadn't cured these animals. It'd just made them a little less feral in appearance. Made them more human.

Charged up, Camille glanced around, needing to

know where Griff was. Whether he was in a position to attack.

Could she take all of them alone?

Not that there was much choice. Ike had called the police, but they'd just laughed at him. And all the on-call lab guards were too afraid to help.

It was up to her.

A giant hand landed on her shoulder, spun her around.

"Come," bellowed the bald bouncer from the door.

He had a friend with him. Two big dopes who had no idea what was about to go down.

"You've got four vampires in here," she yelled over the music, "so don't screw with me."

They both paused, laughed, glancing at each other as if asking, "Did she say *vampire?* Nah. Couldn't have."

Laying hands on her, they started to drag her away into the relatively empty velvet lobby.

"I'm in no mood for this," she muttered, drawing out the machete and the stake at the same time, brandishing them.

They backed away, hands up.

Right into another body.

Griff.

Camille's adrenaline flared, awakened by the sight of something that had taken over the man she loved.

With minimal effort, he picked them both up by the scruffs of their shirts, banged their heads together in an explosion of red, then tossed them away. Around them, the few lingering patrons scattered, screaming.

Done, he turned back to her. "Hey."

It was his usual greeting, that casual, sexy word that meant he'd been thinking about her all day.

But now it was a mockery.

She tried to separate this thing from her boyfriend. These golden eyes from Griff Montfort's deep-brown ones.

"Hey." She'd spit it out. Rejecting what he now was.

Still, she couldn't strike. Couldn't move.

Somewhere in that body, Griff still lingered. Her Griff.

He smiled, touched the tip of his tongue to a fang. Reminded her of the ecstasy she'd felt earlier in the night when he'd had his mouth on her.

In spite of itself, her body reacted, heating up, moistening, aching.

"Camille," he said, reaching a hand toward her face. "You tasted so good."

Enraged, she dodged his touch, raised the stake, knowing she should just plunge it into his heart right now.

And she would have—maybe—if a pinprick of red light hadn't locked on Griff's chest, right over his heart.

With her gaze, Camille traced the line backward, following its path through the smoke of the room.

Then she gasped in utter shock at the person who was aiming the laser-sighted crossbow at her boyfriend.

Chapter 15

Sarge fixed his sights on the man he wanted to kill more than anything.

Except for Howard, of course.

She was just to the right of his target—Griffie, the object of his revenge dreams.

Good positioning, he thought. After Sarge put an arrow through Vamp Boy, he wanted a good view of Howard's face. Of the realization that she'd made the wrong god-damned choice back in those woods three months ago.

So he took his shot.

But Griffie was fast, even speedier than he'd been as an infant fang freak, when he'd kicked Sarge's ass. The kid literally leaned to the left, avoiding the shot just as if it were a slow-motion bullet.

Nice. A *Matrix*-inspired bloodsucker. Now Sarge's world was complete.

As the arrow *thwapped* off of the club's etched-stone wall, the vamp got this soulful look on his face, then glanced at Camille, who was aiming her stake at him.

Just heave the damned thing, he thought, reloading.

"Camille?" Griffie said, sounding confused.

Oh, no. Not this. Vamp psychology, where they acted all contrite and saved their skin.

Unaffected, Sarge brought up his bow again, catching the Brit's attention. In turn, the kid seemed surprised, then dived behind a red-velvet curtain, disappearing. Sarge humped it over there with his pain-in-the-wanker limp, kicking aside the heavy material while targeting.

Gone. He was freakin' *gone*.

Then Sarge locked on to a square hole near the floor, a missing block of stone. Hell knew where it led.

Screaming cascaded over the pumping music and, suddenly, all the horny customers were crowding the lobby, bowling over Howard, who fought her way toward him.

"Sargent!"

Either in response to Griffie's attempt at screwing with her mind or to her seeing Sarge again, Howard's pale complexion was stark against the red of her loose, wild hair. There was a crimson splash against her pale T-shirt, right under a breast that wasn't wearing a bra.

Sarge's pulse gave a naughty leap, and he glanced away.

A nipple. Big deal.

But he found himself looking again.

She covered herself with the blade of her machete, blocking his pleasure. Then, with what could've been a welcoming smile, she pulled out that adrenaline gun, gave herself a shot.

Machete. Stake. Where the hell were her licorice gun and other science-can-be-fun devices?

"Don't dawdle." She jerked her head toward the dance floor, pushing against the flow of the crowd. "Let's go."

So much for the passionate hello he'd envisioned from that hospital bed. But had that smile meant she was glad to see him? Even a little?

As the club's music abruptly cut off, they entered a pit that was already tinged with the tang of blood. The air was suffused with red light: The throes of purgatory. A cave with bodies flying off ledges, limbs splayed on the ground. Hellfire licking at skin.

A cry from above caught Sarge's attention, a descending squeal of terror. Sarge whipped his bow around as a man's writhing body came at him. With minimal effort, he merely stepped out of the guy's path, blocking out the sickening splash of his death.

Above, a blond vampire hissed down at him, laughing.

Oh, yeah. The hiker chick. He remembered her.

Out of nowhere, an arrow spit through the air, tagging Blondie right between the eyes. Her forehead started steaming, and she cried out in screeching rage while disappearing into a cloud of abandoned blue pajamas.

He barely had time to glance at the shooter before flying into action again. But what he saw froze in his mind like a front-page picture: Howard with her crossbow, eyes haunted, mouth caught in a gape of self-disgust.

Her parents.

Wasting no time, she reloaded while searching the room, then ran into a private alcove where two limp females were stirring awake.

Strigoiaca replacements? Shit, they were back to their old tricks. From his source at the university lab, a cute little assistant who filed reports for Beatrix Grasu, Sarge knew how the female vampires had "humanized" during their forced stay. But old habits died hard, didn't they?

No time for analysis. Instead, a blur of tan clothing caught his attention. Another vamp—the one that used to look like a Gypsy. She was swinging like a jungle monkey from the iron candle sconces on the far wall, dressed like a sheriff or something. Weird-ass vamps.

Sarge aimed just as she swooped down to capture a fleeing woman. Before the laser could lock on to the creature, though, she plunged fangs into the girl's neck.

But he wasn't about to let her make another vamp. He fired, hitting his mark with ease, heart not even skipping a beat. The arrow pierced the beast right in the temple, clean as you please. Felt good to be back in business.

The vamp hadn't even had time to warn the remaining *strigoiaca* with a scream.

Up in smoke the creature went, and all the weeping

victim had to show for it was a lifetime of traumatic stress disorder and some neck wounds.

Not a bad deal when you considered that Sarge had walked away the last time with so much more…and less.

He checked on Camille, who was busy determining the vital signs of the women in the booth while her heated gaze sought the last original vampire. She extracted a cell phone from her back jeans pocket and yelled into it.

Their gazes locked, and he signaled to her.

Two down.

She nodded, went back to jabbering, scanning the room.

Good God, even after laying waste to the blond pajama monster, Howard was still a bleeding heart. *We can still cure these new ones,* she was no doubt thinking. She was even probably chattering with Beatrix about how to play Nurse Angel right now.

Though Sarge knew they'd successfully cured Ana, he still wanted to plant some sense into Howard's brain.

They're vamps, got it? Vamps. *You lucked out once, but look what happened to the four you're chasing tonight.*

He thought she'd finally gotten it when she'd shot that arrow right into Blondie.

But he didn't have the chance to mull it all over. Next thing he knew, there was a tugging at his good leg.

He aimed the crossbow downward, at the man grabbing a handful of Sarge's black fatigues.

"Nu!" the guy yelled, his voice bouncing around

the now emptied disco. His body convulsed, and he blanched.

Dance lights celebrated over his ripped button-down, but half his body had disappeared into a hole in the wall, just as if a snake were dragging this mouse into its lair.

Ah, little Griffie. Come out, come out, wherever you are.

He crept to the hole, easing out his machete as the victim cried out in agony, then jerked still.

As Camille finished her call to Ike, she knew this was a losing battle.

The two club women had clearly been exposed to the virus, and God knew how many other *strigoiaca* were still running around. Sure, Sarge had said two vamps were gone, but they could've changed patterns, already ushering an endless number of victims into their tribe.

Sarge. She still hadn't gotten over the shock of seeing him again, the ecstatic rush that had forced a smile, even though there wasn't much to smile about.

The way he limped around, the perma-scowl he wore… He hated her, and she cringed at the thought of it.

One of the female victims clutched at Camille's wrist and bolted upward. Camille whipped out her stake.

"Nu inteleg," she said. *I don't understand.*

Neither did Camille. Couldn't understand any of it: Why she'd shot Claudia in a passionate fit of revenge. Why it'd relieved her to know that she'd rid the world of one more enemy.

With one hand, Camille seized the woman's arms, then used the other hand to strip off the belt of the victim's jeans and tightly wrap it around her wrists. To the tune of the captive's Romanian complaints, Camille did the same to the second *strigoiaca* candidate, using a leather thong from some curtains for restraints.

Thank God Ike had been standing by back at the lab. He'd be here in a snap with guns from his own collection and sedatives, plus their private ambulance.

Was she doing the right thing by keeping these women alive? Or should she take a clue from all the destruction that'd already happened because of her reluctance to kill?

Camille sucked it up. Maybe she couldn't put down these innocent victims who still had a chance, but she could sure as hell take out another vampire.

Just to be sure the victims would be secured, Camille braced a hand against the shoulder of the first woman.

"Nothing personal," she said in Romanian. Then she punched her, knocking her out.

The second lady suffered the same fate.

Now where was Sarge? Things were awful quiet. Had he taken care of all the vampires?

Camille sprinted to the middle of the dance floor. The lights still winked down in muted rainbow colors, blurring her vision.

But that didn't keep her from finding him.

He was peering into a hole in the wall, positioned over a man who was lying belly down on the floor, mouth gaped in terror, stiff body jarring back and forth.

It was a corpse. And something in that hole was feeding on it.

"Sarge?" She crept nearer to him. Oddly enough, he was making her feel better, not worse.

"I'm taking care of it, Howard."

Okay. She had a bad feeling about *this*. Where had Griff been all this time?

"What's in there, Sarge?" She moved closer, whisking the machete out of its sheath.

"You'll see," he answered with the same warning tone. "Just take care of the *strigoiaca*, and then we'll chat."

"They're still around?"

"Should be one left. Your boyfriend's other woman."

He glanced up at her, smirking wickedly, enjoying her pain. She deserved his acidity.

"Say, give me a hand." He gestured toward the body on the floor. "Pull at him."

Sheathing the machete, she bent down, took the corpse's rigid hands in hers, tugged at his weight.

There was a slight hitch, then his body came free from the hole. Since he should've been heavier, she'd overcompensated in her pull. That caused her to stumble back and fall.

When she looked up, she saw why he'd been so light.

He was no more than a torso, a body ripped in half. Nausea filled her.

Slowly, she slid her gaze back to the hole, to Sarge as he prepared to go in.

Tell me Griff's not in there, she thought.

She and Sarge locked gazes in challenge, the visual contact quickening her pulse.

Crouching, she tensed, ready to dart into the hole and reach Griff before her nemesis did.

But the sound of smacking lips, then a female "Aah," stopped Camille.

Alert, she swung out her machete.

Attracted by the fresh gore, Mina had wandered onto the dance floor. She was dragging her slumped male conquest, blood trailing from one of the private alcoves. Obviously, Mina had been busy feeding there.

With a careless thump, she dropped her former meal, then used those blazing red orbs to inspect this new one.

Being the most ancient vampire, Mina hadn't changed as much as the others, though she'd exhibited signs of growing human intelligence like the rest. Her features were much the same, if not faded by the treatments. Ineffective wings, dulled tongue. But the blood-spattered guard uniform and mouth testified that she was still a killer.

With relish, Mina dived to the corpse, buried her face in his torn stomach, feeding.

She'd ignored Camille completely. Had the lab treatments switched her priorities from keeping the tribe alive to making her a loner? Or did the call of blood override all else?

Didn't matter. Mina would be dust in a second.

"You're the reason for all this crap," Camille said, voice shaking as she glided closer to the feeding monster. "You're a predator who doesn't give a damn about whose life you ruin. You get off on blood. You get off on the kill."

She could've been talking to her parents' murderer.

She *was* talking to him.

From the corner of her eye, she could see Sarge disappear into the hole. Something fisted in her belly.

As if she'd understood everything Camille had said, Mina tilted up her bloodied face from her food, hissed.

Camille chuffed and raised her machete over her head. "Whatever, bitch."

She swung down, and Mina clawed upward, nailing over Camille's stomach. Though Camille grunted with the burn, she followed through with the machete's arc.

But Mina had cleared away. Though her wings and tongue had been made impotent, she still had plenty of weapons: fangs, claws, strength.

Even if her abrasions stung, Camille was able to block out the pain. All she saw was the man who'd killed her parents. The thing that'd changed Griff.

A scapegoat for all that mattered.

She lashed out with the machete, swinging madly. At first, the she-beast merely sidestepped the cuts, smiling in that insane, fangy way.

That only made Camille more determined.

The blade sang through the air—*phu-wop, phu-wop*—as Mina continued to avoid each attack.

By now, Camille's adrenaline shot was wearing off. She was getting weaker, slower, out of breath. Out of time. Ill.

As she missed yet again, the vampire cackled, having a grand old time.

"Play with this," Camille muttered, desperate.

With both hands, she angled the blade upward, and Mina casually stuck her hand out, intending to bat it away.

Phu-whop.

That hand went flying three feet to the right.

As blood sputtered out of the stump, Mina cocked her

head, fascinated. Uncomprehending. She'd survived hundreds of years without encountering her own mortality.

And it was time for that to end.

Camille followed with a downward stroke, and the vampire jerked backward just in time. It almost seemed as if she were calling on her wings to take her away, as if she weren't used to staying light on her feet.

Ruthless, Camille cornered her against a wall.

The monster hissed in earnest, and Camille could see that, in her eyes, she was scared. A crazy laugh bubbled inside Camille's chest, heated by compressed rage, imminent release.

But the vampire wasn't finished trying to survive. She struck out again with her remaining claw, lightning quick, stripping the inside of Camille's wrist to bloody shreds.

Reflexively, she let go of the machete. Steel clattered to the floor, leaving her open to another attack.

And attack she did. Crying out, Camille dodged the blow, the vampire's nails tangling in her necklace instead of flesh.

The ring.

The chain ripped away from her neck, became tangled in the vampire's fingers.

Seeing her holding Griff's gift, just like she'd probably held Griff himself—feeding off him, ruining him—Camille's mind whirred.

Blood on sheets. Blood on Griff's mouth. Blood on Bea's neck.

The vampire struck, fangs extended, aimed at Camille's throat. But…too late.

With a vengeful yell of release, the huntress jerked the wooden stake out of its holder, thrust it forward, impaling Mina.

The creature gurgled, and Camille roared in fury, spiking the vamp further, the sharp end coming out the other side of Mina's body and hitting the stone wall.

Panting, Camille backed off, letting go of the stake, heart jackhammering as she watched Mina choke and stare at the gaping wound.

Don't stop now, Camille thought. The vamps can't continue.

She grabbed the machete from the floor and positioned herself at the vampire's side.

Then, quite simply, she chopped off her head.

Afterward, she didn't dwell on it. Couldn't dwell. Couldn't think about the blood spattering her skin.

Efficiently, she cleaned her weapons, replaced them in their proper holders, picked up the baby ring, inspected the broken chain, stuck it in her front jeans pocket.

Then, exhausted, she wandered over to Ike, who'd arrived just in time to cower from the showdown.

Camille pointed to the unconscious women in the alcove. "I think they're the last of the *strigoiaca*. Get them back to the lab and start treatment right away. Then call the police and tell them to clean this mess." She started walking away, then stopped. "And one more thing."

He nodded.

"Please take out Mina's heart and burn it."

Then, as if the request were on par with asking for a

cup of coffee or for him to take out the trash, Camille said, "Thanks," and walked over to the hole in the wall.

She couldn't think. Couldn't feel. Not if she wanted to survive.

Once there, she crouched down. Waited until the world stopped spinning. She was hardly aware of Ike, dabbing her cuts with the coagulating gel, bandaging her up.

She couldn't feel anything.

It seemed like only minutes later when Sarge crawled out, bloodied and battered.

"Don't even ask," he said.

She didn't.

He stood, hurled his stake to the ground, then shook the rafters with a yelled curse. And, all the while, Camille waited, half of her relieved that he hadn't been successful in killing Griff.

Half of her wanting to do it herself because of what the vampire in him had done to Aunt Bea.

Before the cops showed up at the disco, Ike had seen that the infected women were transported back to the nearby lab and put in isolated cells. He'd also done some cleanup work, shooing Sarge and Camille out the door so they wouldn't get caught in the trap of police questioning.

They had too much work to do yet, and Ike was willing to stay behind and buy them time. Interviews with the detectives could come later, he'd said, after they'd taken care of the male vampire.

Sarge and Camille had hoofed it out of the nightclub, but they had nowhere to go. Griff had made a clean escape.

She followed her rival to his parked Jeep, the street lighting low and insufficient, the summer-night heat gathering on their skin and mixing with the drying blood to make it moist again. She wanted to touch him, make sure he was real. Tell him how sorry she'd been to sacrifice him. Tell him...

What, exactly?

"Sarge, talk to me," she said as he jogged ahead of her. Even with his limp he was in fighting shape.

"No time."

He hopped inside, and she grabbed his door.

Looking very unamused, he asked, "You think I won't start this baby up and drag you along the street like tin cans on a wedding car?"

Anger. She'd felt so much of it, too. It had sapped her, and she was sick of it.

"Sarge." She wouldn't move until he looked at her. "Listen, my tracker won't pick him up unless he's within our proximity, so your instincts might be our only resource right now. I need you."

"Don't count on me," he said, clearly choosing to ignore the tension. All business.

The words were a bolt of emotion, sizzling between them.

God, *did* she need him? And in what way?

She sucked in a breath as his eyes widened. In their depths, she could see such intensity, such fear, that she actually took a step away.

She wasn't ready for this. Sarge? Her?

No way.

Never.

Finally, he looked away, staring at the steering wheel.

"After scrapping with me in that passageway and thinking it was pretty entertaining, that skinny British runt got all apologetic, then squeezed through a hole I couldn't get through and hopped to the streets. While I stupidly tried to follow, getting stuck, by the way, he flagged down a cab, threw out the driver and rode off with a gargoyle flying over the cab's roof. I just know he's somewhere that has roads, Howard. So that's where I'm gonna start."

"Did you mention a gargoyle?"

"A gargoyle."

Camille didn't know what to say for a moment. About anything. She'd definitely seen stranger things lately, felt weirder emotions. "Okay, then. Maybe we should get ahold of a police scanner, listen for carnage. That'd be our best bet to find him."

"Oh." As he turned back to her, she could see that one of Sarge's eyes was already swollen, and there was a nasty gash caked with coagulating gel on his forehead. "So, you're telling me that you're hunting the boyfriend now."

Bea's body flashed in her mind's eye, melding with Sarge's own wounds. "Yeah."

"And when you catch him, what're you going to do? Give him a love tap?"

She couldn't answer.

"Goddammit," he said. "Nothing's changed with you. And don't think I'm idiot enough to let you tag along with me so you can get me wounded again when I move to cut his head off."

"He killed Beatrix." The sentence left an aftershock of grief, and she pursed her lips, holding back the anguish.

A slow burn consumed Sarge as he gripped the steering wheel.

"And," she said softly, "he deserves to be punished. The vampire part of him."

"You think there's any human left in him?" His voice was as bruised as her own conscience. "Even after seeing that body ripped in half when you pulled it out of the wall hole?"

Don't think of it, she told herself. Just survive.

"Sarge." She just wanted to clear the air. To go on. "I'm so sorry for that day."

He reached for the ignition. "Want to say sorry?"

"Yeah."

"Then bring me your boyfriend's heart."

He started the engine, preparing to be on his way and kill Griff without a second thought.

And why shouldn't she let him? Griff had become one of her monsters.

But, deep inside, he was still the guy who made her smile just because he talked in his sleep. Just because of the way his mouth shaped itself into an O when he was thinking of a new way to design an Internet site. Just because of the way he looked at her over breakfast tea.

The Jeep's engines gunned, tires squealing and burning rubber. As it bucked away, Camille launched herself, grabbing onto the rails spanning the rear storage area. Her body caught air, hands losing purchase on the rails, as she held on for dear life.

Sarge skidded the vehicle around a corner, and her legs swung out, flailing. When her boot nicked a lamp-post, she scrambled, diving into the Jeep's back seat.

"Aw, what the hell?" yelled Sarge over the engine. "You're gonna hurt yourself." Then he skidded to a stop, face red as he avoided looking at her again.

Did he care if she smashed into a pole? The realization warmed her, bathed her in guilt, too. Camille climbed into the front, just as if she'd been expected and was a teeny bit tardy.

"Let's find that police radio," she said, wanting to make Sarge more comfortable by avoiding the real subject.

"Don't take those chances."

He thought about what he'd just said, then hunched over the steering wheel, glared at her. "This ain't going to work, you know. Even if you think you're hot stuff for sticking a stake in that other lady vamp. The one who made sweet vampire love to Griffie."

Damn him. He knew his words were lethal. "It wasn't easy killing Mina. Or Claudia."

"The blonde?" Sarge shrugged. "That was good aim. You learned how to shoot a crossbow."

"I had plenty of time to practice." They idled in front of a cemetery, darkness shrouding even the street lamps. Camille glanced at her watch tracker. Nothing. "I see you added laser technology to your beloved crossbow. Doesn't that dull your instinctual fighting methods?"

"I'm not much for all that 'intuition' anymore, just as I noticed you're not using those feel-good sci-fi knockabouts. Looks like we've both lost our faith."

She hated that he was right. Hated that he couldn't stop bringing up her terrible choice in the woods.

"I'll say it again, Sarge. I'm sorry."

"Would you do it again?" he asked, voice low, soft with something that made Camille shift in her seat.

The breath chopped in her lungs as she searched for an answer.

"That's what I thought."

It was dark, and she couldn't be sure, but she thought his eyes clouded a little.

"You seem to have recovered," she said, trying to accentuate the positive. "Except maybe for that leg. But even that doesn't seem to slow you down."

"They used bionic parts on it," he snapped.

He probably wanted to keep up appearances, so she let it go. "I want to make it up to you."

"Howard."

He leaned toward her, face-to-face. His overshadowing bulk, his scent—blood, sweat, grime, musk—got to her. Thrilled her ever so slightly.

Or maybe she was feeling ill again.

"You know what I dreamed about while I was laid up in a hospital bed? You know what kept me going?"

"The lunchtime Jell-O?"

He hovered a breath away. "Not really. It was the thought of pulling Griffie's limbs off one by one."

Stung, Camille blurted out, "You blew your chance tonight, then."

Great going, she thought. Just as you two were getting onto civil ground…

A bitter grin crossed his lips. "It sure as hell won't happen again."

With that, he gunned the Jeep, leaving the conversation dead.

But if there's one thing Camille knew about herself, it was that she wasn't really into letting matters rest in peace.

Chapter 16

As they'd cruised the streets, Camille's watch tracker had been silent, and she'd actually wondered if they weren't moving farther away from Griff rather than toward him.

Then they'd struck pay dirt. Sort of. A cop car had been parked in front of the Cismigiu Gardens, a lone policeman shadowed in the front seat. So Camille had seized the opportunity while Sarge waited in their vehicle.

She'd lured the cop out, hands pressed against the blood on her shirt, pretending to have been attacked. When the poor young lawman had gotten close enough, she'd sprung to the back of him, wrapped her arm around his throat, then squeezed until he'd passed out.

Then the radio had been hers for the taking.

"I hate doing that," she said, hopping back in the car with the squawking communicator. Mainly news from the nightclub. Nothing more. "He just wanted to help me."

Sarge took off, streets a blur of headlights on concrete. "You should be used to working people over."

Another round of guilt seized her, so she didn't offer a comeback.

Instead, they didn't talk at all, just listened to the radio. She knew he wanted its information, too, and that was a big reason he was tolerating her presence. Or was there something more? Something she'd seen that night at the castle in the tunnel when she'd accidentally hugged him?

Forget it, she thought. Just clue into the radio.

Were the police just slow in finding Griff's new victims? Or did the calm have something to do with that so-called gargoyle Sarge had seen chasing down Griff's cab?

Who knew if Griff was still even on a rampage? There'd been a moment in the nightclub when she'd seen the man she loved reappear. Right before he'd dived behind that red-velvet curtain and into the hole in the wall. He'd looked at her with a save-me plea, had said her name as if he couldn't understand what was happening to him.

"Camille?"

She startled, still in her Griff world. But Sarge was the one who'd said her name.

Suspicious of his sudden familiarity, Camille waited for him to continue.

He was watching her as if he cared. Sarge. Caring. That was some sort of oxymoron.

He went back to concentrating on the road, much to her relief.

"When are we going to meet up with Ashe?" she asked, searching for conversation.

He paused. "Ashe retired."

Camille allowed this news to settle. "I thought you were a team."

"He refused to come with me this time."

"Protective Ashe?" Camille recalled the gentle Wiccan, the way he'd taken care of all of them during the castle mission. "What happened?"

Sarge exhaled, as though telling her how he hadn't died would really cramp his style.

Then, busying himself by scanning the streets, Sarge spoke, voice casual. "I thought it was over when your boy wonder chucked me out of that chopper. Remember that, Howard? The first time he tried to kill me?"

"It's crystal clear." Her stomach started doing its acid dance of remorse.

"Well, during my military training, I learned a little something called a spider fall."

"That's what operatives are taught to do when they scale down tall walls," she said, shrugging off Sarge's impressed glance. "I read while Griff was—"

"And that's how I didn't end up in fifty pieces when I fell from the Huey," he said, obviously not wanting to hear about Griff. "I used the tree to control my gravity. But your boyfriend managed to land on his vamp feet, the bastard, and we proceeded to engage."

The beginning of the end, she thought.

He continued. "I have to say, Pretty Boy is one of the tougher vamps I've fought. Besides Nicolae."

"We think it's because of the way the *strigoiaca* blood mixed—"

Sarge held up a finger. "Science talk."

"Oh, yeah." She couldn't help smiling. "Not your bag."

"Right. I've told you, vamps are vamps. It's no use trying to explain them."

If she hadn't come to that same conclusion tonight, she might've argued.

"So…Ashe?" she asked.

"Right." Sarge slowed down at the sight of a deserted car. "He got me to a hospital, tried all his healing powers on me, then when I was able to talk around the holes in my head, he laid into my ego."

Like Sarge, she went on alert while they drew up to the car, but relaxed once she spied two people kissing in the front seat.

Sarge moved on, shaking his head. "There're still people in this world who have the luxury of making out on a dark road."

The affectionate couple brought that striking awareness back to the atmosphere, marking the air with unspoken tension.

Couldn't it just disappear? "Ashe didn't want you to hunt anymore?"

"You got it. He whipped up one last swan song of a protective spell and said he didn't have the strength for anything more. Said he couldn't stand to see me self-destruct. Thought this so-called vengeful mission of mine would end up stealing my soul or something."

"Why? You've hunted before."

"But I've never hunted another human."

The words stunned her. "Is this about me more than Griff?"

"It was." He'd said it so softly she wasn't even sure there had been an answer.

She thought of all the times she'd imagined him following her throughout Bucharest: at the library, the markets, on the streets...

"You were keeping tabs on me, Sarge?"

"Yeah, just limping along the streets, biding my time." He gauged her with a glance. "Waiting."

The way he looked at her made her face heat up. "Did you ever come into the laboratory to—"

Now his eyebrow was raised. Oh. Evidently, that Sarge sighting had been her own doing.

"So you were thinking of me, too, huh, Howard?"

She didn't answer. What could she say?

"Good to know." He laughed, settled into his seat. "A man can only hope."

She tingled a little, and she wasn't liking it. "When you say you were waiting, biding your time, all that James Bond villain nonsense, what exactly did you mean?"

"I meant that I was doing some reconnaissance. Seeing when I could get to your boyfriend...and to you."

"Get to me?"

"Being almost dead gives you a lot of passion. According to what's been written about you in the papers, you should know what I'm talking about. You know about death."

"Too much."

That brought a halt to this discussion. As if sensing her disquiet, he said, "You guys had that lab heavily guarded." He turned the corner, onto a street with green apartment courtyards and wrought-iron fences that cast gnarled shapes. "So, I had to use an alternative means of infiltration. Tina."

"Bea's assistant?" The chippy with the curly brown hair and big blue eyes?

"Jealous?" He sounded hopeful.

She wasn't about to feed his Mount Everest-size ego. "You slept with her for information?"

He shrugged.

Why did it bother her to hear this? Sarge was a normal—well, sort of normal—red-blooded American male. Guys had sex. A lot of it. Everyone knew that.

So what was the big deal?

"Then let me get this straight," she said, speaking through her teeth. Then she loosened her jaw, willing herself to mellow out. "You used Tina to tell you what was happening in the lab. You knew Griff was getting better, and that must've really gotten to you, because you couldn't come in to kill him before all the vampire was washed out of his body. Why didn't you try to storm the fort? I mean, you *were* special ops."

"Thanks for the confidence, but even though I'm damned good at what I do, I'm not stupid."

Just vengeful. "What a plan. Why didn't you just move on to the next vampire the world had to offer, Sarge?"

"Because," he said, heating her with his gaze, "we've got unfinished business between us."

Camille closed her eyes, wishing there hadn't been any subtext to his comment. In her personal darkness, everything jumbled together, confusing her.

"Camille," he said, "why do *you* do it?"

Opening her gaze to the world, she took a deep breath, exhaled. Here it went.

"Because I can't live with myself if another one dies. Everyone I love seems to leave me, almost as if I'm the one who's cursed or something." She cleared her throat of emotion. "If Griff doesn't come back to me, I'll die inside this time. I'm so afraid that will really happen."

The air stilled, laden with silence.

"I'm sorry," he said.

Sorry. She was the one who owed him a million apologies. "Sarge, I—"

"Damn!" He slammed on the brakes, threw open the door. Hopped out of the Jeep. "We can talk later."

Thankful for the interruption, she followed, wielding the machete.

They came upon an abandoned taxi. It'd crashed into a stone wall, the hood steaming, the driver's door open, just as if someone had jumped out and ran away.

"What are the odds?" Sarge said, limping over to it.

He bent inside, ran his hand over the driver's seat. When he reemerged, his fingers were covered with blood.

"Pretty good odds, I'd say." Camille came to stand next to him.

Now they didn't have any leads. The police radio hadn't produced news, and Griff had switched transportation on them. Even her tracker wasn't helping.

This was the end of the line, wasn't it?

"Maybe," she said, "this is hopeless."

She collapsed against the taxi, face tilted to the moon. The tears were coming again, the emotional baptism that would wash her clean before permanent guilt settled in.

Sarge stepped in front of the light. But the golden mist of a street lamp revealed his concern.

Voice soft, he said, "We'll find him, Camille."

"And then what?" She choked, tried so hard to hold back the stinging disappointment, the worry and fear.

For the first time, she really looked into his gaze, past the surface of the emerald color and *into* his eyes. They were a well of deep emotion, fathomless, enigmatic.

Slowly, he bent over her. She held her breath.

Was he going to…?

He dipped down, caught her lips with his, warming her during this cold moment.

At first, she was taken aback by the tender pressure, the soft brush of innocent assassination. Then she closed her eyes, pretending she was somewhere other than a Romanian street, accepting the comfort. The care.

He stroked a callused hand over her cheek, cupped his palm against the curve of it as if in half prayer.

We'll find him, Camille.

And then what? she heard herself ask again.

Forcing open her eyes, she stiffened, pushed away. What was she doing?

Crushed by her rejection, Sarge backed away, posture framed like a wary animal.

Now that she could think again, she realized that his

irises reminded her of something scarier: the leaves of a sunflower. Sharp, green, cutting leaves.

"You shouldn't have done that," she said, words riding the edge of anger.

Anger at herself. Confusion. The memory of the Griff she'd loved was lingering, begging her to still have faith in his redemption.

As Sarge stood there, hands clenched at his sides, Camille's watch tracker started *blumping*.

Blumpblumpblump…

Wait. How could it suddenly have gotten so quick? No time to think about some kiss.

"Timing," Sargent muttered.

Both of them whipped out their machetes and stakes, double fisted, coming back to back with each other. They circled around as her watch grew louder.

"Aw, no." Sarge's deep voice vibrated through his back and into hers, jarring her senses.

"What?"

"You can turn around."

She did, taken aback by what awaited her.

It was the most beautiful man ever, with long white hair. Glowing violet eyes. Shining fangs. Gray robes.

"Hello, Hans," Sarge said, keeping his weapons up.

She did, too, unable to look away from the vampire, shocked that Sarge was conversing with him and not wielding that machete.

Then something Sarge had once told her came back, echoing in her mind.

I've kept a vampire or two alive in my day—if they can help exterminate the worst of them.

Maybe he hadn't been lying to her.

"Elijah," Hans said, voice like the ring of a blade being sharpened.

Elijah? If Camille hadn't been so fixated on the vampire, she would've given Sarge a tough time about having an actual first name. A stately one, too.

The creature spoke again. "You are searching for the vampire who was driving the cab?"

"Yeah," Sarge said. "The one with the gargoyle roof ornament. How'd you guess?"

Elegant, long-fingered hands emerged from Hans's robes. "I am lucky, I suppose. Do you want the boy?"

Camille busted in before Sarge could. "Yes, I do."

Hans glanced from Sarge to Camille, interest sparked. "The boy speaks of a hunter with red hair. I assume I have found her. Come. The vampires will entertain your request."

The vampires? Great. There were *more* of them?

When the street opened beneath Hans's feet, Camille turned to Sarge.

"What the hell is going on?"

As the vampire walked down a set of stairs that faded into darkness, Sarge holstered his weapons, then followed.

"Told ya." Sarge started to disappear below ground level. "You're about to meet some devils I've made a deal with."

Demons, she thought, keeping her own weapons out. Everyone had them.

Shutting down her now silent watch, she trailed Sarge into the black of the unknown, heartbeat screaming in her veins.

* * *

Hans led them on an endless trek belowground, one in which Camille kept her ears peeled for every echoing sound, every ghoulish sight her brain taunted her with during the pitch-black journey.

Her final descent. On the way down, Camille had tried to get Sarge to explain this baffling development, but Hans had shushed her.

Shushed by a vampire. She'd truly hit rock bottom.

The stench of death filled the room Hans led them to, even though the floors and walls were built of white marble. It resembled something from a history textbook, scenes from a Greek senate.

In the stone seats, the other silent vampires rested, dressed in all manner of costume. She was struck by the opulence of their mahogany velvets, luscious blue silks, green satins, all of the material flickering under electric chandelier lights. The only vampire in the room wearing humble robes was Hans. However, he seemed to be the one in charge. The judge in this court.

Sarge seemed relaxed as they stood before the gathering. "You've got our boy?" he asked simply.

Nodding, Hans took a seat and, immediately, a black gargoyle winged over to his chair, resting behind it.

It was the monster from Castle Bethlen's roof, Camille realized. The one she'd taken a shot at with the crossbow and missed. The one Sarge had probably seen flying over Griff's escape taxi.

With a ghastly smile, it blinked at her, made a veering motion with its claw, mocking the arrow she'd shot at it.

"You have both met Radu," Hans said, "though Elijah has never had the pleasure up close. My pet acts as our eyes in Transylvania. And he uses his brain waves to fend off projectiles that are rudely shot at him."

Her first urge was to smart off—Sarge had gotten her in the mood, of course—but one warning glance from her rival changed her mind.

"I won't do it again," she said. There. Peace be with you.

"Certainly, you will not in this chamber." Hans calmly surveyed her stake and machete. "But you are willing to use them if you cannot tame the boy, stop his murderous acts by reminding him he once had a soul?"

Griff biting, blood, his golden eyes fired with murderous intent.

"I'm willing." There. She'd committed. But even a painful swallow couldn't wash away the taste of fear.

"I'll stake him," Sarge added. "Get this over with."

Hans turned to the mercenary. "Griffin does not like you. If this one is to be tamed at all, it would be by someone who can reach his mind and heart. That is not your strong suit, Elijah."

She wondered if they were wrong about that.

But Hans wasn't finished with Sarge. "I hope you will stay so calm for the duration of our meeting. We do not intend to harm your friend. We want her help."

Sarge rested his hands on his hips. "Who's worried? She can take care of herself."

His compliment made her smile a little, but she quickly chased it away. "Why would vampires need help?"

"I should explain," said Hans.

He gestured to the center of the room, where a misty

image appeared. It featured Camille, sitting in a library, hunched over a large book. She recognized it as an ancient account by a monk that detailed the lore of the male Carpathian Mountain vampires.

"You have been curious about us," Hans said.

Us?

Was this the legendary male tribe?

And Sarge *knew* them?

She cast him a dirty look, and he raised an innocent eyebrow.

I tried to tell you, his gesture said.

Another image overtook the library picture. Now there were dark caverns, bright eyes.

"Hundreds of years past," Hans said, "we sheltered ourselves in caves, away from society. The tribe was begun by two pets who escaped from the *strigoiaca*. We have sought to gather our kind ever since, though they are few and far between."

Now she doubled the chiding power of the glare she aimed at Sarge.

"In all my studies," she said, "I never found a connection between you and the Girls."

"It is not important for most humans to know our ways. You have read folklore. Fictions."

Sarge inserted his own mocking commentary. "Yeah, they don't document how these guys upgraded from caves to a marble underground, either. I've never seen this place."

"We do not tell you everything, Elijah. Just enough for you to find Nicolae. Someday, when he resurfaces."

Okay, now this was making sense. Sarge used these vampires to hunt down his Holy Grail—Nicolae. It was like a cop using informants, Camille thought, separating different degrees of evil for a higher purpose.

Had he been hired by these guys to neutralize Nicolae? Why?

The mist picture swirled again, forming the image of a vampire with white hair and a black-streaked white beard, his eyes as dark as bottomless pits.

"Nicolae is rogue," Hans said. "Like me, he is a master vampire, one of two who started our tribe. But Nicolae and I do not share the same philosophy."

"Or the same appetite," added a dark-haired vampire with translucent, unlined skin. His fangs dug into his lower lip as he grimaced at Nicolae's mist picture.

Sarge looked like he'd heard all this before. "Yeah. The philosophy. See, Camille, these guys here don't hunt and kill humans. It sickens them, they say. And when one of their kind—like Nicolae—turns against this code, that vamp is put down like a rabid animal. Keeping any hint of vampirism out of the evening news is pretty important to Hans and the boys."

"And that's why you want Griff?" she asked Hans. "Because he's put your existence in danger?"

The master vampire nodded. "But there is something more. He is our brother. We are all born of *strigoiaca* blood, having sipped from them to survive. But Griffin is different."

His pause spoke volumes. So did Hans's violet eyes versus Griff's wild-gold ones.

Different.

The lab treatments. *Had* she and Beatrix changed his composition into that of an animal?

"He is rogue," the dark-haired vampire said.

The jury all hummed in agreement.

"Just like Nicolae," Sarge said.

From the way the others kept nodding, Camille wondered how often Sarge worked with them. Was he their enforcer?

"Where *is* Griff?" Camille asked, restless to see him. Tame him. If it was even possible now.

Hans calmly bridged his hands below his chin. "Somewhere he cannot kill anymore."

The eerie room picture changed to images of Griff striking at Beatrix in the lab. Of him slashing at Sarge in the disco's passageway.

Dammit, did this vamp need to rub Griff's sins into her heart?

Sarge stepped forward, next to her. A protective gesture, probably because he knew she wanted to go after Hans more than the other way around.

"Camille," he said, "they don't like to put down their own, just like humans consider killing each other to be murder. Getting rid of a tribe member is a last resort. They're asking you to do it for them, if he's beyond taming. You realize that, don't you?"

She took a second to absorb the horror of it. "I realize it. And aren't you their executioner, Sarge? I thought all vampires are scum to you."

"I know how to prioritize."

Hans laughed. The other vampires joined him, breaking their silence. They were like echoes, all connected.

"Elijah wishes we were expendable, but we both want to neutralize Nicolae," the white-haired vampire said. "We are bonded by our mission."

Sarge grunted. Camille sneaked a gaze at him, lingering on the lips that'd caressed hers earlier.

Something like an electric spark zapped through her body. Bad timing. Bad libido. Sure, her heart had been serrated by Griff tonight, but that didn't mean she'd turn somewhere else for comfort.

Definitely not to Sarge.

"Why didn't *you* go after the female *strigoiaca?*" she asked, ignoring her inner soap opera.

As the room picture waved into a blaze of the *strigoiaca's* red eyes and streaming hair, Hans answered.

"The *strigoiaca* were discreet while they existed." He shot both Camille and Sarge a harsh glare. "Though feral, they hunted with order. They confused the villagers with stories of whether they were fiction, or indeed real. Though they disgust us, they were not a danger to our security until tonight's very public bloodbath."

The horror of Griff tearing that man in half in the disco replayed on the room picture, but this time, Camille couldn't look away.

Why had Griff gone animal? she asked herself again. What had they done wrong in the lab?

"Child," Hans said softly, obviously reading her thoughts, "do not attempt to inflict rationality on our existence. Have you wondered why the *strigoiaca* came to Juni instead of any other village last year?"

Petar Vladislav had summoned them out of disrespect for an elder, a know-it-all college boy attitude. That much she'd figured out long ago. But for months, she'd wondered how the females had heard the invitation.

"And," Hans added, "have you wondered about those wolves guarding the castle? What they were?"

"I don't have answers for any of it."

"And you won't," Hans snapped, standing from his marble throne. The gargoyle's wings flapped. Dark applause for its master.

Sarge must've noticed how lost she felt. He stepped in front of her, shielding her, offering the only support she'd accept from him.

"Elijah, do not pretend to go on guard." Hans smiled. "Even your Camille seems to understand that we're too valuable to your ego, too instrumental in finding Nicolae."

Your Camille?

A mysterious shiver traveled her skin. The thought of his possessing her should've given her the hives. But, instead, the idea enticed her a little.

Hell, she just needed someone to watch her back. That was all. And Sarge was here to do it. Surely being kind of grateful for that wasn't against the laws of nature.

"Just give Griffin to Camille for taming," Sarge said.

He'd said "Camille." Not "us." What was he up to?

He glared straight ahead, ignoring her, mouth set in a grim line.

At that moment, Camille's heart cracked, creating another fissure. Was he doing this for her? Why?

Hans stepped forward, robes whispering, gargoyle stepping in each of his light footfalls. "You would make demands of us?"

"This means the world to her," Sarge said softly.

Camille crossed her arms over her chest, holding in the grateful emotion.

"Oh, he is arrogant." Hans turned to his friends, laughing.

They echoed his amusement, right down to the number of "ha-ha's."

"Touching. I like to see you in this position. It is rather torturous for you to be so loyal and tender to this girl, is it not? A change from habit."

Sarge managed to look embarrassed, his rough skin reddening—except for that neck scar. The emotion hadn't claimed that part of him yet.

"Elijah," Hans said, "I know you would love to see my blood spilled for pointing this out."

Ignoring the taunts, Sarge glanced at Camille.

A beat passed, and she finally understood what he was silently saying.

The man you love tried to kill me. Are you going to let him off the hook? Choose him over me again?

He was going to trust her to do this? He was going to let go of his pride and code of living so she could save her own soul?

With a shock, she realized that yes, he'd make the sacrifice. By stepping back, he was enabling her to become whole again, even at the cost of his beliefs.

He was relying on her to do right by him, too.

"Thank you," she whispered.

He bowed his head, still snagging her gaze with such emotion she didn't know if she could contain all of it.

"I think I am going to weep," Hans said mockingly. "The hunter is evolving before our eyes."

"Back off, Hans," she said, tearing her attention away from Sarge. "You said you'd take me to Griffin."

He walked closer, and the gargoyle took off into an adjacent hallway. "You can tame him?"

"Let me try," Camille said, trying not to sound too desperate. For the chance to get Griff back, if it was even possible, she'd do anything. Everything. "Please."

"True, you have tamed Elijah quite nicely," Hans said. "It makes me believe you can accomplish your hopes. But if you should fail, he will need to be put down."

Lord help her. "I understand."

She couldn't believe this was happening. Maybe this was just one of her nightmares.

Or maybe, if she failed, she'd be living another layer of the old one for the rest of her life.

"Elijah," Hans said, "you may go in if she fails."

"I won't need to," he said.

His confidence lit through her, and she knew she could do it. Knew she could save Griff.

Even if that meant she would choose him over Sarge in the end.

"Until then," Hans added, "she is to be with the boy alone. He has spoken of this Camille ever since we jailed him. He has spoken of Elijah, too, and clearly he would do no good in the rehabilitation of him."

Impulsively, Camille blurted, "You won't hurt Sarge?"

While the mercenary's eyes widened in disbelief, Hans seemed quite amused.

"We cannot harm Elijah, unless he should attack first. The spilling of human blood weakens our own souls, Camille, but we will fight to save them if provoked." Stressing his point, he gestured in the shape of a circle. "Besides that, Elijah is walking under the protection of the moon tonight. He will be fine."

Ashe's final spell. That explained why Griff hadn't torn Sarge in half at the disco, too.

"Then lead me to Griff," she said.

As the vampires rose and guided her and Sarge to the hall where the gargoyle had disappeared, Camille and Sarge exchanged glances.

He mouthed, "I've got your back."

Beyond words, she nodded, wanting to say so much more. Say things she couldn't even comprehend right now.

Once in the hallway, Camille tried to stay frosty, on her toes. It was weird, but knowing that Sarge was here, too, pulsed strength into her system.

Like Griff's cage in the lab, this one had a window. The walls were white marble, slick and shiny. But there was no security glass to capture him, just some sort of clear, impenetrable field that allowed her to see inside.

His back was turned while he painted something red on the pristine wall. His T-shirt was torn, his jeans bloodied.

Who was this man? Did she even know him anymore?

She looked closer, hoping to catch some hint of familiarity, some flicker of who he'd been.

When she saw what he was drawing, she fell against the force field, thankful that it had the power to hold her up.

Using his own blood, Griff was recreating the picture he'd sketched of her in the National Gallery when they'd first met.

The girl with the haunted stare.

The girl he said he'd love forever.

Chapter 17

Griffin dipped his finger in the well of blood he'd made from slashing open his inner arm. He was painting Camille, recalling how she'd stared forlornly at *Sunflowers*.

As he paused, assessing his work, a drop of blood winced as it hit the floor.

He took in her blurry image, filling all the voids he'd created inside of himself.

Then the pain arrived. It wrenched apart his head again. Crashed, invaded, forced him to his knees. One of his hands slipped down the wall, blood smearing, leaving a road of carnage like the trail he'd forged tonight.

Razor shreds of memory cut his mind's eye to pieces:

Sinking his teeth into Dr. Grasu's neck. Clawing the vocal cords out of a lab guard as he tried to scream. Gnashing into the waist of a man at a disco, just to quench the thirst that had been growing all night. Ripping the guy's body in half, the blood flowing freely.

Griff gagged. Grappled with himself to take back control.

And he did, thank God. This time.

The insanity had been coming and going, a slide show of reaction. One minute, he'd be standing in front of Camille, her stake aimed at his chest as he regretted what he'd done this time. The next minute, he'd be slurping blood, enjoying the thickness and warmth.

Every time he'd escape from the madness, he'd also physically run away. Into the hole of that nightclub's stone wall. Into the streets of Bucharest to steal a cab.

But there was no escape, here in this new cage. After that gargoyle had brought him to the male vampires, Griff had resigned himself to fate.

No more human blood, the males had told him. You're a bad vampire for wanting it.

Reaching up toward Camille's picture, Griff burned to bring it to life. To hold her near, never letting go.

From behind him, he heard a fuzzy sound—like a telly station shutting down for the night. Then her voice.

"Your blood."

Griff glanced behind him, exhausted by a mind that wouldn't allow him to catch up with his cravings. His mouth watered at the sight of her inside his room, dressed in those jeans, that white, red-stained top, those bloodied arm bandages. Her smooth, luscious skin.

Her sharpened weapons.

"I gave you that wound beneath your breast," he said.

"Yes, you did." She walked closer, clutching her machete and stake, gaze wary as she checked his eyes. At that, she seemed to stand off a bit. "You did a lot of wounding tonight."

He fisted the hand he'd used for drawing. This wasn't how Lady Tex used to look at him. "I don't want to do it anymore. I don't want to kill any more people."

That was a lie. Even now, he was shaking. Wanting.

"You murdered Beatrix." Her tone reflected an inner rage. "For that alone, I want to rip you up."

"I'm sorry. God forgive me, I'm really so sorry."

"Sorry doesn't have anything to do with resurrection. My sorries never brought anyone back to life."

His sight scrambled again, a fast-forward through a clipped reel of red meat and disco lights.

Battle it, he thought. Don't let it claim you. Battle…

After a moment, he had the urges beaten. The beast of need slid back into the dark corners of his mind. Waiting.

So tired. He focused on Camille, who was crouching near him, still on alert.

"I see that you can fight it," she said.

He could barely talk. "Yes."

An indiscernible emotion crossed her face. Fear? Love? Hate? "I came here to see if I had it in me to put you down. But—" she clenched her teeth "—you've made this a little tough, Griff. Sometimes you're still the man I loved."

Loved. As in love no more?

Grasping the shirt material over his heart, he covered the area of his body that hurt the most. "You want to kill me, Tex?"

She searched for an answer.

Death. A way out. With death, he wouldn't have to see her growing hatred flower for him. Wouldn't have to become something inhuman. Insane.

Seeing her fall out of love with him would kill him anyway.

"The vampires," she said, "are going to terminate you unless I walk out of this room with you a changed man. Am I too late? Because I can't look past what you did."

Her gaze slid to the wall's blood-painted image, lingered, then settled on his cut arm. A tear gushed down her cheek.

"It always heals within moments. See?" He showed her the wound that had almost mended itself. "It became faster throughout the night."

"Oh…God…" she whispered.

He didn't mean to torture her just by existing.

Don't worry, whispered a voice from that dark corner of his mind. *You can make her love you again. Forever.*

"Tex." He crept nearer to her, wanting to brush away the sadness from her cheeks. His movements put him in the position to see the window into his cell.

They were standing there. His vampire brothers.

Sargent.

The possessive mercenary was watching Camille, and Griff couldn't help growling, showing fang.

"Griff." Her word was a command.

"He's in love with you, too," he said.

Face falling, Camille tossed a glance over her shoulder. Sargent flattened a hand against the invisible barrier, blasting Griff with a hateful look.

"You're imagining things," Camille said, voice doubtful. Did she feel the same way?

"Bring *him* in here."

"If your vamp fan club had wanted you immediately dead, they would've sent Sarge instead of me."

"So you're not going to—?"

She held up the stake, twisting it safely sideways, but still demanding silence. "I don't want to. But you're like a baby rattlesnake right now. You're dangerous because you don't know how to control your poison. I did think there might be a way to condition your behavior, but now I just don't know."

A lack of belief. It forced his eyes closed. This would be the rest of his life: White cages. Solitude.

"I can't help doing it, Tex." He opened his gaze, showed her his stained hands, the dried blood of innocents crusted under his fingernails. "Murder."

Pain jogged through her gaze, and Camille lowered her head. When she glanced up again, she had hardened herself.

Griff kept his hands up, punishing himself with reality.

Now, in his advancing degradation, even the scent of the old blood was wafting through him, suffusing him with addiction. It hadn't been this bad earlier.

His mind went crimson again, a liquid curtain of red heat blowing over his sight.

Want. Want. Want. *I want.*

"Water!" she yelled. "Can't I get the blood off?"

It was no surprise to Griffin when a fall of moisture sluiced down the marble wall. These ancient vampires had told him that, with training, he would someday manipulate his surroundings, as well. That he would be at peace in their ranks, imitating their ways and existing on animal blood for sustenance.

The type of blood that didn't fulfill.

Slowly, the water washed away his picture of Camille in a smear of diluted scarlet.

She didn't question the small miracle of vampire power; instead, she sheathed her stake and led one of Griff's hands under the stream, cleaning him thoroughly. Then she did the same with the other hand as he lavished her with a loving gaze.

"That's a start," she said, inspecting his eyes, judging him. "We'll wash it all off."

How? They both still had blood on their clothing. All the same, Camille's determination calmed him.

Even if blood would always be on his hands.

His eyes were back to that warm almond brown she used to adore so much.

Camille kept holding on to his jittery hand. The hand of a user gone cold turkey. A hand that, once upon a time, had stroked the valleys and peaks of her body.

She could barely stand to look at the beast who'd murdered Bea, but then again—even though she knew it was wrong—that's all she wanted to do: look at him. Take him in as an elixir for all the tragedy they'd shared.

Right now, even though his fight against the inner vampire was obvious, he was in control. Remorseful. Human. It almost made her think she could still save him.

But how many times would she try a cure? How many times would she fail?

"Know what?" he asked, sitting against the wall after the water dried, resting his eyes, leaning his head back against the marble as if listening to a silent symphony in his head.

"Open your eyes, Griff." His irises were the barometer. Brown or gold. Safety or danger.

His gaze stayed shuttered. "We could always be together, no matter what happens."

She gripped the stake for strength. "I did want to be with you. Always. Back when you weren't killing people."

"There are ways of getting back what we used to have."

He finally opened his eyes. They looked normal, except for a faint shine. But maybe that was from the lights outside the cell. A reflection.

She reluctantly inched out the stake, just in case.

There are ways, he'd said.

The words hung between them, beads of blood shivering, ready to drop and explode.

Was he talking about having her make the ultimate sacrifice? Having him turn her so they could always be together with similar codes and cravings?

He couldn't be serious. If she turned vamp, she'd murder, too. Sure, she'd be able to forget her parents and Bea. Shedding blood would be in her nature, if she were like him. Her memories would be cleansed.

Camille couldn't help thinking about it. She peered at Sarge, who was outside the room scraping both hands over the barrier of silence, trying to get to her.

Life as a vampire. It was everything Sarge hated. Everything she'd fought against her whole life. Darkness. Death.

She turned back to Griff, remembering that sweet smile. Those puppy eyes. The nights they'd spent just lying in each other's arms without a word because they knew what the other was thinking.

But, dammit, she couldn't forget everything else. Tonight's events mingled like a bad formula, imploding, causing her to hold her stomach, to collapse into herself.

Curious, Griff got to his hands and knees, causing Camille to raise her weapons against him. He cocked his head at her.

"Think of it." His voice was lower, warped. "You'd be around to keep me in check. I'd be around to keep you happy. It's a change of lifestyle, certainly…"

His voice withered into a growl as he locked on to Sarge in the window. Chin lowered, Griff watched the hunter engage in a silent, one-sided argument with the vampires.

"The first thing we'll do," he said, "is kill that bastard."

Without rushing, she turned around to find Griff fully changed. Eyes golden, wild. Not that she was shocked.

Heart sinking, she raised her stake, angled her machete.

But, split-second quick, the new vampire leaped up, smashed away her weapons, then palmed a hand behind her head, tilting back her neck with superior strength.

Helpless, she could only say, "Don't you turn me."

He laughed, breath dampening her sensitive skin.

"Neither of us has been able to hold on to what we've loved, wouldn't you say? This is our chance."

"No." She pushed against the feral vampire who'd taken Griff over. "Bring him back."

In answer, the vampire scraped fangs over her jugular, playing with her. Camille jerked away, but the creature was too strong. His grip tightened, making her wince.

"Don't fight," he whispered. "You'll see that the blood fills you up so you don't have to think about your pain. Just what you've always needed, Camille."

This time, when she pushed at the vamp, she tried to be crafty, using a Krav Maga move to free herself. Quickly, she raised her arms, cupped her hands, hooked down on his wrists to grab them away.

If it'd worked, she would've darted backward, out of his reach. But seconds later, he was still holding her in the kiss-of-death position.

The male vampires were giving her every chance to tame him, weren't they? They weren't going to allow Sarge to come in here until she utterly failed. But she'd already known that. And nothing could've stopped her from trying to help Griff one last time.

He arched back his neck, swooped his fangs toward her jugular. Executing one last, lucky squirm, she managed to get away, then lash out with a chop to his windpipe. Fighting for breath, she dashed to her machete.

Unfortunately, his shoe stomped down on the handle just before she grabbed it. Too fast.

He coughed, rubbed his sore neck, his flaring eyes boring heat into her. "I want you to want this."

She stood, facing him down. "Bring back Griff."

Pausing, he seemed to consider her request. But then he merely shrugged. "Can't find him."

With a blast of speed, he zoomed at her, gripping a handful of her hair.

Springing out of instinct, she maneuvered away, chopped at his neck again, then pushed both hands down on one shoulder to bring him forward and knee him in the groin.

He fell forward, groaning. Camille jumped back, seeking a weapon on the floor.

Though she'd hated to do it, she'd hoped his crotch would be vulnerable since he'd exhibited a sex drive earlier in the night. And she'd been right. This time.

As she crawled on the floor for her stake, Sarge went ballistic on the other side of the barrier, pacing back and forth, punching the air and yelling. The vampires merely ignored him, engrossed in her reindeer games.

With more confidence than she actually had, she clutched the wooden weapon, held it up so they all could see that she was still in the running. So she could show Sarge that she hadn't let either of them down.

Panting, Griff got to his knees, eyes sizzling. "The more you escape, the more I want to catch you. You'll make a brilliant vampire."

Then he rocketed toward her again, a blur of motion. He belted into her, winging her across the marble. With a lung-crunching smack, she crashed into the wall, smashing her face, her chest, her legs. The stake popped out of her grip. Bungled to the floor.

I have no weapons, she thought, groggy.

Her nose was numb. Blood trickled from her nostrils. Her bones felt like crushed grain, and her hipbone stung because something in her pocket had jammed into her skin.

She felt the shape of the object. Took it out and rolled to her other side where she could face her monster.

Their baby ring.

Think, Camille, think.

Like Ashe's crucifix. She'd never believed it could work, but it'd left its mark on Griff. How? It was an object.

But one imbued with meaning.

For real serious situations, Sarge had told her.

Ten feet away, Griff was hunched and ready. First he walked at her. Ran. Flew.

Sucking in a last-ditch breath, she held out the baby ring, hoping he'd see it before he tore into her.

As he spied the new weapon, he lost momentum, skidding along the floor, straight for her.

For protection, Griff had once told her, securing it around her neck with the chain.

Concentrating all her faith and love into the sacred talisman, she brandished it, pressed it into his neck as he froze and banged into the marble wall next to her.

A burning hiss of steam accompanied her energized

yell as she tamed him, reduced him to an unmoving vampire with his fingers clawed, his mouth locked in a scowl.

But how long could she keep him here like this?

"Remember when we rode the tube all day and you put your hands over my eyes, making me point out our next stop on the underground map?" Her whole body was quaking, a victim of fear. Her voice rose with every word. "Remember our first kiss? We were walking in the Camden Market and, out of the blue, you just turned to me and held my face. It was so soft and wonderful, that kiss. Do you remember?"

She'd screamed out that last part. The ring had branded away layers of his skin, but she didn't remove it.

A sob flamed through her lungs. "Griffin Montfort? Griff? You come back to me!"

He closed his eyes, hands falling to his temples, mouth contorting in anguish. "I remember."

Too afraid to hope the real Griff was back, she didn't move, kept captivating him with the ring.

Moaning, he opened his eyes again. Brown. Deep, dark, beautiful, swimming under a sheen of moisture.

"I hurt you," he said.

"You're back?"

He blinked. A tear sped down his temple. "It's killing me, Tex."

She moved the ring an inch away from his skin, but still kept it in front of her. A shield.

"No, it's not our ring." Griff gave her a look so steeped in sadness that her chest tightened. "The insanity. Every hour, my mind shuts me out a bit more. Help me?"

"You mean by adjusting the serum or—?"

"No." His voice softened, hoarse. "End it."

For a moment, she couldn't move, couldn't respond. She thought of the suicidal cut in his arm that he'd been using to paint her picture.

"You said you'd do anything for me, Tex."

She scrambled away, nearer to her weapons, almost afraid to use them now. She was afraid of what his death would do to her. "You're asking me to kill you?"

I can't. I should, but I love the man who used to be you.

Couldn't he understand that saving him meant redemption?

"Don't be sad," he said, still slumped on the marble. "Remember, you can do away with the vampirism, but you can't get rid of what I did. What I enjoyed and craved. You know you can't live with that."

It was true. Some little part of her would always know he had a killer in him, even if he was cured.

"Hate to say it," Griff added, smiling the way he used to, "but you'd be better off with that Sarge bloke. He's got the potential to be much more human than I can be now."

"He's just as bad." No. That wasn't true.

"He's got a choice. I don't."

"Just…stop talking. Please." She couldn't take it anymore, because he was saying everything young Camille would've said—the girl who'd found her parents' bodies in an artful arrangement of silence and death.

"Do you still love me?" he said.

Her voice clutched, riding a sob. "Yes. I love you so much that I can't imagine life without you."

"Then do it. Show me how much you love me." His look beseeched her. "Let me go."

"I need to think...." What had happened to the slayer she'd become tonight? Where had the righteous anger gone?

"I can't do it myself." Griff ignored her plea. "Do it before—"

Voice grinding to a halt, he battled, pushing his head into the floor. His neck was still steaming from his new mark—the one next to his crucifix scar.

"Hold on, Griff," she said, knowing she was being stubborn, stupid. Too much in love.

"Now!" He folded into himself, grabbing his knees, drawing them up to his chest. He screamed, fighting whatever was taking him over. "Now, Tex!"

It was coming back. The vampire.

As she scrambled for the nearest weapon—the machete—she clutched the ring, pushed it out in front of her. To the left, Sarge pounded against the invisible barrier.

He wanted her to put the ring away. To kill.

Could she complete this act of mercy? Her love for Griff, measured in the biggest sacrifice she could make?

Within seconds, the vamp was upon her. The golden-eyed beast. Springing to its feet, laughing in her face.

"Too slow," he said in a lower, warped voice.

Grabbing the machete, she thrust the ring at the beast

and, with a roll of the eyes, he swiped her hand away. The ring went clattering to the floor, spinning. Useless.

"You know he's not coming back," the vampire said, cocking its head. "So what does that piece of tin mean?"

"Everything!"

Pissed as hell, he pinned her to the floor, buried his fangs in her neck. Camille bucked back from the piercing agony, the shock of actually being bitten.

In the distance, she could hear a roar of disbelief.

She grunted, raised her blade, but the monster vised her wrist in his grip. Strong. Too strong.

With every greedy suck, the life slipped out of her, leaving her dizzy and discombobulated.

It's over? I couldn't do it?

Then the room filled with that weird fritzing blip she'd heard when the male vamps had lowered the barrier for her. She knew who'd entered.

Pushing at the vamp with waning strength, Camille could only watch as Sarge burst into the room.

Even as Griff still sucked from her, she glared at her fellow hunter, baring her teeth.

Let me finish it.

"Dammit, Camille," Sarge said. His voice wavered, face drained of its usual color. "Let it go."

She forced out a desperate, garbled plea to him. "If you care about me at all, you'll let me do this."

The vamp disconnected from her neck, ignoring Sarge altogether. *"Mine."*

Grabbing the machete, he sat up, straddling her. Then he made a big show of the whole process, taking the blade, cutting his lip. The kiss of immortality.

"You'd better hurry, Howard," Sarge yelled, coming to stand behind the vamp, machete raised for the kill. "Do what you're going to do *now*, goddammit."

His tensed body swam in her vision and, in a flashing, slow-motion instant, she realized how much love could leave you a victim.

Love.

To be a killer, you have to be a little in love with death.

Sarge had told her that. And he'd been right.

Griff had become a bringer of death. He *was* death—the end of her dreams, her naivete.... She did love death, then. Literally. But did she love it—Griff—enough to be a killer? Did she love him enough to end his pain?

God, yes.

Drawing on every bit of remaining energy, she roared, springing upright, grabbing the machete from the vampire and carrying through to a standing position.

Her blood dripped from his mouth as he flared upward to his feet. The ultimate predator.

"I love you, Griffin," she said, cocking her weapon. "Wherever you are."

And with a vengeful cry, she heaved the blade forward, through the vamp's heart. Gouging away a part of her soul at the same time.

Out of the corner of her eye, she could see Sarge relax, stumble backward, giving her the space she needed to complete herself.

To take herself apart with every passing second.

Golden eyes fading to brown, Griff dropped to his knees, hands spread out in supplication. "You did it."

"Yeah."

It was a sob. One sob. That's all she allowed herself before falling to her own knees before him.

Since she was numb anyway, she wanted to touch him, one last time. Nothing could hurt her now.

Bringing his forehead to hers, she couldn't talk around the choking burn of her throat. The blinding tears.

His body gave way, and he crumpled face first to the floor. She scooped him up, just as she'd done to Bea earlier in the night, cradling him. Willing him to stay. Willing things to be as they were before Juni.

"I love you, Tex."

She raised her head from his, wanting to kiss him one last time, to bring him back to life like they did in fairy tales.

But his eyes were beginning to glow again, proving this wasn't even close to a happy ending.

Couldn't she remember him as *her* Griff, not the damned vampire? Couldn't she at least have that to keep?

Don't think. Just do. Or die.

Before the monster could take over, she summoned her courage, took hold of the machete, pulled it out of his heart, then pushed the body away. Swinging downward, she aimed for the monster's head.

And did it.

Turning away from the corpse, she screamed, a young girl who'd lost her parents one New York day. Her soul pulled out of her with the sound as it bounced around the room, seeking escape.

She screamed until her throat was dry and only the vibration of sheer horror was left. After that, she could only cry, her heart trying to crawl up through her throat, her hands covering her face so she could keep the pain to herself.

Minutes…hours…sometime later, someone took her into his strong arms. Pressed the baby ring into her hand.

She didn't even have to look up to know that it was Sarge.

Epilogue

New York, three months later

Sarge stood at the bottom of the concrete police station stairs, watching the paparazzi attack Camille.

Camera flashes lit her calm expression, her formfitting black designer skirt suit and boots, the red hair worn in a sleek, behind-the-ears style. Although she'd had surgery to fix the nose she'd broken in Bucharest at the vampire underground battle with Griff, it still listed off to one side a touch.

She was so damned beautiful.

"As you know," she said, answering one of the photographer's questions, "my parents have been deceased for twelve years. I'm here to see if the police will aid me in bringing the killer to justice by warming up this cold case."

A shower of "Ms. Howard"s followed her progress up the steps. One particularly exuberant reporter hopped in front of her. To Camille's credit, she didn't chop him in the throat as Sarge had once seen her do to Griff.

Poor kid, may he rest in peace.

"Ms. Howard," the photographer asked, "everyone knows there was no evidence in this case. What if the cops can't find any this time, either?"

He flashed a bulb in her face, but Camille didn't startle.

That's my girl, thought Sarge.

"Then I'm going after the culprit," she said, "with or without the NYPD."

A twinge of concern knotted in Sarge's belly.

Next to Sarge, Eva Godea, whom Camille had hired as a personal assistant because they'd "been close" in Romania, tapped Sarge's arm. "I am relieved you are here."

Of course he'd come. It was Camille.

He tugged at the collar of his T-shirt, just to give him something to do. "I thought this might be important. You sounded worried."

"Fairly. She has not moved away from her thoughts of revenge. Ever since Griffin…"

Sarge knew. After accepting what she needed to do to save her boyfriend's soul, she'd become more resolute in wanting to set the world right.

He'd done what he could, but her wounds from Griffin's death were still fresh. It was tough knowing the woman you loved was suffering and wouldn't let you hold her, soothe her. Would only allow you to communicate with phone calls.

And the thing of it was, Sarge knew he could make her feel better if she'd just allow him in.

"She was always a warrior," he said, watching Camille withstand another round of pictures. "Just look. These camera-toting jackals would have *me* running for the hills."

Done with small talk, Sarge started walking up the stairs to join Camille, but Ms. Godea hadn't finished.

"You will make her see happiness, Mr. Sargent. No matter what she says."

Right, Sarge thought, hearing his boot heels make uneven echoes on the concrete. Stubborn Howard. She was still going after that doctorate degree, dedicating her life to learning about all varieties of vamps, calling herself an "aspiring vampirologist" now. She still hunted for answers about the male vampires who'd literally dissolved into air after she'd neutralized Griffin. Not that Sarge knew a lot about them, either. They were reluctant allies, but he'd see them again when Nicolae resurfaced.

He passed her, caught her eye. Caught the glint of the baby ring she still wore on the chain around her neck. As one more camera flash lit her like the shine of a full moon, she smiled, the tips of her mouth rising gently.

"I need to be going," she said to the paparazzi.

"Ms. Howard!" they yelled. "Can you finally tell us where you've been for the past year?"

But she'd deftly moved on, matching Sarge's strides as they approached the station door.

"Fancy seeing you again," she said.

"Ms. Godea called me. I thought I could stick around while all this crap was going down. Offer moral support."

"I keep telling you. I'm fine." She got the door, motioned him in before her. "But thank you."

She'd said so many thank-you's to him, thought Camille, pulse racing even at the sight of her former rival. She'd told him she was fine over the phone, and in her head every night as she slept in her empty bed.

Actually, they both called each other frequently. She kept him up to date about how, upon further research, she and Ike had discovered that Griff's cell pattern had been minutely off. Slightly inhuman. It'd taken them a month to find the aberration. This meant that Griff's killing spree was her fault. She and Bea had created a monster.

Damn her for being arrogant enough to do it, but now she was going to catch one to make up for her errors.

Taking the weight of the door from her, Sarge held it open and ushered her into the officious lobby before him.

Touched by his chivalrous gesture, Camille took a moment to survey her surprising supporter: the rough-and-tumble brown hair, the squinted eyes, the faded jeans instead of well-worked fatigues.

Brutal, but workable.

What she really wanted to do was tug on his shirt, pull him into a hug. She knew exactly why he was here. To see that she didn't lose her soul to this case by going after the murderer as she'd done with Griff.

He didn't need to say it out loud: he wanted to see that she remained human.

And truthfully, she might need his help this time around. She wasn't ashamed to admit that she kind of missed him. They were a great team, right? That was why she found herself thinking about him so often, battling the desire to see him again.

As he watched her pass, his green eyes went soft with an emotion she couldn't handle right now.

We could be a great team in so many ways, his gaze was saying.

She touched her baby ring, felt the weight of it around her neck, over her heart.

Every good vampire hunter carried a crucifix. And now, so did she. Camille Howard could make it on her own.

Right?

"Camille." Sarge allowed the door to close behind them and tentatively rested his fingers on the small of her back. "You okay?"

"Always." His touch was sending warmth up her spine, sensitizing her skin, making her keenly aware of him towering above her.

His hand feathered up her back, coming to rest at the nape of her neck. "Whatever you need, I'm here."

"I know, Elijah." She smiled at the name, liking it. A lot.

Lifting his eyebrows, he seemed amused. "My given name. I thought 'Sarge' created the proper distance."

"It's a quality name." She relaxed under the pressure of his hand, thinking she could get used to this. Someday. "It's got character."

Just like you.

He looked so thrilled that she turned away, thinking she should've kept their dealings as impersonal as usual.

More emotional turmoil was *not* on her agenda.

"I've got to get this done." She moved toward a reception counter that was manned by a blond female cop.

He didn't follow, just hung back, uninvited.

"Hey," she said.

Hey, said the ghost of Griff from his home in the shadows of her heart.

Camille swallowed, chasing away the ache, the tragedy of losing his love.

But Sarge still waited, sticking his hands in his pockets, looking out of place on the fringes of her world.

Warmth wrapped around Griff's shadows, covering them like sleeping memories.

"You comin' or what?" she asked.

A grin tugged at his mouth, and he shrugged, stepped forward. "Just wanted to be invited, is all."

"You—" she smiled, held out her hand to him "—are so difficult."

He stared at her open palm for a moment, then raised an arrogant brow. "Just glad to be wanted."

And, as he stepped to her side at the counter, he slipped his hand into hers.

Entering into another battle.

Together.

* * * * *

SPOTLIGHT

"Debra Webb's fast-paced thriller will make you shiver in passion and fear...."—*Romantic Times*

Dying To Play
Debra Webb

When FBI agent Trace Callahan arrives in Atlanta to investigate a baffling series of multiple homicides, deputy chief of detectives Elaine Jentzen isn't prepared for the immediate attraction between them. And as they hunt to find the killer known as the Gamekeeper, it seems that Trace is singled out as his next victim...unless Elaine can stop the Gamekeeper before it's too late.

Available January 2005.

Exclusive Bonus Features:
Author Interview
Sneak Preview...
and more!

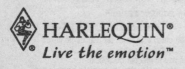

HARLEQUIN®
Live the emotion™

Wells

™ Silhouette®
BOMBSHELL™

COMING NEXT MONTH

#29 PERSONAL ENEMY—Sylvie Kurtz

When security specialist Adria Caskey's undercover plan to
ruin the man who had destroyed her family went awry, she
found herself protecting the man she loathed most in the
world. But as a cunning stalker drew them into a trap,
her sense of duty battled her desire for revenge....

#30 CONTACT—Evelyn Vaughn
Athena Force

Anonymous police contact Faith Corbett had been a psychic
all her life, but now her undercover work had put her in a serial
killer's sights. As she raced to save innocent lives, she had to
confront the dark secrets about her psychic gift, her family and
the skeptical detective who challenged her at every turn....

#31 THE MEDUSA PROJECT—Cindy Dees

Major Vanessa Blake had the chance to be part of the first
all-female Special Ops team in the U.S. military through
the Medusa Project. Only trouble was, the man charged
with training the women was under orders to make sure
they failed. But when their commander disappeared in
enemy territory, Vanessa and the Medusas were the only
people the government could turn to to retrieve him and
expose a deadly terrorist plot.

#32 THE SPY WORE RED—Wendy Rosnau
Spy Games

When Quest agent Nadja Stefn accepted a mission to
terminate an international assassin and seize his future-kill
files, she had another agenda: finding the child who was
ripped from her at birth. But she hadn't counted on
working with her ex-lover, Bjorn, agent extraordinaire—
and unbeknownst to him, her child's father.

SBCNM0105